Jude
x

Catherine Ryan Hyde, an acclaimed novelist and award-winning short story writer, is the author of several novels including, most recently, *Love in the Present Tense*. *Pay it Forward* was named an ALA Book of the Year and made into a feature film starring Kevin Spacey and Helen Hunt. Catherine lives in Cambria, California.

D1424979

Critical praise for *Love in the Present Tense*

'A sweet and honest look at the pains and pleasures of
love, and who could not fall in love with Leonard –
what a beautifully drawn character'
Jane Green

'A remarkable story of the magic of love'
Daily Express

'Full of cinematic imagery and haunting prose'
Bolton Evening News

'A work of art . . . enchanting'
San Francisco Chronicle

'Hyde excels in her story of a love that transcends time,
place and human weakness'
Publishers Weekly

'Haunting'
Washington Post

Critical praise for *Pay it Forward*

'Hyde's book delivers a profound vision: The simple magic of the human heart'
San Francisco Chronicle

'Heartwarming, funny, and bittersweet . . . A quiet, steady masterpiece with an incandescent ending'
Kirkus Reviews

'*Pay it Forward* is reminiscent of Frank Capra's *It's a Wonderful Life*. Like the [Capra] film, this novel has a steely core of gritty reality beneath its optimism . . . It takes courage to write so unabashedly hopeful a story in such cynical times'
Amazon.com

'The story is a quick read, told with lean sentences and an edge . . . Hyde pulls off a poignant, gutsy ending without bathos'
Los Angeles Times

'The philosophy behind the book is so intriguing, and the optimism so contagious . . . a book that lingers long after the last page is turned'
Denver Post

'Catherine Ryan Hyde accomplishes a very difficult job, with an easy, beneficent wisdom about the ways of the world'
Chicago Tribune

Also by Catherine Ryan Hyde

FUNERALS FOR HORSES
EARTHQUAKE WEATHER
ELECTRIC GOD
WALTER'S PURPLE HEART
BECOMING CHLOE
LOVE IN THE PRESENT TENSE

Pay it Forward

Catherine Ryan Hyde

BLACK SWAN

TRANSWORLD PUBLISHERS
61–63 Uxbridge Road, London W5 5SA
A Random House Group Company
www.rbooks.co.uk

PAY IT FORWARD
A BLACK SWAN BOOK: 9780552774253

Originally published in hardcover in 1999 by Simon & Schuster, Inc.
First published in Great Britain in 2000 by Simon & Schuster
Black Swan edition published 2007

A CIP catalogue record for this book
is available from the British Library

Addresses for Random House Group Ltd companies outside the UK
can be found at: www.randomhouse.co.uk
The Random House Group Ltd Reg. No. 954009

The Random House Group Ltd makes every effort to ensure that the papers
used in its books are made from trees that have been legally sourced from
well-managed and credibly certified forests. Our paper procurement policy
can be found at: www.randomhouse.co.uk/paper.htm

Typeset in 11½/15½pt Bembo by
Kestrel Data, Exeter, Devon
Printed in the UK by
CPI Cox & Wyman, Reading, RG1 8EX

2 4 6 8 10 9 7 5 3 1

For Vance

PROLOGUE

October 2002

Maybe someday I'll have kids of my own. I hope so. If I do, they'll probably ask what part I played in the movement that changed the world. And because I'm not the person I once was, I'll tell them the truth. My part was nothing. I did nothing. I was just the guy in the corner taking notes.

My name is Chris Chandler and I'm an investigative reporter. Or at least I was. Until I found out that actions have consequences, and not everything is under my control. Until I found out that I couldn't change the world at all, but a seemingly ordinary twelve-year-old boy could change the world completely – for the better, and forever – working with nothing but his own altruism, one good idea, and a couple of years. And a big sacrifice.

And a splash of publicity. That's where I came in.

I can tell you how it all started.

It started with a teacher who moved to Atascadero, California, to teach social studies to junior high school students. A teacher nobody knew very well, because they couldn't get past his face. Because it was hard to look at his face.

It started with a boy who didn't seem all that remarkable on the outside, but who could see past his teacher's face.

It started with an assignment that this teacher had given out a hundred times before, with no startling results. But that assignment in the hands of that boy caused a seed to be planted, and after that nothing in the world would ever be the same. Nor would anybody want it to be.

And I can tell you what it became. In fact, I'll tell you a story that will help you understand how big it grew.

About a week ago my car stalled in a busy intersection, and it wouldn't start again no matter how many times I tried. It was rush hour, and I thought I was in a hurry. I thought I had something important to do, and it couldn't wait. So I was standing in the middle of the intersection looking under the hood, which was a misguided effort because I can't fix cars. What did I think I would see?

I'd been expecting this. It was an old car. It was as good as gone.

A man came up behind me, a stranger.

'Let's get it off to the side of the road,' he said. 'Here. I'll help you push.' When we got it – and ourselves – to safety he handed me the keys to his car. A nice silver Acura, barely two years old. 'You can have mine,' he said. 'We'll trade.'

He didn't give me the car as a loan. He gave it to me as a gift. He took my address, so he could send me the title. And he did send the title; it just arrived today.

'A great deal of generosity has come into my life lately,' the note said, 'so I felt I could take your old car and use it as a trade-in. I can well afford something new, so why not give as good as I've received?'

That's what kind of world it's become. No, actually it's more. It's become even more. It's not just the kind of world in which a total stranger will give me his car as a gift. It's the kind of world in which the day I received that gift was not dramatically different from all other days. Such generosity has become the way of things. It's become commonplace.

So this much I understand well enough to relate: it started as an extra credit assignment for a social studies class and turned into a world where no one goes hungry, no one is cold, no one is without a job or a ride or a loan.

And yet at first people needed to know more. Somehow it was not enough that a boy barely in his teens was able to change the world. Somehow it had to be known why the world could change at just that moment, why it could not have changed a moment sooner, what Trevor brought to that moment, and why it was the very thing that moment required.

And that, unfortunately, is the part I can't explain.

I was there. Every step of the way I was there. But I was a different person then. I was looking in all the wrong places. I thought it was just a story, and the story was all that mattered. I cared about Trevor, but by the time I cared about him enough it was too late. I thought I cared about my work, but I didn't know what my work could really mean until it was over. I wanted to make lots of money. I did make lots of money. I gave it all away.

I don't know who I was then, but I know who I am now. Trevor changed me, too.

I thought Reuben would have the answers. Reuben St Clair, the teacher who started it all. He was closer to Trevor than anybody except maybe Trevor's mother, Arlene. And Reuben was looking in all the right places, I think. And I believe he was paying attention.

So, after the fact, when it was my job to write books about the movement, I asked Reuben two important questions.

'What was it about Trevor that made him different?' I asked.

Reuben thought carefully and then said, 'The thing about Trevor was that he was just like everybody else, except for the part of him that wasn't.'

I didn't even ask what part that was. I'm learning.

Then I asked, 'When you first handed out that now-famous assignment, did you think that one of your students would actually change the world?'

And Reuben replied, 'No, I thought they all would. But perhaps in smaller ways.'

I'm becoming someone who asks fewer questions. Not everything can be dissected and understood. Not everything has a simple answer. That's why I'm not a reporter any-more. When you lose interest in questions, you're out of a job. That's okay. I wasn't as good at it as I should have been. I didn't bring anything special to the game.

People gradually stopped needing to know why. We adjust quickly to change, even as we rant and rail and swear we never will. And everybody likes a change if it's a change for the better. And no one likes to dwell on the past if the past is ugly and everything is finally going well.

The most important thing I can add from my own observations is this: knowing it started from unremarkable circumstances should be a comfort to us all. Because it proves that you don't need much to change the entire world for the better. You can start with the most ordinary ingredients. You can start with the world you've got.

Pay It
Forward

Chapter One

REUBEN

January 1992

The woman smiled so politely that he felt offended.

'Let me tell Principal Morgan that you're here, Mr St Clair. She'll want to talk with you.' She walked two steps, turned back. 'She likes to talk to everyone, I mean. Any new teacher.'

'Of course.'

He should have been used to this by now.

More than three minutes later she emerged from the principal's office, smiling too widely. Too openly. People always display far too much acceptance, he'd noticed, when they are having trouble mustering any for real.

'Go right on in, Mr St Clair. She'll see you.'

'Thank you.'

The principal appeared to be about ten years older than he, with a great deal of dark hair, worn up, a Caucasian and attractive. And attractive women always made him hurt, literally, a long pain that started high up in his solar plexus and radiated downward through his gut. As if he had just asked this attractive woman to the theater, only to be told, You must be joking.

'We are so pleased to meet you face-to-face, Mr St Clair.' Then she flushed, as if the mention of the word 'face' had been an unforgivable faux pas.

'Please call me Reuben.'

'Reuben, yes. And I'm Anne.'

She met him with a steady, head-on gaze, and at no time appeared startled. So she had been verbally prepared by her assistant. And somehow the only thing worse than an unprepared reaction was the obviously rehearsed absence of one.

He hated these moments so.

He was, by his own admission, a man who should stay in one place. But the same factors that made it hard to start over made it hard to stay.

She motioned toward a chair and he sat. Crossed his legs. The crease of his slacks was neatly, carefully pressed. He'd chosen his tie the previous night, to go well with the suit. He was a demon about grooming, although he knew no one would ever really see. He appreciated these habits in himself, even if, or because, no one else did.

'I'm not quite what you were expecting, am I, Anne?'

The use of her first name brought it back, but more acutely. It was very hard to talk to an attractive woman.

'In what respect?'

'Please don't do this. You must appreciate how many

times I've replayed this same scene. I can't bear to talk around an obvious issue.'

She tried to establish eye contact, as one normally would when addressing a coworker in conversation, but she could not make it stick. 'I understand,' she said.

I doubt it, he said, but not out loud.

'It is human nature,' he said out loud, 'to form a picture of someone in your mind. You read a résumé and an application, and you see I'm forty-four, a black male, a war veteran with a good educational background. And you think you see me. And because you are not prejudiced, you hire this black man to move to your town, teach at your school. But now I arrive to test the limits of your open mind. It's easy not to be prejudiced against a black man, because we have all seen hundreds of those.'

'If you think your position is in any jeopardy, Reuben, you're worrying for nothing.'

'Do you really have this little talk with everyone?'

'Of course I do.'

'Before they even address their first class?'

Pause. 'Not necessarily. I just thought we might discuss the subject of . . . initial adjustment.'

'You worry that my appearance will alarm the students.'

'What has your experience been with that in the past?'

'The students are always easy, Anne. This is the difficult moment. Always.'

'I understand.'

'With all respect, I'm not sure you do,' he said. Out loud.

*   *   *

19

At his former school, in Cincinnati, Reuben had a friend named Louis Tartaglia. Lou had a special way of addressing an unfamiliar class. He would enter, on that first morning, with a yardstick in his hand. Walk right into the flap and fray. They like to test a teacher, you see, at first. This yardstick was Lou's own, bought and carried in with him. A rather thin, cheap one. He always bought the same brand at the same store. Then he would ask for silence, which he never received on the first request. After counting to three, he would bring this yardstick up over his head and smack it down on the desktop in such a way that it would break in two. The free half would fly up into the air behind him, hit the blackboard, and clatter to the floor. Then, in the audible silence to follow, he would say, simply, 'Thank you.' And would have no trouble with the class after that.

Reuben warned him that someday a piece would fly in the wrong direction and hit a student, causing a world of problems, but it had always worked as planned, so far as he knew.

'It boils down to unpredictability,' Lou explained. 'Once they see you as unpredictable, you hold the cards.'

Then he asked what Reuben did to quiet an unfamiliar and unruly class, and Reuben replied that he had never experienced the problem; he had never been greeted by anything but stony silence and was never assumed to be predictable.

'Oh. Right,' Lou said, as if he should have known better. And he should have.

*   *   *

20

Reuben stood before them, for the first time, both grateful for and resentful of their silence. Outside the windows on his right was California, a place he'd never been before. The trees were different; the sky did not say winter as it had when he'd started the long drive from Cincinnati. He wouldn't say from home, because it was not his home, not really. And neither was this. And he'd grown tired of feeling like a stranger.

He performed a quick head count, seats per row, number of rows. 'Since I can see you're all here,' he said, 'we will dispense with the roll call.'

It seemed to break a spell, that he spoke, and the students shifted a bit, made eye contact with one another. Whispered across aisles. Neither better nor worse than usual. To encourage this normality, he turned away to write his name on the board. *Mr St Clair*. Also wrote it out underneath, *Saint Clair*, as an aid to pronunciation. Then paused before turning back, so they would have time to finish reading his name.

In his mind, his plan, he thought he'd start right off with the assignment. But it caved from under him, like skidding down the side of a sand dune. He was not Lou, and sometimes people needed to know him first. Sometimes he was startling enough on his own, before his ideas even showed themselves.

'Maybe we should spend this first day,' he said, 'just talking. Since you don't know me at all. We can start by talking about appearances. How we feel about people because of how they look. There are no rules. You can say anything you want.'

Apparently they did not believe him yet, because they said the same things they might have with their parents looking on. To his disappointment.

Then, in what he supposed was an attempt at humor, a boy in the back row asked if he was a pirate.

'No,' he said. 'I'm not. I'm a teacher.'

'I thought only pirates wore eye patches.'

'People who have lost eyes wear eye patches. Whether they are pirates or not is beside the point.'

The class filed out, to his relief, and he looked up to see a boy standing in front of his desk. A thin white boy, but very dark-haired, possibly part Hispanic, who said, 'Hi.'

'Hello.'

'What happened to your face?'

Reuben smiled, which was rare for him, being self-conscious about the lopsided effect. He pulled a chair around so the boy could sit facing him and motioned for him to sit, which he did without hesitation. 'What's your name?'

'Trevor.'

'Trevor what?'

'McKinney. Did I hurt your feelings?'

'No, Trevor. You didn't.'

'My mom says I shouldn't ask people things like that, because it might hurt their feelings. She says you should act like you didn't notice.'

'Well, what your mom doesn't know, Trevor, because she's never been in my shoes, is that if you act like you didn't notice, I still know that you did. And then it feels strange that we can't talk about it when we're both thinking about it. Know what I mean?'

'I think so. So, what happened?'

'I was injured in a war.'

'In Vietnam?'

'That's right.'

'My daddy was in Vietnam. He says it's a hellhole.'

'I would tend to agree. Even though I was only there for seven weeks.'

'My daddy was there two years.'

'Was he injured?'

'Maybe a little. I think he has a sore knee.'

'I was supposed to stay two years, but I got hurt so badly that I had to come home. So, in a way I was lucky that I didn't have to stay, and in a way your daddy was lucky because he didn't get hurt that badly. If you know what I mean.' The boy didn't look too sure that he did. 'Maybe someday I'll meet your dad. Maybe on parents' night.'

'I don't think so. We don't know where he is. What's under the eye patch?'

'Nothing.'

'How can it be nothing?'

'It's like nothing was ever there. Do you want to see?'

'You bet.'

Reuben took off the patch.

No one seemed to know quite what he meant by 'nothing', until they saw it. No one seemed prepared for the shock of 'nothing' where there would be an eye on everyone else they had ever met. The boy's head rocked back a little, then he nodded. Kids were easier. Reuben replaced the patch.

'Sorry about your face. But you know, it's only just that one side. The other side looks real good.'

'Thank you, Trevor. I think you are the first person to offer me that compliment.'

'Well, see ya.'

'Good-bye, Trevor.'

Reuben moved to the window and looked out over the front lawn. Watched students clump and talk and run on the grass, until Trevor appeared, trotting down the front steps.

It was ingrained in Reuben to defend this moment, and he could not have returned to his desk if he'd tried. This he could not release. He needed to know if Trevor would run up to the other boys to flaunt his new knowledge. To collect on any bets or tell any tales, which Reuben would not hear, only imagine from his second-floor perch, his face flushing under the imagined words. But Trevor trotted past the boys without so much as a glance, stopping to speak to no one.

It was almost time for Reuben's second class to arrive. So he had to get started, preparing himself to do it all over again.

From *The Other Faces Behind the Movement*
by Chris Chandler

There is nothing monstrous or grotesque about my face. I get to state this with a certain objectivity, being perhaps the only one capable of such. I am the only one used to seeing it, because I am the only one who dares, with the help of a shaving mirror, to openly stare.

I have undergone eleven operations, all in all, to repair what was, at one time, unsightly damage. The area that was my left eye, and the lost bone and muscle under cheek and brow, have been neatly covered with skin removed from my thigh. I have endured numerous skin grafts and plastic surgery. Only a few of these were necessary for health or function. Most were intended to make me an easier individual to meet. The final result is a smooth, complete absence of an eye, as if one had never existed; a great loss of muscle and mass in cheek and neck; and obvious nerve damage to the left corner of my mouth. It is dead, so to speak, and droops. But after many years of remedial diction therapy, my speech is fairly easily understood.

So, in a sense it is not what people see in my face that disturbs them, but rather what they expect to see and do not.

I also have minimal use of my left arm, which is foreshortened and thin from resulting atrophy. My guess is that people rarely notice this until I've been around awhile, because my face tends to steal the show.

I have worked in schools, lounged in staff rooms, where a Band-Aid draws comment and requires explanation. Richie, what did you do to your hand? A cast on an extremity becomes a story told for six weeks, multiplied by the number of employees. Well, I was on a ladder, see, preparing to clean my storm drains . . .

So, it seems odd to me that no one will ask. If they suddenly did and I were forced to repeat the story, I might decide I had liked things better before. But it's not so much that they don't ask, but why they don't ask, as if I am an unspeakable tragedy, as new and shocking to myself as to them.

Occasionally my left arm will draw comment, always the same one. 'How lucky that it was your left.' But even this supposed consolation is misguided, because I am left-handed, by nature if not by practice.

Until I was shipped home from overseas, I had a fiancée. I still have pictures of us together. We were a handsome couple – ask anyone. To someone who wasn't there, it might seem as if my fiancée must have been a coldhearted woman. Surely she could have married me just the same. I wish Eleanor had been a coldhearted woman, or even that I could pretend such to be the case, but unfortunately I was there. The real truth is hard to re-create. The real truth is that we both agreed so staunchly not to see it or care about it that it was all we could see, nor had we time left over to care about anything else.

Eleanor was a strong woman, which no doubt contributed to our defeat.

She is married now and lives with her husband in Detroit. She is a plastic surgeon. I haven't entirely decided how much significance to attribute to these facts.

Any of them.

From *The Diary of Trevor*

I saw this weird thing on the news a couple of days ago. This little kid over in England who has this, like . . . condition. Nothing hurts him. Every time they showed a shot of him, he was wearing a crash helmet and elbow pads and knee pads. 'Cause I guess he would hurt himself. I mean, why wouldn't he? How would he know?

First I thought, Whoa. Lucky. But then I wasn't that sure.

When I was little I asked my mom why we have pain. Like, what's it for? She said it's so we don't stand around with our hands on a hot stove. She said it's to teach us. But she said by the time the pain kicks in, it's pretty much too late, and that's what parents are here for. And that's what she's here for. To teach me. So I don't touch the hot stove in the first place.

Sometimes I think my mom has that condition, too. Only on the inside where nobody sees it but me and maybe Loretta and definitely Bonnie. Except, I know she hurts.

But she still has her hand on that hot stove. On the inside, I mean. And I don't think they make helmets or pads for stuff like that.

I wish I could teach her.

Chapter Two

ARLENE

Ricky never exactly came home, not like she thought he would, but the truck did. Only not like she thought it would. It had been rolled a few times; all in all it looked worse than she felt. Only, it ran. Well, it idled. It's one thing to start up and run, quite another to actually get somewhere.

Much as she hated that damned Ford extra cab for imitating her own current condition, she could have forgiven it that. Potentially she could. It was the way it kept her awake at night. Especially now, when she'd taken a second job, at the Laser Lounge, to keep up the payments. And since it was the truck's fault that she didn't get to bed until three, it at least could have let her sleep. Surely that would not have been asking too much.

Yet there she was again at the window, double-checking the way moonlight slid off the vehicle's spooky shape. The way its silvery reflection broke where the paint broke.

Only Ricky could screw up a truck that bad and walk away. At least, it would stand to reason that he had walked away, seeing that the truck was found and Ricky was not.

Dragged off by coyotes? Stop, Arlene, just get ahold of yourself. He's sitting in a bar somewhere, talking that same sweet line to some poor girl ain't learned yet what it all adds up to. Or what it all don't add up to.

Unless, of course, he limped away, not sauntered off, maybe dragged himself to a hospital, maybe got out okay, maybe died, far from anything to tie him to a Ford extra cab, far from any ties to hometown news.

So there could be a grave somewhere, but how would Arlene know? And even if she did, she could not know which one or where. Even if she bought flowers for Ricky out of her tip money, she would never know where to put them.

Flowers can be a bad thing, a bad thought, if you don't even know where to lay them down. Just stop, Arlene. Just go back to bed.

And she did, but fell victim to a dream in which Ricky had been living just outside the town for months and months and never bothered to contact her with his whereabouts.

Which made her cross to the window again to blame the damn truck for keeping her awake.

★　　★　　★

31

'So then, what if I get it home and it's bent? I just spent two hunnerd dollars on nothin'?'

'You just said yourself it's reinforced over that door, so you can roll the damn truck and the door don't get bent.'

'I'm just sayin' what if, though. That's all I'm sayin'.'

'Tell you what. I'll hold your check for a couple, three days. You can't get it to go on your truck, you bring it back.'

'Yeah. I guess. One seventy-five.'

'Get outta my driveway you're gonna jack me around.'

'Okay, two hunnerd.' With a little smile.

Guys like it when you talk to them like that. For some damned reason.

He leaned on the mangled Ford's hood and lit a smoke. Marlboro Red, same as Ricky used to smoke, like she wouldn't have known that without looking. Seemed this world, this town, was just full of men cut from Ricky's same pattern. Seemed so to her, anyway. Which is why she felt drawn to this guy, this Doug or Duane or whatever the hell he said, her first customer.

And she knew that was why, and that there would be more if she were to bother to dig for it. She knew if she asked him he would say his daddy whupped him harder than most and that he has been on his own from some ungodly young age. She knew if she were to take off his T-shirt he would have a tattoo on his shoulder, with a name too faded to read. Someone he knew for a month or two when he was too young to know that forever only goes for the scars. And the blue ink you have allowed under the skin.

And it made her feel tired to be attracted to Doug. Duane.

Later she would say to her best friend, Loretta, 'I no longer think I lack judgment about men. I will never again say my instincts are poor, no sir, because how do I keep finding this same guy over and over? I am beginning to think I have a very keen sense of judgment, only it would seem that it is on somebody else's side.'

For the time she seemed content to watch his big arm muscles breaking loose the bolts on the door hinge and to feel tired knowing that part of her was scoping out the next big life mess before she had even cleared the rubble of the last one from her normally tidy driveway.

Before she could finish this dampening thought, Cheryl Wilcox, Ricky's ex-wife, pulled up into Arlene's driveway to thank her for being a two-faced slut.

And it wasn't even 9 a.m.

From *Those Who Knew Trevor Speak*
by Chris Chandler (1999)

I don't want to disappoint everybody. It wasn't exactly the Immaculate Conception. Just one of those risks you let happen sometimes. Probably seems kind of stupid and careless now, after the fact. Still, thank God it worked out the way it did, right?

I'm not saying I didn't toy with the mention of precautions, somewhere along in that evening, but the thought didn't go no farther than that. Seemed like any poorly thought-out words might've broken up that moment. Brought everybody home to their own good sense. And if you want to see a man come to his senses, try saying something like, Do you happen to carry a rubber in your wallet? Did I mention I'm not on the pill?

Besides, him and his wife, Cheryl, they'd been trying to get pregnant forever. Never thought it was all her fault. Why would I? Never really thought it was something more likely to happen to those who don't try, no matter how many people it might've happened to just that way, and maybe in my head I knew it.

He was married. At first. It's kind of complicated.

So, anyway, what I did say was to complain that we would never be able to go dancing. Maybe if we'd lived in New York City, maybe then, but not in Atascadero; you could not. Not where everybody knew everybody, at least to the point of knowing who rightfully matches up with who.

'You wanta go dancin'?' he said. 'I'll take you dancin'.' And he did. Drove us up somewhere along the Cuesta Grade, looking down over the lights of the town, which I must say looked kind of nice from so much distance. We got out of that old sedan, and he reached back in and turned the key to accessory, which I guess he should not have done, because it ran his battery down, not that we cared at the time. Or later, come to think of it.

He tried three stations for a slow number, and then the next thing I knew, well, it's kind of hard to explain. It's like the whole world was all his hand in the small of my back, nothing bigger than that, nor ever would be. And when he dipped me, the warm feel of his breath on my neck, which had always been there and would never entirely move along. It was something that was keyed to fit on the manufacture, and I'm not sure it's our fault we discovered it too late, after the exchanging of rings elsewhere and vows one might live to regret. It was like a map, I decided. You know, with red lines to divide up the states, and blue lines for the rivers, and brown folds for a mountain range. Which is more important: this deal we all make that Idaho stops being Idaho right here, or the mountains and rivers that were there before anybody took to tracing?

It's like there was always a me and Ricky, and I was sure there always would be. Even if I didn't know exactly where he took that love. I mean, when he was gone. I thought it was there, and I would wager he could feel the weight of it, whether he was traveling or holding still for a change. I'm gettin' off the subject. Everybody wants to know about that night.

When we made love for that first time I felt like I'd lost something, even before it was over. I thought, There is nothing here for me to keep. Nothing that is really my very own when all this is over.

But I was wrong. I got something to keep.

$\star$ $\star$ $\star$

35

Cheryl stood in her living room. Said, 'Don't you got anything to drink around here?'

And she did, although her sponsor had warned her to throw it away. Sooner or later I got to be around it, though, she'd said to her sponsor, who is named Bonnie. Later is one thing, though, Bonnie said. You only got five days under your belt. Only not anymore she didn't, because she took down two glasses.

Bonnie also said, time to make your amends, clean up the wreckage of your past, which is why Arlene invited Ricky's ex-wife into her house in the first place. To apologize for sleeping with Ricky while he was still married to her. For that nine or ten years of overlap.

Otherwise, when Cheryl pulled into her driveway to thank her for being a two-faced slut, she might have just said you're welcome and let Cheryl scream on out of there leaving some bad-smelling rubber dust for a souvenir. In her old days she just might have. Then smiled at Duane like nothing had ever happened. Seen what his plans were for the evening.

But here Doug had gone off with his trial-offer truck door, Cheryl was standing in her living room, and it was all her sponsor, Bonnie's, fault. Later, when she was good and drunk, she'd have to call Bonnie up to tell her just that.

Cheryl said, 'I believe you know where he is and you just ain't telling me.'

Arlene said, 'If I knew where he was, I wouldn't be parting out that truck to get maybe one-third of my lost monies back. I'd find him and tell the loan collector where and shove that sorry piece of junk you know where and let them take the depreciation out of *his* sorry ass.'

Cheryl said, 'It's what you get for cosigning. You got just what you deserved.'

Arlene started to say something back but couldn't think what it should be and worried maybe it would be a bad, weak-sounding something no matter how carefully she thought it up. So instead she poured two fingers of good old José Cuervo. The one man in her life who never told lies, so you always knew what you would get. And you could never say you didn't know. Then she said, 'I brought you in here to say I was sorry.'

And Cheryl said, 'Yeah. That's what I always say about you. You'd have to be pretty damn sorry, coming in my house like you did, like a guest, eating my dinner like you was my friend. Being all nice to me.'

Arlene stopped to consider this, how she'd lost points for niceness. 'Why you just telling me all this now?'

Cheryl took a big breath, the kind people do when you've hit a crack, a seam where they're prone to bend from some of the collisions they've absorbed. Lately everybody reminded Arlene of that piece of expensive trash in her driveway: rolled a few times, and nobody's doors fit quite right anymore.

Cheryl said, 'When I heard the truck come here, I thought—'

'You thought what? That he was here with it?'

'Maybe.'

What is it about Ricky, she could not help but wonder,

that makes women wish he'd come back and mess things up some more? 'Well, he ain't.'

'Yeah. I see that now.'

The door opened. Arlene's boy came spilling in. His hair was a mess, which was Arlene's own fault, because in her hurry to start parting out that disaster in her driveway she'd left the boy more or less to his own devices. Part of the seat was ripped out of his blue jeans, but Arlene didn't even want to know about that. Yet. And at least he had on clean underwear, thank God.

'Trevor, where you been?'

'Over at Joe's.'

'Did I say you could go to Joe's?'

'No.' Downcast eyes, which Arlene thought he might practice in the mirror. He knew who this was in the living room with Momma, but not why. But he knew it was not for fun. Kids know. 'Sorry.' His eyes on her drinking glass. No judgment, just a silent taking in, too grown-up for a boy his age, knowing certain things, like why grown-ups try. And how damned unlikely they are to succeed.

'That's okay. Go on back there now.'

'I just got home.'

'Will you mind me for once?'

And he did, without back talk. Arlene made a mental note to take him out for an ice cream later, the usual fallback for any out-of-sorts behavior on her part; as a result they ate a lot of ice cream. The door slamming behind him made Arlene ache with a separateness from him, like she still hadn't gotten over the cutting of that cord in the first place.

Arlene filled both glasses again. 'Thanks for not saying nothing in front of the boy.'

'He looks so much like Ricky.'

'He ain't. Ricky's.'

'Spitting image.'

'He's twelve. I only took up with Ricky ten years back.'

She felt as though Bonnie were looking over her shoulder, reminding. This was not the honesty that would help her set a course to a whole new life. But it was such an old lie, and so hard to shake after all those years of telling. That lie fit so well after all this time.

'I see him in that boy.'

'Well, you're seeing what ain't there.' *Or what you wanted for yourself and never got.* What we don't get, we see everywhere we look. What we won't let ourselves do, be, we refuse to tolerate in any other living soul. Arlene was beginning to notice this.

Nine o'clock that same evening Bonnie came unannounced to her door.

'I know how this looks,' Arlene said. 'But I was just thinking to call you.'

'I thought you might want to talk.'

'You got some kind of ESP?'

'Not as I know of. Got a message on my machine from your boy.'

This sudden news made Arlene cry, for reasons she could not entirely sort out. Lately the tears seemed to hover just below the surface, and any little jolt would bring them up, like when a sudden burst of laughter or fright made it hard to hold her bladder, especially if she'd been holding it too long as it was.

Bonnie brought herself through the door, all 315 pounds of herself, and folded herself around Arlene like a big pillow, smothering her in a not entirely unlikable way.

After a while they went through the cabinets and poured all the liquor down the sink.

'I'll just start all over again tomorrow. Maybe get it right this time.'

'What's wrong with right now? You can start over any old time of the day, you know.'

'I guess.'

Bonnie followed behind her to the bedroom window and looked out with Arlene into her driveway, across the moonlit wreckage of everything that had once seemed worth anything. Almost as though Arlene, who could never find the words just right, would show Bonnie the problem. The ghost. Like to say, If you were haunted by the likes of that, who's to say you'd do much better?

Bonnie nodded slowly.

'Hear them trees?' Arlene said.

'What about 'em?'

'They been singing to me at night. So clear and plain I can't get no sleep anymore. Ricky songs. Can't you hear that? I swear, before that damn truck come home they never

40

sang those songs. They sang something, I guess. But not that.'

'That's just the wind, girl.'

'To you, maybe.'

Bonnie tucked her into bed. 'I'll come back to check on you in the morning.'

'Oh, I'll be right here.'

And Bonnie left her alone with all that singing.

She got up after a time. Let herself into Trevor's room. Sat on the edge of his bed and brushed all that curly black hair off of his forehead.

'You okay, Momma?' He had not been awake, but came up into those words like he'd been filling a place in his sleep all concerned with her welfare.

'You're the one good thing I ever did.' She said this to him a lot.

'Aw, Mom.' He always said this same thing back.

When she left him, his eyes were still open. Like maybe he heard it, too.

From *The Diary of Trevor*

Sometimes I think my father never went to Vietnam. I don't even know why I think that. I just do.

Joe's father went to Vietnam, and he tells stories. And you can tell, just by the stories, that he really did go.

I think my father maybe just says things sometimes that he thinks will make people proud of him or feel sorry for him.

My mom feels sorry for him because he went to Vietnam. She says no wonder he has problems. So I don't tell her that I think maybe he never did.

Mr St Clair is so cool. I don't care what Arnie says. I think he's great, and I'm gonna do such a great job on that assignment Mr St Clair won't even be able to believe it.

Chapter Three

JERRY

He spent the night in a Dumpster behind the auto parts store, not two blocks from the place he planned to be at 9 a.m. Even in his sleep there was hopefulness. Something he'd been missing for a while.

But when he woke, the whole thing seemed too much like a job interview for his taste. The prospect of it made his stomach feel weird. Like he knew in some part of himself how it would be. Just like so many other things. Just around the corner, just beyond his fingertips. A line that cuts off one or two people ahead of him.

And when he'd first read it, it had made him feel so good. So he read it again.

It was in his shirt pocket, folded. The newsprint smeared by the sweat of his hands. Rumpled. But he could read it just the same.

FREE MONEY AND OTHER HELP FOR SOMEONE DOWN ON LUCK. COME TO CORNER TRAFFIC WAY AND EL CAMINO REAL. SATURDAY MORNING 9:00.

He couldn't get the feeling back, though.

He used to have it all the time, the feeling that whatever-is-up-there — 'whatever' because words like 'God' made him edgy — was looking right at him when something was said. Or as in this case, read. And maybe because he didn't feel it anymore, maybe that's why he'd come to this, why he'd sunk so low.

When the sky and what's in it don't know you exist, then what's left to you? Just this damn world, the part of it right under your nose, with no more promise or meaning than what you see. What you do with your day.

And he did almost nothing anymore, except the repetition of the same necessary steps. Get his hands on some money, spend it all in one place.

He couldn't get that meaning back. Now he read that little ad and knew that lots of others probably had read it, too. That he would be standing in a long line.

But he set off just the same.

He looked in the window of the parts store, saw it was only seven-thirty. But he went to wait at that corner anyway, as if a real line would form and he could secure an early place.

But before he even got to the corner, he saw he was late. Later than he thought. There were seventeen people already there. So, with an irksome feeling of competition chewing at his gut like little mouse teeth, he stood with them. Nobody met anybody else's eye.

It gets so damned cold in Atascadero. That's what he kept thinking. *This is supposed to be California, right? Sunny*

California. During the day maybe, but here at night it could be thirty degrees. Some of these people had gloves. But he did not. So he rubbed his hands together to keep warm. And busy.

They were almost all men, he noticed, waiting; the one exception was a woman with no front teeth. Some looked better than he did, some worse. He had that thought, then doubted it. Doubted his own perception of how he looked. It had been a while since he'd looked in a mirror.

And then it hit him.

I'm looking in a mirror right now.

So he saw himself clearly for maybe the first time since everything went south, and sour. Saw his own image in the company he kept. These were his peers. It made him want to leave, and he almost did. But three more guys showed up and he decided he had just as much right to free money as they did.

He didn't know if it was nine o'clock yet, but it seemed like it must be. Forty-eight people were gathered on the corner, not counting himself.

A boy twelve, thirteen years old rode up on a bike, an old beach cruiser. Jerry was surprised that there weren't more kids waiting, because kids like free money. Along with everybody else. But the kid didn't act like he'd come to wait.

The kid looked at the crowd. The crowd looked at him.

Maybe because he was the only one so far who didn't keep his eyes down on the pavement. The kid's eyes scanned around like he was counting. His forehead all furrowed down into a frown. Then he said, 'Holy cow. Are you all here for the ad?'

He said it in a kind of official way, and some heads came up. Listening to him, sort of. Thinking he might know something. And some others got defensive, and you could almost smell it. Like who was this little punk, anyway, to address them?

A few people nodded.

'Holy cow.' He said it again. Shook his head. 'I only wanted one guy.'

Then this big bald guy walked up. Said, 'You did that ad?'

Jerry knew this big guy. Not knew him, but knew enough to keep away. A high-profile bum around town. Made a lot of waves.

But the kid didn't know to lie low around the big bum, so he said, 'Yeah, I did.'

Big bum said, 'Well, that's it, then.' And almost everybody left, following him like he was the messiah or something. Whether he meant he thought there was no money, or wouldn't take it from a kid, Jerry didn't know. Didn't know if the guys leaving did, either. Just went where they were told to go. Elsewhere.

Jerry could hear them grumbling as they pushed by. But he was not leaving, not jumping to any conclusions. Most of the grumblings added up to something like, 'Shoulda knowed it was all a gag.' That or, 'Real funny, kid.'

The kid just stood there awhile. Kind of relieved, Jerry thought, because now there were only ten or eleven left. A little more manageable crowd.

Jerry walked up to the kid. Nice. Humble, not like to scare him. 'So, *is* it a joke?'

'No, it's for real. I got a paper route, and I make thirty-five dollars a week, and I want to give it to somebody. Who'll, like, get a job and not need it after a while. Just to get 'em started, you know? Like food and something better to wear, and some bus fare. Or whatever.'

And somebody behind Jerry, some voice over his shoulder, said, 'Yeah, but which somebody?'

Yeah. That was the problem.

The kid thought this over for a bit. Then he said he had some paper in his book bag, and he asked everybody to write out why they thought it should be them.

And when he said that, six people left.

Kid said, 'I wonder what happened to them.'

And the lady with no front teeth, she said, 'What makes you think everybody can write?'

It was clear from the look on the kid's face that he never would have thought of that.

Why I think I deserve the money, by Jerry Busconi

Well, for starters, I will not say I deserve it better than anybody. Because, who is to say?

I am not a perfect person, and maybe somebody else will say they are. And you are a smart kid. I bet you are. And you will know they are handing you a line. I am being honest.

I know you said you wanted somebody down on his luck. But you know what? It is all bull. Luck has nothing to do with this. Look at all these people who showed up today. We are a bunch of bums. They will say it is bad luck. But I won't sell you a line, kid. We did this to ourselves.

Me, I have a problem sometimes. With drugs. This is my own fault. Nobody else's. Not my mother. Not God or the government. They did not stick a needle in my arm. I did this to myself. But I have not had any drugs for a few weeks now. I been clean.

I lost some stuff because of my problems. A car, even though it was not a very good one. And my apartment. And then I went to jail, and they did not hold my job for when I got out.

But I got lots of things I can do. I got skills. I have worked in wrecking yards, and in body shops, and I have even worked as a mechanic. I am a good mechanic. It's not that I'm not. But, used to, you could go in kind of scruffy and dirty. For a mechanics job no one would mind.

But now times is hard, and guys show up for the same job. Dressed good, and some even got a state license. So they say, fill out this form. Which I can do. Cause as you see, I can read and write pretty good. But then they say, put down your number. We'll call you if you get the job.

But the dumpster where I been staying ain't got a phone. So I say, I'm just getting settled in. And they say, put your address, then. We'll send you a postcard.

And they know, then. That you are on the street. And I guess they figure you got problems, stuff they don't know nothing about.

And, well, I guess I do. Like I said.

But if I had a chance at a job now, I would not screw it up like I have done before. It would be different this time.

These other people, look at them. They have got used to their situation. They expect to sleep on the street. And I guess that is okay with them.

But it is not okay with me. I don't think I quite sunk that low. Anyway, not yet.

So if you go with me, you won't be sorry.

I guess that's all I got to say.

Also, thank you. I never knowed no kid who gave money away. I had a job at your age, and I spent the money on me. You must be a good kid.

I guess that's all now. Thanks for your time.

When Jerry looked up, everybody else except the kid had gone.

Chapter Four

ARLENE

It was not even seven o'clock, and therefore a scandalous hour of the morning, especially when a damned Ford extra cab had kept you awake half the night. Someone was shaking her shoulder, and without being exactly conscious, she knew by instinct that it was her boy.

'Momma? Are you awake?'

'Yeah.'

'Can Jerry come in and take a shower?'

She blinked and squinted at the clock. She had another half an hour to sleep. Nothing should have been happening now. A dream maybe, but that's it. 'Who's Jerry?'

'My friend.'

She hadn't known Trevor to have any friends named Jerry, and now she had forgotten the original request.

'Use your own judgment. I'll be up in a half hour.'

She folded a pillow around her head, and that was the last thing she remembered until the alarm clock went off and she threw the pillow at it. She was not mad at the alarm, she was mad at the damn truck and at Ricky, but one had suffered enough abuse as it stood, and the other was not around.

A few minutes later, as she set a bowl of hot cereal in front of the boy, a total stranger popped out of the hall and into the kitchen. She was all set to scream but felt too embarrassed to follow through, maybe because, out of the three of them, she was the only one who seemed the least bit surprised.

She figured the man to be in his forties, at least, short, clean shaven, with a receding hairline, and he was wearing brand-new blue jeans and a stiff-looking denim shirt.

'Who the hell are you?'

He didn't answer fast enough, so Trevor said, 'It's Jerry, Mom. Remember you said he could come in and take a shower?'

'I said that?'

'Yeah.'

'When did I say that?'

'Right before you woke up.'

Meanwhile Jerry had said nothing in his own defense or otherwise, but apparently was a smart enough man to know when and where he was not wanted, because he began to creep sideways toward the door. 'Thank you kindly, ma'am,' he said with his hand on the knob, and Trevor asked him, of all the damned things for a kid to say, if he needed money for the bus. The man held out a handful of change. Held it out like war medals or rubies, something a damn sight more important than quarters and dimes, that's for sure. 'I saved it, see? From my clothes money.'

And Trevor said, 'I hope you get the job.' And then after the door had closed behind him, Trevor looked up at Arlene like nothing at all had just transpired and said, 'You know your mouth's hanging open?'

But when he saw the look on her face he hunkered down over his hot cereal and concentrated on stirring in the sugar.

'Trevor, who the hell was that?'

'I told you. Jerry.'

'Who the hell is Jerry?'

'My friend.'

'I did not say he could come in here and take no shower.'

'Yeah, you did. You said I should use my own judgment.'

She had no memory of saying this, but it rang true, in that it was what she would have said if she was really just trying to stay asleep. Unless the boy was smart enough to know that's what she would have said, and proceeded with his story from there. But it was too early in the morning to sort between things that happened and those that allegedly did, so she said only this: 'If your judgment is to let a strange man into our bathroom to shower, then I do believe your judgment needs a tune-up.'

He tried to argue again that the man was not a stranger, but rather his friend Jerry, but Arlene was not having any of it. She told him only to eat up and get on to school, and that she did not want to see Jerry in the house anymore, ever, not under any circumstances, not even if hell froze over, no way, José.

The minute Trevor was out the door she regretted having forgotten to ask why he offered Jerry money for the bus.

She went straight to the bathroom, which the man had left surprisingly neat, and commenced to sterilize every exposed surface.

Maybe three days later, maybe four, Arlene arrived home after working at the Laser Lounge until 3 a.m. to discover someone in the driveway tinkering with a light on the wrecked truck. And the fact that she pulled up in front of her own house did not seem to dissuade him from his work.

She had been afraid of this, being gone as much as she was. Every time someone came to see the truck and then drove away without buying something, she was half afraid they would come back in the night and take what they wanted. And now look.

She slipped into the house and into her bedroom closet, where Ricky's twelve-gauge shotgun sat on the shelf, right where he'd left it. In a locked case, because boys are curious. It had always given her a good feeling, it being there, not so much because she expected to use it but because she firmly believed Ricky would have taken it were he not planning a return trip. She pulled it out from its case, wrapped in a big old towel as Ricky always kept it, and when the towel fell away, the moonlight from the window turned the black gunmetal a beautiful deep blue. It smelled of gun oil and reminded her of Ricky, of watching him cleaning it in front of the TV at night.

She loaded the breech with three rounds of less-than-lethal bird shot, and with a big, deep breath kicked the back door open directly onto the driveway, where the man crouched, working by the light of a metal lamp clipped onto the bumper. And plugged in somewhere in her own garage. Which made her madder, somehow – that some low-life sneak thief would use her electricity to see better while robbing her blind.

He jumped up and turned to face her in the dark, and she finally got to do it, and it felt as good as she thought it would, cocking the weapon with that big, powerful *shuck-shuck* sound, and the reaction of fear that sound was bound to produce.

Talking about that sound, Ricky told her once, 'You seen them cartoons where a guy runs right through a wall and leaves a hole just his shape in the wall behind him? Well, that could happen.'

Only this man held his ground. 'Please don't shoot, ma'am. It's only me.'

'Only you who?'

'Jerry.'

Oh, damn it all to hell. 'What the hell you takin' off my truck?' she said without lowering the shotgun.

'Everything, ma'am. I been stacking parts in the garage. Trevor told me you were parting out. You can get a lot more money that way. Did you know that? You got to give a price break if the people has to pull them parts on their own.'

'So you're just trying to help out,' she said, in tone that made it clear she didn't think so.

'Yes, ma'am.'

'At three o'clock in the morning.'

'Yes, ma'am. I got me a job now during the day, at the Quicky Lube & Tune a few miles down on the Camino. So if I'm going to help out, it's got to be at night.'

She couldn't see his face as well as she'd have liked, dark as it was, but his voice sounded pretty matter-of-fact, and the whole incident was beginning to get under her skin. Lowering the shotgun, picking up his little work light, she walked to the garage to see for herself. He had parts stacked all neat in there, with a door and a bumper and seats. And he had things labeled with something like a grease pencil: *Driver's Side. Front. Rear.*

She stepped out again and shone the light straight at him. He threw a hand up to shield his eyes.

'Did I ask you to help?'

'No, ma'am. But it's something I'm good at. I used to work at a wrecking yard. And the boy's helped me out a lot.'

'Trevor been giving you money?'

'Yes, ma'am. Just to help me get on my feet. You know, to get cleaned up enough to get a job again. Like that.'

'And now you got a job, you gonna pay him that money back?'

'No, ma'am. I'm not allowed to. I have to pay it forward.'

'"Pay it forward"? What the hell does that mean?'

He seemed surprised that she was not familiar with the term. And meanwhile it had become something like a normal conversation, with Arlene not entirely having the upper hand, and the fact that she couldn't get mad at him pissed her off but good.

'You don't know about that? You oughta talk to him. I'm surprised he didn't tell you about it. Something he's working on for social studies class. He could explain it better, though. You know, if you got ten bucks to rent a hoist, I'll pull that engine and put it up on blocks and tarp it. Save you a bundle.'

'No offense to you personally, but I told Trevor I did not want you around the house.'

'I thought you told him you didn't want me in the house.'

'What the hell's the difference?'

'Well. The difference is, one way I'm in the house. And the other way I'm out of it.'

'Excuse me. I think I better go have a talk with my boy.'

But Trevor was so sleepy all he could say was, 'Hi, Momma,' and, 'Is everything okay?' and when she told him Jerry was out in the driveway taking the truck apart he said, 'That's good.'

And she couldn't be upset with him. He was just like his father in that respect.

★   ★   ★

Because it is always so much easier to blow off steam to a stranger, she went down to Trevor's school to have a talk with this Mr St Clair. She went to the office first thing, before class started in the morning, hoping she would not even run into Trevor and that he would never have to know she'd been there. The office lady told her to go right up.

She got halfway through the door into his classroom, stopped, and misplaced all that good steam she had built up.

First of all – though it wasn't the most important part – he was black. She did not feel so very different about black people – it wasn't that. It was more that she tried so hard to bend over backward to show she wasn't like that. After a while it became hard to act natural. So she would try harder. And there you have a losing battle if ever there was one. Trying hard to act natural. That can have you chasing your tail until long after the sun goes down.

So, right off the bat it made him hard to yell at. He might think she fancied herself better than him, where really it was more that it was her boy, and also her tax dollars paying his salary. Any teacher's salary, that is.

So he looked up, and she still had nothing to say. Nothing. One hundred percent card-carrying speechless. And not mostly over any racial issues, either, but more because she had never seen a man with only half a face. It's one of those things. Takes a minute to adjust to. And she knew if she took even one minute more he would notice that she had noticed his unfortunate scarring, which would be just plain rude. This whole scene had all gone very smoothly in her mind on the way to school, where she had been angry, articulate, and really quite good.

She moved through the room toward his desk, feeling small, feeling like twenty-five years ago, when these desks were too big to fit her. And he was still waiting for something to be said.

'What's "Paying Forward?"'

'Excuse me?'

'That expression. "Paying Forward." What does it mean?'

'I give up. What does it mean?' He seemed mildly curious toward her, slightly amused, and as a result, miles above her, making her feel small and ignorant. He was a big man, and not only in physical stature, although that too.

'That's what you are supposed to tell me.'

'I would love to, madam, if I knew. If you don't mind my asking, who are you?'

'Oh, did I forget to say that? Excuse me. Arlene McKinney.' She reached her hand out and he shook it. Trying not to look at his face, she noticed that his left arm was deformed somehow, the wrong size, which gave her the shivers for just a second. 'My boy is in your social studies class. Trevor.'

Something came onto his face then, a positive recognition, which, being connected in some way to her boy, made her like this man better. 'Trevor, yes. I like Trevor. I particularly like him. Very honest and direct.'

Arlene tried for a little sarcastic laugh, but it came out a snort, a pig sound, and she could feel her face turn red because of it. 'Yeah, he's all of that, all right. Only, you say it like it's a good thing.'

'It is, I think. Now, what's this about Paying Forward? I'm supposed to know something about that?'

Actually, she'd been hoping for a laugh, a smile, something besides his businesslike manner; a bad sense was forming of Mr St Clair looking down his nose at her in some way she could never entirely prove. 'It has something to do with an assignment you gave out. That's what Trevor said. He said it was a project for your social studies class.'

'Ah, yes. The Assignment.' He moved to the blackboard and she swung out of his way, as though there were a big wind around him that kept her from getting too close. 'I'll write it out for you, exactly as I did for the class. It's very simple.' And he did.

THINK OF AN IDEA FOR WORLD CHANGE, AND PUT IT INTO ACTION.

He set his chalk down and turned back. 'That's all it is. This "Paying Forward" must be Trevor's own idea.'

'That's all it is? That's all?' Arlene could feel a pressure building around her ears, that clean, satisfying anger she'd come here to vent. 'You just want them to change the world. That's all. Well, I'm glad you didn't give them anything hard.'

'Mrs McKinney—'

'Miss McKinney. I am on my own. Now, you listen here. Trevor is twelve years old. And you want him to change the world. I never heard such bull.'

'First of all, it's a voluntary assignment. For extra credit. If a student finds the idea overwhelming, he or she need not participate. Second of all, what I want is for the students to reexamine their role in the world and think of ways one person can make a difference. It's a very healthy exercise.'

'So is climbing Mount Everest, but that might be too much for the poor little guy, too. Did you know Trevor has taken a bum under his wing and brought him into my house? This man could be a rapist or a child molester or an alcoholic.' She wanted to say more but was busy thinking that since she herself was an alcoholic, that might have been a bad example. 'What do you suggest I do about the problems you've caused?'

'I suggest that you talk to him. Lay down the house rules. Tell him when his efforts on this project conflict with your safety and comfort. You do talk to him, don't you?'

'What the hell kind of question is that? Of course I talk to him.'

'It just seems odd that you would come all the way down here to find out what "Paying Forward" is. When Trevor could tell you.'

Leaving the room was becoming a more and more appealing option. 'I guess this was a mistake.' Obviously nothing was being accomplished here, except for the on-going process that was making Arlene feel stupid and small.

'Miss McKinney?' His voice hit her back a few steps into a long stride to safety and freedom.

She almost kept walking, but like ignoring a ringing phone, it was too contrary to human nature. She spun around to face this man, whom she openly, immediately disliked, and not because of his face or his color, either.

'What?'

'I hope you'll forgive my asking this. But is Trevor's father dead?'

Arlene blinked as though she had been slapped. 'No. Of course not.' *I hope not.* 'Did Trevor tell you that?'

'No. He said something strange. He said, "We don't know where he is." I thought maybe he was being euphemistic.'

'Well, we *don't* know where he is.'

'Oh. Well, I'm sorry. I just wondered.'

Bewildered now, she struck for the door, and nothing could have stopped her. What a way to feel like a complete idiot.

Not only did she just admit that the father of her child hadn't so much as sent a Christmas card home, but now she'd have to go find a dictionary and look up the word 'euphemistic.' See what he'd just accused her son of being.

It better not have been an insult – that's all she could think.

From *The Diary of Trevor*

Sometimes I think this idea is gonna be so great. And maybe it is. But then other times I remember other things I thought would be great. Like when I was real young. Like ten or something. And now that I'm big I can see what a crock it is. So then I think, What if this all bombs out? Then Mr St Clair won't be all impressed with me. And then in a few years I'll look back and think, Boy, was I stupid.

It's really hard to know what's a good idea when you're growing and these ideas don't hold still and neither do you.

Mom hates Jerry. Which is funny, because he's a lot like Dad. Except Dad is cleaner. But if Mom would let Jerry in the house, he'd be cleaner too. Maybe if she didn't keep letting Dad in he'd look just like Jerry. Maybe, wherever he is, he already does.

Chapter Five

JERRY

He was just getting set to bunk down for the night, and there she was. Like the damn police. Or the landlord of a building whose cellar he might try to use for shelter. Like she'd made up her mind. He was a bug and she didn't want her damn place infested.

He'd just gotten done on the truck. Taking the engine loose. Not from its mounts, but unhooking all the smog and the wiring. All of which there was way too much of. Not like the old days. The way they made them anymore, like a piece of crap.

And he'd gone into the garage. Rolled out an old Oriental rug in a corner. Against a wall. Barely got his eyes closed.

She came in, flipped on the lights. Made him blink.

'It's only me, ma'am. Jerry. Just takin' a quick break. Just a nap. Then I'll get some more work done on your truck.'

'I know you been living here, in my garage.'

'No, ma'am. Just a quick nap.'

'Then where are you staying?'

'Down at the shop where I work. They let me sleep on the couch in the waiting room.'

'Get up. I'll drive you down there.'

Damn. There were two bad things about the way she treated him. One was, she was so damn pretty. Didn't look old enough to have a kid Trevor's age. Late twenties from the look. And real small and cute, built like a little doll. Until she opened her mouth. Personality like an amazon, someone ten times her size. But she was so damn pretty. If they were in a bar together and he had enough money on him to buy them both a drink . . . if things weren't like this, like they really were right now . . . it wasn't so out of the question. The other bad thing about her treating him like vermin was that he couldn't really hold it against her. Couldn't argue against it, because how? With what?

Getting into her car, her in the driver's seat, the dome light on as he got in beside her, he saw her face clear. Looking at her, he thought, You and me, we're not so very different, and maybe you know it. But he knew better than to say it out loud.

They drove in silence down the Camino, the main street of town. A ghost town at this hour. The street was long and deserted, with traffic lights changing color for no reason he could see.

'Damn good car you got here.' Old green Dodge Dart. Serve you forever if you took care of it. Hell, even if you didn't.

64

'That supposed to be some kind of sarcastic?'

'No, ma'am. I mean it for a fact. That slant six engine, best they ever made. Couldn't kill it if you tried.'

'You might want to, though. Sometimes.'

What you got out of her was always harder, colder than what you were set to expect. Pretty lady, though. Cute.

'I know you don't like me.'

'It's not that.'

'What, then?'

'Look. Jerry.' Standing at a red light, idling. Even though there was no one around. No one to go on the green while they waited. 'I'm trying to raise that boy on my own. No help from nobody. I can't watch him all the time.'

'I don't mean no harm to your son.'

'You don't *mean* none.' Light turned, squeal of her tires. Just hit the gas too sudden.

She pulled up in front of the Quicky Lube & Tune.

It was cold out there. He didn't want to get out. Kind of thought he wouldn't have to. Anymore. No more sleeping out in the cold. He didn't really have the key to the shop. Would never in a million years have told his bosses he needed that couch to sleep on.

'Thanks for the ride, ma'am.'

'I don't have anything against you personally. I don't.'

'Right. Whatever.'

He stepped out of the warm car. Into the wind. A minute later she was behind him.

'Look, Jerry. In a different world, who knows? We could have been friends even. It's just that—'

He spun around. She had to look at his face. Only for a second, then at his shoes. If only she wouldn't have looked at his shoes. He hadn't had enough money to replace the old sneakers. Saw a great pair of lace-up work boots but couldn't afford them. But tomorrow. Tomorrow would be payday. No, today. It was after 3 a.m. Later today, work boots.

'Pleased to hear you say that, ma'am. The way you been acting, I'da thought only one of us is people.'

'I never meant that.'

'Never *meant* it.'

She turned to go back to the car. He turned to watch her go. So they both saw it. Like a long streak, starting at the top of the sky. Drifting down, but fast. Lighting up the night like lightning. A ball of fire with a tail.

'Holy cow,' she said. 'Did you see that? What was that, a comet?'

'Meteor maybe, I don't know. When I was a kid, we used to call that a falling star. I used to think if you saw one, you'd get your wish. You know, like all your dreams'd come true?'

She turned back to look at him. All softness in her face. Maybe it had never occurred to her that bums used to be kids. Or wanted their dreams to come true, like everybody.

She said, 'Don't you hate moments like this?'

'What moments is those, ma'am?'

'When you get that feeling like we're all just the same?'

'No, ma'am. I like 'em.'

'Well, good luck.'

'Ma'am?'

'What?'

'I get my first paycheck today. And I'll go get a cheap room. Be out of your hair. Your boy won't be sorry he made the effort. I don't think you will either. I'll do just what I'm supposed to do. Pass it along, you know.'

She stood there a long time, like she was trying to decide whether to say something or not. And she said it. 'Will you explain to me about that? How that Paying Forward thing goes?'

He kind of blinked. 'Didn't he tell you?'

'I didn't exactly ask.'

From *Those Who Knew Trevor Speak*

So, I explained Paying Forward to her. I got me a stick. Sketched it out in the dirt. In the dark. We both had to squint to see. It was cold, but she had a choice. Could have been home in a warm house. That made a difference. How do I know why?

I drew them three circles. And explained them. Like the kid explained them to me. 'See, this one, that's me,' I said. 'These other two, I don't know. Two other somebodies, I guess. That he's gonna help. See, the trick is, it's something big. A big help. Like you wouldn't do for just anybody. Maybe your mother or your sister. But not nobody else. He does that for me. I got to do it for three others. Other two, they got to do for three others. Those nine others, they got to do it for three others. Each. That makes twenty-seven.'

Now, I ain't so good with math. But that kid, he worked it out. It gets real big real fast. Like you can't believe how fast. Up in the thousands in no time.

So I'm on my knees there. Drawing all these circles in the dirt. Counting by threes. Running out of dirt. You can't believe how fast. And you know, it happened again. And we both saw it. A big comet, or whatever. Did I mention about that first comet we saw? I guess I did. So we see another comet. Falling star. Falling, shooting, I don't know. But I ain't never seen two all in one night. It was kind of spooky.

We're looking at these circles, thinking this whole thing could be great. Except it won't be. Because, well, we all know it won't. Because people, they are no good. They won't really pay it forward. They will take your help, but that's all.

I know we were both thinking that. And then the sky lit up again. That big comet. The second one, I mean. I ain't sayin' there was a third. Maybe I made it sound that way. But two, anyway. That's a lot. Spooky.

You know, it's a big world out there. Bigger than we think.

Then she starts to tell me it's hard for her to talk to that kid. I couldn't believe it. Telling me. Me. She says he's just like his father that way. She hates to question him. Can't get mad at him. Don't want to seem like she don't trust him. So things just go by. She just lets 'em go by. She told me all this. It's like we were . . . I don't know . . . communicating. For the first time. About all kinds of stuff. It was so amazing. I told her I was gonna do big things. Maybe not big to somebody else. But from where I was. Get me an apartment. Drive a Dodge Dart. She said I could have hers. Dirt cheap. I told her again how it was payday. Payday. The day everything changes.

After a while it was all the same stuff we was saying. Over and over. But I liked it anyway. After a while she went home. But after that, the night was, like . . . different. Like . . . not so . . . you know . . . cold. Or something.

At nine-thirty he got his paycheck. Didn't have to stay and work that day or the next. So he took it to the bank.

Way over $100, cash in his hand.

Time to buy work boots.

He stood at the bus stop a while. Too long. But it was a nice day. He could walk down to the Kmart. Walking with all that money, that big lump in his pocket. And he'd earned it, too. A whole new day. Comets in the night, who knows?

Then he walked by Stanley's, that little bar he used to like. Thought a beer would go nice. Good day, pocket full of money. If you can't take a minute to celebrate over a beer, then why? Then what was it all for?

And he was right. It went down real nice.

Saw two of the guys, too. That he knew when he was mostly on his feet. And now he was on them again. And they never had to know otherwise. They wanted to know where he'd been. San Francisco, he said, because he'd always wanted to go there.

Bought them each a beer so they would know he could. So they would see that roll come out of his pocket, unfold real nice. Bought himself another so they would see he was in no hurry. No place he really had to be.

Yes sir. New day for sure.

They played a game of pool or two, for money. Then one of them phoned up Tito, a guy they used to know. Told him Jerry was loaded. Come on down.

He did, with some product.

Said to Jerry, 'I know you looking to buy. Don't tell me you don't got a taste for the stuff.'

'Not no more,' Jerry said.

'Oh, come on.'

So they played a few more games of pool. The other three went into the bathroom to fix. That didn't seem fair. They could and he couldn't, how is that fair?

I mean, what is the point, really? Why have a whole new world all caught up in rules? Where you can't even feel good. Have what you like. So he had another beer, and Tito came back out. And Jerry said maybe just a dime bag. Not enough to get in trouble on. Not so much that he couldn't afford the boots.

It was his day off. After all. Had to borrow a rig off Tito, didn't even have his own. Didn't know how much he missed that little sting, that needle sting, till he felt it again.

Then it was closing time. How could that be? It was just yesterday morning a minute ago. What day was it now?

Then it was a whole day later in a Denny's, drinking coffee. Hungry now, with stubble on his face. Sick. Feeling bad.

Breakfast, that would have gone good. But he couldn't have any. Because that cup of coffee had tapped him out.

Dug deep in his pockets twice, but it was no use. That money was all used up.

Chapter Six

REUBEN

When he arrived in his classroom on a Monday morning, Trevor was already seated. He'd taken a place in the front row, which he had never done before. They looked at each other briefly, Reuben sensing something unsaid on the boy's part.

'What's on your mind this morning, Trevor?'

'Mr St Clair? Are you married?'

'No. I'm not.'

'Do you ever wish you were?'

Reuben remembered Trevor's mother standing in his classroom, remembered something she'd said when he referred to her son as very honest and direct: 'Yeah, he's all of that, all right. Only, you say it like it's a good thing.' In fact, Reuben remembered Trevor's mother often. At odd moments, with no seeming connection, she would return in memory. How, like a little storm cloud, she'd blown into his classroom one morning.

'That's a hard question to answer, Trevor. I mean, there's marriage and then there's marriage.'

'Huh?'

'There are good ones and bad ones.'

'Do you sometimes wish you had a good one?'

'Okay, I give up. What's this all about?'

'Nothing. I just wondered.'

Mary Anne Telmin wandered in. Not surprising that she would be the next to arrive. She was the only other student that Reuben knew for sure had accepted his extra credit assignment, because she'd stayed after class one day and described it at great length. A recycling project. She was a cute, popular girl, very white, very potential cheerleader, about which Reuben tried to hold an open mind. But her approach to his class and assignment seemed insincere and staged, reminding him that Trevor's project remained secret.

And a good secret it might prove to be. Paying Forward. He should have asked about that before the rest of the class began to arrive, but Trevor's agenda had thrown him off his game.

After class Trevor filed out last and Reuben raised a hand to flag him down, opened his mouth to call Trevor's name. But once again Trevor proved quicker on the draw.

'I want to talk to you again,' Trevor said, turning and stopping in front of Reuben's desk. He jammed his hands deep into his pockets and waited until the last of the other students had gone. Little sweeps of his eyes and a slight rocking on his heels revealed something, but Reuben wasn't sure he could properly decipher it. A little nervousness maybe.

Finally, convinced that they were alone, Trevor said, 'My mom wants to know if you'll come to dinner tomorrow night.'

'She said that?'

'Yeah. She said that.'

And that little place in Reuben, the one he could never properly train, jumped up to meet her kindness, despite his caution. Maybe she didn't dislike him as much as he thought. But even Reuben's heart could sense when something didn't fit.

'Why does she want me to come to dinner?'

'I dunno. Why not?'

'She doesn't like me very much.'

'You met my mom?'

'I met her temper, yes.'

'Well . . . maybe she wants to talk about Jerry. My friend Jerry. He's part of my project. But she doesn't like him. At all. I think she wants you to help her, you know. Sort of work it out. About that.'

This invitation was becoming grounded now, in Reuben's mind, in something that made sense and fit with everything else he knew so far. 'Couldn't we have a little private parent-teacher conference here at school?'

'Oh. Here at school. Well. I asked her. But she said, you

know. She works so hard and all. Two jobs. She just said it would be nice if you could come over.'

'I guess that would be okay. What time?'

'Uh. I'll have to ask her. I'll let you know tomorrow.'

The following morning, early, just before his first class, it happened again. Lightning striking twice in the same place.

She was angry again, and Reuben wondered if she had ever settled down in between. He didn't even have to open his mouth this time, because her anger was all prearranged and complete, needing only to be delivered. Reuben admired that in her. Envied it, actually, maybe even felt tempted to ask for lessons. She'd be a good tutor in righteous indignation for people like Reuben, who had no natural talent in the field.

And she was pretty, but not the kind that made him hurt.

'Why did you tell my boy we had to meet at my house?'

'I didn't. I didn't say we had to meet at all.'

'You didn't?' She stopped in midcharge, obviously thrown, her anger a sudden liability, all fired up with no target. 'Trevor told me to make chicken fajitas because you were coming for dinner. Because you wanted to talk to me about his project.'

'Really?' Interesting. 'He told me that *you* invited *me* over for dinner, and he thought it was because you wanted to talk to *me* about his project.'

'Well, what the hell's he doing, then?' she said disconnectedly, as if Reuben were not in the room at all.

'Maybe he wants to talk to both of us about the project.'

'But why not here at school?'

'He said you work two jobs and it would be easier if I came to the house.'

'I'm here, aren't I?'

'I'm only telling you what he said.'

'Oh. Okay. Why's he trying to get you over, then?'

It would be a risk to say it, but Reuben guessed that he probably would anyway. It would get her going again, most likely, which was okay, because he didn't mind her anger. It was clean and open and you could always see it coming.

'Yesterday morning he asked me if I was married. And then he asked me if I'd like to be.'

'So?'

'I'm just speculating.'

'He was probably just curious. I'm telling you that kid don't never know when to keep shut.'

'I just thought . . .'

'What?'

'I just thought he might be trying to fix us up.'

'Us?'

She seemed to freeze in place, everything running across her face at once, waiting to be read. Another risk, another defacing for which he'd left himself open. Us? You must be joking.

'I realize we're the world's most unlikely couple, but after all, he is just a boy.'

He watched her stumble back up through herself, clumsily, to a place that could speak again. 'Trevor would never do such a thing. He knows his daddy is gonna come home.'

'Just speculating.'

'Why did you even say you would come to dinner?'

'I felt guilty after you left last time. You were asking me to help straighten out some problems that might have been caused by my assignment. I'm afraid I was a little dismissive.'

A beam of morning sun slanting through the window caught Arlene and made her brighter than anything else in the room. It glowed on a strip of bare midriff below her lacy tank top. Untanned, vulnerable skin, like a china doll's. Something fragile, relegated to the shelf for fear of breakage in handling. She appeared so vulnerable until she opened her mouth. 'I know you don't like me.' It was the last thing Reuben expected her to say, especially as he admired her. He felt transparent at almost all times, yet his intentions never seemed to be correctly read by those around him. Not even at close range.

'What makes you think that?'

She made that noise again, that rude little snort. 'You just said we're the most unlikely couple in the world. What does that mean, if you're not looking down on me?'

It means I assumed you were looking down on me. It means I knew you were thinking it, so I had to say it. But Reuben couldn't bring himself to give those answers, so she went on.

'You think I'm too stupid to see the way you look down

on me? Well, I may not have your education and I may not talk good like you, but that don't mean I'm stupid.'

'I never said you were stupid.'

'You didn't have to.'

'I never thought it either. It never occurred to me to wonder how much education you have. I think you're being overly sensitive.'

'What the hell would you know about what I'm feeling?'

'When it comes to oversensitivity, I'm something of an expert. Anyway, none of this was my idea, and if you don't want me in your house I won't come.'

'Uh, no. You know what? That's okay. Truth is . . .' Reuben knew from her pause, the strain in her face, that if she ever finished this sentence, she'd tell him something difficult. Something that was hard for her to say to anyone, but particularly to him. 'Truth is, I'm not doing so good talking to him about this. I could use the help. Six o'clock?'

From *Those Who Knew Trevor Speak*

I went to her house. It wasn't at all what I expected. Her house. Well, any of it, but I meant her house. And that made me examine my own expectations and admit that perhaps in some small way I *had* been guilty of looking down on her. Though God knows I never meant to.

It was a modest house, but scrupulously clean inside and out, and fussed over, and tended. No plant life growing over the walkway. Not a single streak on those white-trimmed windowpanes. Except for a wrecked truck in the driveway, every part of her home existence brought back an expression my mother used to use in reference to herself: house proud.

I never expected her to remind me of my mother.

The whole thing made me nervous. Her pride in her home reminded me of the pride that flew behind all that rage of hers. Which made me feel overmatched and overwhelmed, as if I'd relinquished strength by meeting on her home turf.

She answered the door looking distressingly nice. She was wearing this blousy, cottony dress in a flower print, as if she took dinner guests rather seriously. I stepped into her living room, holding flowers that I couldn't bring myself to give her. Frozen. Every part of me frozen. For the longest time neither of us could seem to talk about anything.

And then Trevor showed up, thank God.

As soon as Arlene cleared the dinner dishes from the table, Trevor ran to his room and got his calculator. He'd put off explaining his project all through dinner because, he said, it was too hard to explain without a calculator.

'This all started with something Daddy taught me.'

Arlene's ears perked up at that and she pulled her chair around, as if to watch the calculator over his shoulder.

'Remember that riddle he used to do? Remember that, Mom?'

'Well, I don't know honey. He knew a lot of riddles.'

Reuben's stomach felt warm and nicely full. He watched them both across the table, feeling surprisingly relaxed. The flowers he'd brought her sat in a vase on the table. Not roses – that would have been too personal, too much. A mix of dried flowers and sunny things, daisies and the like, which he'd presented with an apology for having made a bad first impression. Intended only as a friendly gesture, it had embarrassed her and made them both feel awkward. It had been a mistake, one he'd take back if he could, and every glance at them sitting in the porcelain vase reminded him that he could not.

'Remember that one about working for thirty days?'

'No, Trevor, I don't think I do.'

Their voices seemed a little distant to Reuben, who felt himself becoming disconnected from the scene in a subtle way.

'Remember, he said if you were going to work for somebody for thirty days, and you had a choice – you could take a hundred dollars a day, or you could take a dollar the first day, and then it would be doubled every day. I said I'd take a hundred dollars a day. But he said I'd lose out. So I worked it out on my calculator. A hundred dollars a day for thirty days is three thousand dollars. But if you double that dollar every day, you'd make over five hundred million on your last day. Not to mention everything between. That's how I thought of my idea for Mr St Clair's class. You see, I do something real good for three people. And then when they ask how they can pay it back, I say they have to *pay it forward*. To three more people. Each. So nine people get helped. Then those people have to do twenty-seven.' He turned on the calculator, punched in a few numbers. 'Then it sort of spreads out, see. To eighty-one. Then two hundred forty-three. Then seven hundred twenty-nine. Then two thousand, one hundred eighty-seven. See how big it gets?'

'But, honey. There's just one little problem with that.'

'What, Mom?'

'I'm sure Mr St Clair will explain it to you.'

Reuben jumped at the mention of his name. 'I will?'

'Yes. Tell him what's wrong with the plan.'

'I think your mother is upset because, even though it's good to want to help Jerry, she's . . . worried. About that situation.'

'No, no. Not that. Trevor, I know I gave you a hard time about Jerry, but then I had a long talk with him. And I might've been wrong about him. He's a pretty nice guy. Besides, I think he got a place to live. He hasn't been around for a few days.'

Trevor's forehead furrowed down and he clicked off the calculator. 'Actually. He sort of got arrested.'

'For what?' Arlene said suddenly, and sounding startled. Reuben saw, for a brief flash, her genuine disappointment, sensed some thin cord between her and this faceless man. Something that might have caused her, just for an instant, to be on Jerry's team.

'I'm not sure. I went by his work. They said he never came back after they paid him. They said he got picked up on some kind of violation.'

'Honey, I'm sorry. See, that is the very part Mr St Clair is about to explain to you.'

Reuben took his napkin off his lap and threw it on the table. This pattern between Arlene and her son – it had not only come deadly clear, it had come around to bite him. Here's Mr St Clair, son, to tell you all the things you don't want to hear. *I'm sorry, Miss McKinney. If you want your son to believe that people are basically selfish and unresponsive, you'll have to tell him so yourself.* He smiled tightly and shook his head, saying nothing.

She fixed him with a look that burned in silence, but he was not afraid of her anger, or so he intended to prove to them both; so he noted instead that her eyes were almost the same color of brown as her short, baby-fine hair.

'Well, Trevor,' she said. 'I think it's a good project. Tell us some more about it.'

So Trevor explained, with the help of his calculator, how big this thing could become. Somewhere around the sixteenth level, at which he'd involved 43,046,721 people, the calculator proved smaller than Trevor's optimism. But he was convinced that in just a few more levels the numbers would be larger than the population of the world. 'Then you know what happens?'

Arlene looked to Reuben but he didn't care to guess, wanting to hear it straight from Trevor's obviously active brain.

'No, honey. What?'

'Then everybody gets helped more than once. And then it gets bigger even faster.'

'What do you think, Mr St Clair?' Arlene clearly wanted something from him, but he wasn't sure from minute to minute what that something might be.

'I think it's a noble idea, Trevor. A big effort. Big efforts lead to good grades. How do you feel about the fact that Jerry got arrested?'

Trevor sighed. From the look on Arlene's face, Reuben had done his job correctly for a change.

'It's okay, I guess. Except I just have to start all over, is all. It's okay, though. I already got other ideas.'

'Like what, honey?' Arlene asked in that sugary voice she slipped into when questioning her own son.

'It's a secret. Can I be excused?'

Arlene caught Reuben's eye again, begging for something. As if she could not just say, No, young man, we are not done here. Reuben only shrugged.

'Okay, run along, then, honey.'

Trevor charged in the direction of his bedroom, but as he barreled by Reuben's seat, Reuben took him gently by the sleeve and pulled him over close enough that Arlene, on the other side of the table, hopefully would not hear.

'You can't orchestrate love, Trevor.'

'What's "orchestrate"?'

'You can't make it happen for somebody else.'

'Doesn't that have something to do with music?'

'Not always.'

'Oh. You can't, huh? I mean. Oh. Okay. That wasn't my idea, though. Anyway.'

'Just checking.'

Reuben loosed his sleeve and he disappeared.

Reuben looked up to see Arlene glaring across the table with that mixture of stress and anger and rocket fuel to which he was becoming nicely accustomed.

'What'd you say to him?'

'It's a secret. May I be excused?'

From *The Diary of Trevor*

Mom and Mr St Clair like each other. I just know it. What I can't figure out is, why don't they know it? It's right there, and I just feel like shaking them and saying, Oh, just admit it. Mr St Clair would be nice to her, I think. I think he'd give his entire heart to somebody who would say, You know, that's a nice half a face you got there. You know, like the glass is half full instead of, well, you know. He's sad about his face. I think if he wasn't, he could admit it better when he liked somebody. But then my mom has a great face and she's doing it too. Go figure.

What if the world really changed because of my project? Wouldn't that be the coolest thing? Then everybody would say, Who cares about his face, he's the best teacher in the world, that's what matters. That would be so cool.

I think the best shot I got now for my project is Mrs Greenberg. Jerry got arrested and Mr St Clair says you can't orchestrate love, which made it sound like I was trying to wave a baton around or something. But so far it looks like he's right.

But a garden. A garden holds still for all that orchestra stuff.

Chapter Seven

MRS GREENBERG

Her late husband, Martin, had believed in miracles, but the cancer took him just the same. Since he'd gone, she'd tried to bring that belief around again, thinking it to be natural to the family, divinely intended to live in her little blue-gray house.

And this evening, for the first time in years, it sat on the porch swing with her as she sipped her iced tea. It smiled for her and through her, and she smiled back.

A miracle in the shape of her garden.

Lately she'd begun to dream of waking up, stretching and flexing through the pain in her arthritic joints, easing to the window to discover that, as if by magic, the garden was once again whole. And now, in the dusk of a cool spring evening, the garden was whole. Trimmed, the grass mowed, beds laid with fresh cedar chips, freshly raked, bags of leaves and trimmings bundled at the curb, soon to be trash-day history.

Not an unexplained miracle, exactly, because she'd watched the neighbor boy do it all, day after day. Barely a head taller than he, she'd stood at his side and shown him the junctions at which rosebushes begged to be trimmed and the aphids to be sprayed, and the weeds that had to come out, and the ground cover meant to be cut back, watered, encouraged to flourish.

But miracles can and do have middlemen, she decided, and then she noticed that her iced tea tasted sweeter than usual that night, though made to the same proportions, and that the cold glass did not ache her arthritis the way it usually did.

And as if to dampen this perfect balance just the moment she'd discovered it, her son, Richard Green, came up the walk for his bimonthly visit.

How a woman named Greenberg had a son named Green was beyond her, but it was his legal name, though she would never call him by it. He had turned his back on the name of his father, her late husband, as if in shame, and the thought of it swept through her scalp the way a migraine would, every time, dividing her brain for the exquisite ache to follow. He walked like James Dean, or half like him, with all of the ego and none of the grace, and every time he came to visit he looked more and more like Elvis, with his big, unruly sideburns. Even on a cool spring night he wore those sleeveless muscle tees – unflattering to his hairy shoulders – and sunglasses, despite the fading light.

He'd been a smart boy, Richard, a brilliant boy, but seemingly with no payoff, unlike the neighbor boy, who appeared quite simple, and average in intelligence, yet seemed to prove otherwise with his very willingness to be where he was needed.

At forty-two, Richard was not a willing man, nor was he serious, unless anxious counts, and not particularly cheerful or helpful. But maybe intelligence is not associated with cheerful willingness; too bad she could not trade in Richard's intelligence at this late date. Seemed its only real purpose was to lose him every job he ever tried, being too good as he was for all of them. And she had no more money to lend him, and would not if she could.

He stood on her porch step, a cigarette tucked high in the crook of his first two fingers.

'Hi, Mom.'

'So? What do you think?'

'About what?'

'The garden.'

He spun on the heels of his two-tone leather boots and flipped his dark glasses up to the top of his thin hairline.

'Shit. You paid somebody. I told you I'd do it.'

'I didn't pay.'

'You did it yourself? Come on. You can't even make a fist.'

'The neighbor boy did it for free.'

'Very funny.'

'He did.'

'It must've taken hours.'

'He's been working for days. You haven't been around.'

'I told you I'd do it.'

'Yes. You told me. But you didn't do it.'

'Shit.'

He walked inside and flipped on the TV to a *M*A*S*H* rerun, and though she called after him to extinguish his cigarette, he failed to hear her or pretended not to.

And then, when she followed him in and sprayed all around the clean living room area with pine-scent Glade, he complained bitterly about the smell and said it made him cough.

At first he'd just come by to talk, and that was good enough, and Mrs Greenberg had never expected more.

She was right near the end of his paper route, which he changed around just a little so her house would be the very last. He'd leave his big, heavy old bicycle on its side on her lawn and bring the paper right to her door and knock, knowing as he did that it was a bother for her to go out after it. She was so pleased by his thoughtful attention that she always offered him a glass of cherry Kool-Aid, which she bought specially for him, and he'd sit at her kitchen table and talk to her. About school mostly, and football, and then a special project he had thought up for his social studies class, and how he needed more people he could help, and she said she had some gardening to be done, though she couldn't afford to pay much.

He said she wasn't to pay anything at all to him, and what she paid to others needn't be money, unless that was what she had plenty of. And then he drew some circles for her on a piece of paper, with her name in one, and told her about Paying Forward.

'It's like random acts of kindness,' she'd said, but he disagreed. It was not random, not at all, and therein lay its beauty, built right into the sweet organization of the deal.

It was a foggy Saturday morning when he came by, six o'clock sharp as promised, and they stood in the mist in the front yard, the blue-gray paint peeling from her worried little house, and the smell of damp in the air, and little drips from the oak trees overhead cool in her hair.

He touched the roses as if they were puppies with their eyes still closed, or rare old books edged in gold leaf, and she knew he'd love her garden and it would love him back. And that something was being returned to her which had been away too long and had kept too much of her away with it.

'How is the project going so far?' she said, because she could see it was important to him, a subject he liked to talk a lot about.

His brow furrowed and he said, 'Not so good, Mrs Greenberg. Not so good.' He said, 'Do you think that maybe people won't really pay it forward? That maybe they'll just say they will, or even sort of mean to, but maybe something'll go wrong, or maybe they'll just never get around to it?'

She knew it was a genuine problem in his mind, one of those Santa Claus crossroads of childhood that shape or destroy a person's faith forevermore, and this boy was too good to turn astray.

So she said, 'I can only in truth speak for myself, Trevor, and say that I really will get around to it, and take it every bit as seriously as I know you do.'

She could still remember his smile.

He worked so hard that day, and wouldn't even stop for a Kool-Aid break but once, and when he finished she tried to slip a five-dollar bill in his hand, above and beyond and in no way connected to paying it forward, but he wouldn't hear of it.

He worked all weekend, and four after-school and after-paper-route days on the garden, and said next week he would come around and paint her fence and window boxes and porch railing with two fresh coats of white.

She wondered if her son, Richard, would notice the difference.

She walked to the grocery store slowly, loosening her tight joints and muscles as they warmed to the strain. Just to get out of the house. Imagine the sadness in that, when your son comes to visit and you mostly wish to be somewhere else.

It was late dusk on the Camino, with the car headlights glowing spooky in the half-light as she pulled her little two-wheeled wire cart behind her over the sidewalk cracks. Mrs Greenberg always took the same route to the same store, being comforted by sameness.

Terri was working as a checker that evening and Matt as

a bagger, two of her favorite people in the world. No more than twenty, either one of them, but quick with a smile for an older woman, no condescension, always thinking to ask about her day, her arthritis, and still listening when she gave the answer.

She bought twelve cans of cat food and a five-pound bag of dry cat chow, for the strays who counted on her, and cherry Kool-Aid for the boy, and Richard's favorite brand of beer, and tea and skinless chicken breasts and bran cereal for herself.

All the while thinking, Terri and Matt, that's two who probably could be counted on to pass it along, and maybe that nice lady at the North County Cat Shelter would make a fitting third. Richard would have a cow, but maybe tough love was just what he needed, and with that thought fresh in her mind, she returned to the cooler and put his beer back on the shelf. He could drink Kool-Aid or iced tea, or go home and take his smoke and his money problems with him.

'Good evening, Mrs Greenberg,' Terri said, running the groceries across the scanner. 'I drove by your house today. The garden looks wonderful.'

It pleased her in an uplifting way, like a dance with a good-looking boy in high school, that someone besides herself should notice and care.

'Isn't it wonderful?' she said. 'Trevor McKinney did all that. Such a good boy. Do you know him?'

Terri didn't imagine that she did, but it obviously pleased her to see Mrs Greenberg so beaming, and Matt too, who mirrored back her own smile as he bagged her cat food.

He had one of those modern hairstyles, Matt, a handsome boy with hair shaved high up onto his scalp, and longer on top, but always clean, with a fresh look to say, I'm modern, not a punk.

'Nice to see you so happy tonight, Mrs Greenberg.' He loaded her little cart carefully so it would balance just right.

It would be nice to see Matt happy, too, though by design she would not be around to see it. Young people needed a little nest egg, for college maybe, though it would not be enough for tuition, maybe books and clothes, or whatever they might choose to spend it for, because she felt they could both be trusted.

And that nice lady at the cat shelter, she would put it right back into spaying and neutering and other vet costs. No doubting her priorities.

Yes, she thought, back out in the crisp, clean-smelling night. It's right. She'd make the calls first thing in the morning.

Her chest first began to hurt on the way home. Not her heart, but more her lungs, like a bad congestion, and she stopped often to catch her breath. She was not such an old woman, she had to remind herself, just over retirement age, but since losing Martin her body seemed to turn in on itself, as though it couldn't wait. As though her immunities no longer cared to protect her but meant to hasten her along.

94

The arthritis had tripled its hold since then, and she'd catch any little thing that was going around.

Stopping often to rest, she took a detour, which she never did, by Trevor McKinney's house. Such a nice little house, with a curvy shingle roof, heavy with vegetation but never overgrown looking. Too bad about that twisted, awful thing in her driveway looking like the spooky remains of an ugly death on the highway. Mrs Greenberg imagined his mother must want it gone, want the simple beauty of her place back, maybe even dreamed of it the way she herself had dreamed for her garden.

They had company tonight, she saw, stopping for breath at the walkway. A white Volkswagen Beetle, nicely cared for, parked out front. A new boyfriend. Good. She'd seen the old one, didn't think much of the type.

And she could see, through the window, into the brightly lit dining room, the right side of his face in profile. A well-dressed black man, so handsome and refined.

Well, good, then. Good for them.

Mrs Greenberg hoped Trevor's mother wouldn't listen to anybody, wouldn't let any small minds get in her way. They had tried to tell her not to marry Martin, because he was a Jewish boy, but she wouldn't listen, and he'd been the best husband a woman could ask for. A good man is a good man.

Maybe Trevor's mother would get married. Nice for the boy if she did. She'd never met Trevor's mother but knew she would like her, because look what she had produced with her own womb and her loving care. A boy who could

95

love a garden for a sick, arthritic woman who couldn't love it enough.

'You have a good woman there,' she said quietly, out loud, to the handsome, refined man in the window, who of course did not hear. 'A good woman with a good boy. You take care of them. I know you will.'

When she arrived home at last, winded and sore chested, Richard was blissfully gone.

She took a hot bath and laid herself, coughing, to bed, knowing that whatever happened now, the garden was tended. The porch would take a coat of paint. Tomorrow she'd make some calls, some arrangements. After that it didn't matter.

Even if the thing that latched onto her next was a bad one – pneumonia, or the Asian flu. Even if she couldn't pull through this time, it wouldn't matter. Everything was tended, or would be by then.

Sleep felt heavy and all consuming, like the comforting mouth of death as she imagined it, holding as it did her Martin and a long, much-deserved rest.

Chapter Eight

ARLENE

She slipped in to say good night to Trevor the minute Mr St Clair left. And he didn't leave a moment too soon. What was it, anyway, about that man that always made her feel she was missing the boat on something, and why couldn't she shake the notion that he was doing it on purpose?

Trevor lay on his bed, doing homework in his lap.

'Gotta go to work, honey. You still got the number by the phone?'

'Sure, Mom.'

'And Loretta's?'

'Know it by heart. You know I'm not scared. I never am.'

'I know, honey. But I am.'

'I'm a big kid, Mom.'

'You sure are, honey. That you are.'

She sat on the edge of his bed combing curly strands of hair off his forehead with her fingers. She knew he probably didn't like it, smacking as it did of the preening one gives a much younger child, but he did not complain.

He looked so much like his daddy it was spooky, even with his eyes cast down, and if he'd raised them right at that moment to look into her own, she might have had to look away. He never did, though.

'Honey?'

'Yeah, Mom?'

'You weren't trying to . . .'

'What?'

'No. Never mind. I gotta go.'

'No, really. What?'

'You weren't trying to . . . like . . . fix me up with Mr St Clair. Were you? I was pretty sure you weren't.'

Those Ricky eyes came up to find her and she somehow didn't pull away. 'Why? Don't you like him?'

It hit her in the stomach like a fastball, something she could really feel, to know that he had. Even though she wasn't sure why it should seem so important. And then, looking down at Trevor's homework, she saw the sheet of paper with Trevor's idea sketched out on it. Circles like the ones Jerry had drawn in the dirt, between comets, when they both believed for a flash of a moment that a life could really change.

Or maybe even two lives.

The circles were blank, all except the top three. The first wave. One had Jerry's name written inside, then scratched out, which made Arlene suddenly, overwhelmingly sad, as if his chance had gone up just that quickly. The second said

98

Mr St Clair, also scratched out, which also made her feel something, though she could neither name it nor get along with it. The third said *Mrs Greenberg*, which thankfully meant nothing at all. At least this Mrs Greenberg wasn't on her way over with flowers – at least, not as far as Arlene knew.

Her own words didn't sound quite right at first. 'Well, actually, Trevor, no. I don't think I do like him. He makes me kind of nervous. Why? Do you like him?'

'Yeah. Sure I do.'

'Why?'

'I don't know. I think it's because you can say things to him. And then he says things back. Just real simple like that. Whatever you think of, you can just say. That's good, right?'

'Well, I guess so, but . . . honey, I just don't get why you would do that.'

'I think he's lonely, Mom. And I know you are. And you always said you don't judge people by how they look.'

'No. That's right. You don't.' She learned so much from these little talks with her son. He always swore he'd learned it from her and was only mirroring it back, but somehow the wisdom of her own advice surprised her as it came out of his mouth, and left her wondering if she was wise enough to heed it. It happened this way every time. 'And it's not that at all, honey, it's not about looks in any way, it's just that, well, you know as well as anybody that your daddy'll be back one of these days.'

He didn't answer at first, just looked up at her with an

expression that crystallized like ice around her diaphragm and made it hard for her to breathe. If pressed to put words to it, she'd be tempted to call it a look of pity, but surely he hadn't meant it to be as harsh as all that. 'Mom.' She so didn't want to hear the next thing he'd say, but felt too tongue-tied to stave it off. 'Mom. It's been more'n a year.'

'So?'

'Mom. He's not coming back.'

And she'd been so careful to never let those words pollute her home, not even in the chasm of her own tired brain, not even in the silence of four o'clock in the sleepless morning. But now here they were, having to be fought with desperate means.

So Arlene did something she'd never done, not in twelve years; she raised the back of her hand to her own son and cracked him across the mouth. She tried to stop the hand before it quite hit home, but it was too mindless by then, too bent on relief, or maybe the signal didn't go through in time.

He looked at her without recrimination, without adding one tiny stick of kindling to the shame that already threatened to burn her at the stake.

She'd never hit Trevor, promised herself she never would.

And then, to make matters worse, so unequipped was she to deal with her own shame that she spun on her heels and left him alone.

★　　★　　★

The smoke made her eyes burn, like it did every working night of her life, like it had since the truck had come home alone and unusable, unsalable, but still fully financed.

Conway Twitty blasted on the jukebox, which she didn't like one bit, and which, relieved only by loud voices and the clinking of beer bottles, seemed to add to her already foul mood.

The sound of bottles, the smell of beer – it was one tiny step from all she could take, every night. Now and then she'd get a whiff of it, taste that first cold slug in her mouth, so real, so clear, without ever meaning to imagine it, without any warning whatsoever. Twenty days it had been, and every night seemed harder than the night before.

Half the time she'd call Bonnie at 3 a.m., wake her out of a sound sleep, and Bonnie would say, 'Girl, quit that damn job,' but that was easy for Bonnie to say, because where was Arlene supposed to find another one?

Frustrating as all hell it was, the whole deal, and she hated herself like crazy for taking it out on her boy.

Hitting might have been in her blood now, like a dog who's killed his first chicken and so acquired the taste. Because every time that loud redneck with the beard and tattoos leaned out of his booth and patted her butt, the back of her hand wanted to forget itself one more time, only this time it would be wonderful. And he did it every time she passed his booth. Her eyes kept darting to the clock, hoping for a moment free to call Trevor before he fell asleep, but that moment wouldn't seem to come.

And if one more time she had to scream to be heard over

the din, if one more time she had to ask for an order to be screamed again, only to hear it no better than the time before, well, she just didn't know what she would do. She wanted to know what she would do, but really there was nothing.

Years ago, maybe then. 'Options' was not such a useless word. But now there was the boy to think about. Suicide, homicide, telling the boss to shove it, they were all off the menu for years, maybe forever. Still, she could have gotten by on one job if not for that damn truck.

And then she screwed up the order for table nine. Bud, Coors, what the hell was the big difference anyway for a table of slobs too drunk to taste?

She sidled up behind Maggie, said she was taking five, bad timing or no. She hated to work with Maggie, nice a girl as she was, helpful and sweet as she was, because Maggie was a big, horsey girl, built funny, whom nobody wanted to pinch, leaving more insult for Arlene to duck and bear.

She used the phone in the kitchen, an overwhelming freeway of body traffic, usually the same few bodies, none of whom seemed to mind the shimmery heat over the fryer or the smell of hot grease near as much as she did.

Trevor picked up on the fourth ring, right before her cardiac arrest set in. 'Honey. You okay?'

'Sure, Mom. I'm always okay.'

'Were you asleep?'

'Not yet. I'll go in a minute, though. I was reading that World War Two book.'

'Trevor, I am so sorry. I mean, I am just so, so sorry. I mean, I am so ashamed that I hit you, I just cannot say.' She paused, hoping for something, anything, that would relieve her of the duty to continue. 'If there's ever anything I can do to make it up. Anything at all.'

'Well.'

'Anything.'

'I don't think you'd go for it.'

'Anything.'

'Will you take me to visit Jerry?'

Wow. That big, huh? Don't you hate moments like this, she'd said to Jerry, where it seems that we're all pretty much the same? No, Jerry liked them. Apparently another moment Arlene hated was on its way home. The kind in which you see the person who let you down bad, really messed up everything, and right there in his eyes is you. All you see is the same disappointment and stress you know yourself, nothing to explain how a well-intentioned person could cause all that harm.

Like when Ricky came around after reconciling with his wife, Cheryl, a hateful, miserable thing to do, and he looked like the same man around the eyes, only a little more tired, a little more worried and beaten down.

'Do you even know where he is, honey?'

'We could find out.'

'Okay. Okay, I will, but I gotta get back to work now, Trevor. You be a good boy. Brush your teeth.'

'Mom.'

And Arlene hung up quickly, saved from having to admit

103

she treated him like a three-year-old every time she left him alone at night.

The swinging kitchen door opened at the strike of her shoulder, opened to the sound of Randy Travis too loud and the smell of beer and sweaty men too strong. Hours too long, paychecks too small. Never enough sleep. *Just hold on till three, Arlene.* And then, in the wake of that wisdom, try not to notice that it's an impossible world away, and when and if it ever does come, it will only lead to tomorrow, another working day. Another no-beer day.

The woman in the front cubicle of the county jail wore her blood red nails so long she had to type with the eraser end of a pencil. She sat with her legs crossed, in a tight, short skirt, chewing her gum with clicking sounds Arlene found irritating. Arlene tightened her grip on Trevor's shoulder.

'Name?'

'Arlene McKinney.'

'And you're here to visit . . .'

'Jerry Busconi.'

'Can I see some ID, please?'

Arlene slid her driver's license across the counter, which she hated to do because the picture made her look so bad. In fact, she thought the woman might have smirked a tiny bit at her expense, though she knew she probably imagined the slight after all.

'Wait in there, please,' the woman said, sliding the license back and gesturing with one amazing nail.

It seemed like a simple enough request. Until Arlene tried. And discovered that she and Trevor would not wait alone, as she had imagined, but in a room filled with dirty children, a snoring old man with his mouth open. Women with ankle bracelets, real or tattooed, teeth stained with tobacco and eyes stained bloodshot with disillusionment. And shy women who looked at the floor as if waiting to be hit, with fussy babies and runny-nosed toddlers.

And no more chairs. But a promise is just that, so she stood with Trevor in a corner, clutching at his sleeve, and wondered if these people would think Jerry was her husband, and if so, why she minded so much that they would.

Ten minutes ticked by, each feeling like a day, then they were allowed into a room with a long table, a long line of chairs, Plexi-glas dividers, and telephones. Just like in the movies. Men in two-piece orange suits filed in on the other side, picked up their phones, and women cried and held their hands to the glass just like in the movies.

A few more long minutes.

No new prisoners, no Jerry, just more waiting, more holding Trevor's arm, maybe tightly enough to hurt.

A guard shuffled by behind the divider, behind the row of men Arlene wished were not so familiar around the eyes. She leaned forward and tapped on the glass, and the uniformed man picked up the phone. 'Problem?'

'What happened to Jerry Busconi?'

'He's not coming out.'

'What do you mean, he's not coming out? My son and I came all the way down here to visit him.'

'Can't make him take a visitor. Said he wasn't in the mood.'

Wasn't in the mood. Jerry Busconi wasn't in the mood to see the boy who was always in the mood to give him all the proceeds of his own hard after-school work. Mood, it takes. That's rich. Yeah, that's a good one. 'Can I leave a note?'

'Front desk.'

'Thanks.'

Jerry,

I cannot bring myself to say dear because right at the moment you are not dear to me at all. I can forgive you for getting busted because we all screw up and I am no exception. But this little boy who helped you and counted on you came down here to see how you were, and you were not in the mood. Which I think makes you eighteen different kinds of chicken shit.

It's always easy to get mad on his behalf, in fact it's sort of a specialty of mine, but truth is I'm mad at what you did to me, too. Telling me all your hopes and dreams so I couldn't not like you, because this would be a whole lot easier if I had never liked or trusted you, but you have taken even that small comfort away from me.

I don't trust many people, and then when I make an exception, seems it's always the wrong one.

Get your sorry butt out of this place as soon as you can and then do what you said you would do for my boy, and his school project, which is very important to him.

But you won't, I know, because you are a hop-head, which I could forgive, because people can change, even though it seems they never do, but if you can't face us today, that says a lot about what you will do later.

I don't believe in shooting stars, and if I ever had, I would not believe in them no more, and that is what you have done to this family.

Think about that while you're doing prison laundry at the state pen, where they say you are going on the next bus out.

My boy would like to write something on this note when I'm done, which I am.

Arlene McKinney

Hi Jerry,

Hope you are okay and the food is not too terrible. Do you get to watch TV? Will you write me a letter from the state pen? Nobody ever did before.

Well, gotta go. Mom's pissed.

Your friend,
Trevor

From *The Diary of Trevor*

I wonder where people go when they die. They have to go somewhere. Right?

I mean, it would be just too weird to think about Mrs Greenberg not being anywhere. That would just be too sad.

So, I've decided that she's still out there somewhere. Because I've decided I can think whatever I want about it. Because I've noticed that everybody thinks something different about it. So I figure that means you can think what you want.

Course that means I'm gonna have to keep that garden real nice. And the cats! Geez! I just thought. Somebody's gonna have to keep feeding all those wild cats. I wonder how much cat food costs.

Anyway. You know what? Even this way, it's still sad.

Chapter Nine

REUBEN

He'd been in this house for three months, but nothing was unpacked. Almost nothing. The big bed was set up, made, and comfortable, so he spent a lot of time on it, grading papers, eating off his lap, and watching the news.

He made his way through the sea of boxes to the kitchen, took a small carton of ice cream out of the freezer, and proceeded to eat standing up, right out of the carton, with a plastic spoon, the cat weaving around and through his legs. It made him feel lonely, but then, so did unpacking.

The phone rang and proved difficult to find.

It was Trevor.

'Is it okay that I called you at home? I got the number from information.'

'Is something wrong, Trevor?'

'Yeah.'

'Are you in some kind of trouble? Is your mother there?'

'It's nothing like that. I'm okay. It's just my project. It's not going so good. At all. It just got a lot worse. Something bad happened. Can I talk to you about it?'

'Of course you can, Trevor.'

'Good. Where do you live?'

Reuben hadn't expected that. He let the receiver slip down and looked around. 'Maybe I could meet you somewhere, Trevor, like the park. Or the library.'

'It's okay. I'll ride my bike over. Where do you live?'

So Reuben gave him the address, on Rosita, just off San Anselmo, thinking as he did that this was not the fifties, where public trust was such that a student could go into a teacher's home without anyone getting a crazy and wrong idea. But he had not thought it through fast enough or well enough, because Trevor was off the phone and on his way.

They could talk on the front porch.

To be extra safe, he called Trevor's mother, who was listed in the phone book, to explain where Trevor was and why. She wasn't home, and Reuben had no idea if she worked on Saturdays, but he left a message on her answering machine. Just in case.

Then he looked down and realized he was in sweats, and unshaven. He managed to change into clean jeans and a white shirt and shave before Trevor arrived. It didn't take very long. He grew beard only on the right side of his face.

★   ★   ★

Trevor dumped his bike on its side on Reuben's lawn. Reuben realized he had never seen Trevor upset, so far as he knew.

He stood on the bottom porch step in khaki shorts and a 49ers T-shirt. 'Mrs Greenberg died.'

'I'm so sorry, Trevor,' he said, offering the boy a straight-backed chair on the porch. 'Come sit down and tell me about her. Who she was to you.'

'She was for my project. She was, like, my last chance.' Then he stopped himself, as if ashamed, and took the chair offered him. 'That didn't sound right. I didn't mean I was upset about my project. I mean, when she died and all. It's not that. It's both. I mean, she really was going to pay it forward. She told me. And then she died. I went over to her house this morning. I always take the paper right up to her door. But the last couple days, it's like she's not home. But she's always home. So today it was Saturday, so I just waited. And then the mailman came, and he said she hadn't taken the mail out of her box for three days. He said her monthly check was in there and it wasn't like her not to get it right away. So then we knocked on her neighbor's door, and they called her son, and he came over and opened the door. And she was in bed, just like she was sleeping. Only she wasn't sleeping. She was dead.'

Trevor stopped for a breath.

This was a difficult moment for Reuben. Any moment that required him to be emotionally helpful, to offer solace or understanding, was a hard moment. Not that he didn't have any. Just getting it from the inside of himself to the inside of someone else, that was the tricky part.

'I'm sorry, Trevor. That must have been hard for you.'

'The project is almost due. Jerry got sent to the state pen. He wouldn't even come out when we went to visit. And my mom still thinks my daddy is gonna come back. The whole thing is a bust, Mr St Clair.'

'I'm not sure I follow the part about your mother.' He halfway did but hoped Trevor might elaborate.

'Oh. Well. It doesn't matter. But what am I gonna do for my project?'

Reuben shook his head. It hurt to watch the idealism get kicked out of somebody. Almost as much as it had hurt when he'd lost his own. 'I guess you just report your effort. I'm grading on effort, not results.'

'I wanted results.'

'I know you did, Trevor.'

He watched the boy pick at a seam on the cuff of his shorts.

'I didn't just want a good grade. I really wanted the world to get better.'

'I know you did. It's a tough assignment. That's part of its lesson, I'm afraid. We all want to change the world, and sometimes we need to learn that it's harder than we think.'

'I really do feel bad about Mrs Greenberg, though. She was a nice lady. I don't think she was really old. I mean, sort of old. But not that old. We used to talk.'

Reuben looked up to see an old green Dodge Dart pull up to the curb and Arlene McKinney step out. It twisted into an already sore place in his gut to see her unexpectedly.

She was the closest he'd come to a date in years, a failed attempt at romance, but he'd never intended to put himself in that position and neither had she. It hadn't been a real date, but now the awkwardness was real.

He watched her march up the walkway, up the steps to his porch. Purpose plastered on to cover human frailty. All outward confidence. And it struck him then, for the first time, how much alike they really were.

I know you don't like me, she'd said. I know you're looking down on me. So there it was. He acted defensive toward her because he assumed she found him ugly. She acted defensive toward him because she assumed he found her stupid.

It was such a stunning moment he wanted to share it with her. In that split second he felt he might have been able to communicate this realization, if they'd been alone.

He couldn't remember the last time he'd seen himself in someone else. It changed him, this simple observation, like being jostled off the edge of a tall building, causing him to wonder if it was too late to get his old isolation back.

'Now, Trevor,' she said. 'I bet Mr St Clair's got better things to do than hear about your troubles on a nice Saturday morning like this one. You can talk to *me*, you know.'

'You weren't home.' Trevor studied his scuffed high-tops.

'I didn't mind, Miss McKinney. Really. I just wanted you to know where he was.'

'Well, I thank you for that, but we'll just be going now.'

She motioned with a hand to her son, who followed her off the porch obediently.

'Arlene.' He hadn't known he was about to call her back, had never intended to use her first name. She must have been surprised too. She spun around, looked at him for the longest time. Really looked at him, as though seeing something she hadn't seen before. Which she was. And it made him uncomfortable to feel so transparent.

'Trevor, wait for me in the car,' she said quietly, and rejoined Reuben on the porch.

She stood strangely close. Reuben's chest felt heavy with the expectancy of the moment. The notion that he could express his revelation was gone now; still, he had no choice but to try.

'When you first met me. And you thought I was looking down my nose at you. I just want you to know something.'

She waited patiently, face slightly turned up to him. She reflected a pleasant expectance. She didn't dislike him. She just wanted him to like her. It was right there on her face.

'I have a hard time meeting people. I'm very sensitive about— Well. I tend to think I repel people. I mean, I do. But. I was being defensive. That's what I'm trying to say. I wasn't looking down on you. I was being defensive because I thought you were looking down on me.'

'Really?' A skinless, unguarded question.

'Really.'

'Well, thank you. That's nice.' She moved to the porch rail, glanced at the car and her waiting son. 'No, really, that's nice. I appreciate that you told me that. It's kind of funny, really. I mean, here we are being all cold to each other. You don't think I'm dumb? Really?'

'Not at all.'

'I don't talk good like you. Talk well, I mean. I could, I guess. I know how to talk right. I just sorta got out of the habit. Maybe you could come over for dinner again some night.'

'Maybe.'

Maybe? Reuben felt surprised to hear himself say it. Maybe. Actually, he'd wanted to say no. Now that she had turned her eyes up to him, hopeful and childlike, flattered to win his approval, he could not get far enough away from her.

She stared at him for a moment, then marched purposefully back to her car and drove off without comment.

So. There it is, Reuben thought, his mind caught in a brand of resigned irony. There it was, there it goes.

What a relief, to know that nothing ever really changes.

From *The Other Faces Behind the Movement*

My friend Lou, from Cincinnati, was gay. We'd go out for a beer and talk sometimes, in the evening, about our respective problems. Lou's problem was he had a bad habit of falling for guys who were not. Gay, that is. And my problem was I tended to be . . . what's the word I'm searching for? Picked up, befriended, latched on to, by attractive women who liked me and found me safe. Safe.

115

That's just how every lonely, sexually deprived man wants a woman to see him, right? Safe. They'd ask me out to the movies, to dinner. Exactly like dating. If it differed in any way from dating, I'd like someone to explain how. At the end of the evening I'd get a kiss on the cheek. Always the same cheek.

The hormones would rage. In me, that is. And right around the time I was hopelessly, relentlessly in love and having trouble hiding it, she would say something along the lines of, 'I like you as a friend, Reuben. We have such a nice friendship. Let's not spoil it.' Nice women, in most cases, so I had to assume they had no idea how cruel they had been. Because if any one of them had been monster enough to do that much damage on purpose, I think I would have known.

Anyway, Lou and I tipped a few one night. I didn't even know he was gay at the time. I told him the easiest stories to tell, older, less painful. The kind you can laugh at just a little because those 'years to come' have already come. 'You have no idea how that feels,' I said, not realizing who I was saying it to. 'Nobody does. To have that depth of emotion for someone and to know that they would find your feelings utterly repulsive.'

And Lou laughed and ordered another beer, and told me a story of his own. And then I knew. And I knew as well that he knew how it felt.

'Why straight guys?' I asked.

He shrugged. 'I don't know. There're just so damn many *more* of them.'

116

I got quiet for a long time, and then I said, 'Lou. You didn't mean me, did you? You weren't saying you had those feelings about me?'

Not that I would have been repelled if he had – I certainly wouldn't have stopped being his friend – but I needed to know, to be sure I wasn't being insensitive without realizing.

'Hell no, Reub,' he said. 'You're way too ugly for me. I think we should just be friends.'

'Well, good. That would have been utterly repulsive.'

We got to laughing then, and the sound of his laughter when he got going was so funny and silly it made me laugh just to hear it. I'd try to stop, but just when I'd get it under control, he'd break up again and we'd go for another round.

And then we fell serious, just like that, and I was so tired, more tired than I'd ever been in my life, and I wanted to go home. As if all of a sudden I realized: it's not so goddamned funny.

That should have been a safe, comfortable end to everything, but the following Thursday evening he ran into her at the market. Just dropped into a longish line with his ice cream and his TV dinners and found himself looking at the back of her head.

It seemed to Reuben as though one could look at the back of someone else's head quietly, without being noticed, but apparently he did it wrong, because she immediately turned around.

'Oh, you,' she said, and that was it. She turned back, and they both waited in excruciating silence, watching Terri and Matt scan and bag groceries, as if finding their simple movements fascinating.

She looked briefly over her shoulder at Reuben on her way out of the store.

Then she was gone, and he breathed deeply, a man just having found his way to safety from grave and immediate danger.

He found her in the parking lot, leaning on his car.

'You know what your problem is?' she said.

It was the old Arlene, and it felt good to Reuben to have her back, that little lightning bolt of indignation all ready to read him the riot act about one thing or another.

'No. I don't. What is my problem?'

'Your problem is, you're so quick to think nobody wants you, you don't even give 'em a chance. I couldn't reject you if I tried. You're too fast for me.'

'Thank you, Arlene. That was very informative.'

He moved for his driver's door, and she peeled away, out of his trajectory, as he knew she would. He set his groceries on the passenger seat, got in, and slammed the door. But she wasn't gone. She stood by his window as he fired up the little engine, and before he could drive away she tapped on the glass.

He rolled the window halfway down.

'So,' she said. 'You want to go out, or what?'

'Yes and no.'

'What the hell kind of answer is that?'

'The honest kind. What do you want me to say?'

'I want you to say, "I'm not doing nothing on Sunday night, Arlene. Maybe you and me could take in a movie or something."'

Reuben sighed. He put the Volkswagen in gear, popped it out again. 'Arlene, would you like to go to a movie this Sunday?'

He didn't mean it to, but it came out sounding petulant, like a little boy who's just been ordered to apologize when he wasn't feeling one bit sorry.

'Yes, I would. But I bet I'm gonna be sorry I ever started with this.'

'I'll put a couple of dollars on that, too,' Reuben said, but he was half a block away before he said it.

Chapter Ten

ARLENE

Loretta sat in Arlene's kitchen, drinking coffee and brushing tons of thick blond hair back from her forehead. Arlene figured if she had that much hair she'd fool around with it too, but she never would, and also that she could be a blonde just as easy as Loretta but would prefer to go along with what nature intended.

Arlene said, 'Did I mention he's black?'

Loretta said, 'No.'

'Oh. He's black.'

'So?'

'I don't know. I just mentioned it.'

'Do you care?'

'I don't know. No. I just mentioned it, is all. I told you about his face, though.'

'More times than I could count. That bothers you.'

'No. Not really. At first, maybe.'

'Coulda fooled me.'

'After a while, I just kinda got used to it. I don't think about it much anymore.'

'But what about when you're, like, close, though? Does it bother you then?'

Arlene jumped out of her chair to wash her cup in the sink, even though half the coffee was still in it, waiting to be drunk. Over her shoulder she said, 'Well. To be real honest with you. We ain't never been that close.'

'What about when he kisses you?' Loretta waited patiently for her answer; in fact, Arlene was surprised by how long it took her to give up. 'You ain't gonna tell me you never kissed him.'

'I ain't?'

'You been out with him four times. Don't you think that might start to hurt his feelings after a while?'

'Well, I know you won't believe this, Loretta.' She dumped her coffee and sat back down, leaning close and talking low, a girl-type conspiracy. 'It's not me that's holding out.'

'You're right. I don't believe you. Say. Now, don't get this question wrong. I ain't dared to ask it yet. What you dating this guy for, anyway? You give up on Ricky?'

'Of course not.'

'Why, then?'

'Why do you think? How can you even ask me that? It's been over a year, Loretta. Don't you think I got needs? Besides, serves Ricky right if he comes back and I been with somebody else. It's what he gets.'

Loretta rocked back in her chair, more dramatically than was absolutely necessary. 'Uh-oh.'

'Uh-oh what?'

'That's, like, the worst reason to date a guy I ever heard.'

'What is? I didn't say anything about a reason.'

''Cause it would serve Ricky right.'

'Hypothetically speaking.'

'So this guy's just for sex in the meantime?'

'Yeah, I know how guys just hate that.'

'Some guys might hate it.'

'Not no guy I ever met.'

Arlene looked up suddenly to see Trevor standing in the kitchen doorway. 'Trevor, how long you been standing there?'

'I just woke up.'

'Don't sneak up on a body like that.'

'I just came for breakfast.'

'Get on out and play, would you?'

'I haven't had my breakfast.'

'Oh. Right. Sit down, let me fix you something.'

Trevor shook his head in apparent bewilderment and settled at the table, leaning his chin on both hands.

Loretta said, 'Well, anyway. Can't use a guy for what he won't give you.'

Trevor perked up his ears. 'Who you talking about?'

'This don't concern you, Trevor. And Loretta, little pitchers have big ears, if you catch my drift.'

Loretta shrugged and refilled her own cup at the Mr

Coffee machine. 'Anyway. Sounds like a personal problem to me. If I were you, I'd be talking to Bonnie.'

'Nothing to talk about, Loretta. Just drop it.'

She set two toaster waffles in front of her boy, then ran down the hall and called Bonnie on the bedroom phone. The machine picked up and Arlene left a message saying she had a personal problem she'd like to discuss.

She cut her way through Bonnie's little double-wide mobile home, through knickknacks and home crafts and needle-point and feathers and pottery and blown glass and porcelain clowns. Bonnie liked things and kept plenty of them around the house so things would never be in short supply. Arlene made herself comfortable on the soft couch in a nest of embroidered pillows.

Bonnie said, 'So. You finally quit the damn Laser Lounge.'

'Yeah. Guy come and bought the engine off me for eight hundred dollars, so I got two months ahead on the pay-ments.'

'And in two months? Then what?'

'Cross that bridge when I come to it. Least I'll get caught up on my sleep before I gotta worry. That's not what I come to talk about.'

'How can you be having relationship problems? I thought we said no new relationships in your first year.'

Arlene sighed and studied the ceiling. 'Well, I'm sorry, Bonnie, but for one time I didn't do what you told me.'

'For one time?' Bonnie's sharp voice cut the air like a siren. If there'd been dogs in the yard, Arlene figured they'd howl along, but there were no dogs allowed in Bonnie's mobile home park. 'Girl, where'd you learn to count? You don't never do what I told you. What about Ricky?'

'You see him around here?'

'No, but what if we do?'

'Cross that bridge when we come to it too.'

'In other words, just go on a spending spree and worry about the bills when they get in.'

'I didn't say that.'

'It's what I heard. So, what's the problem?'

'Well. I been out with this guy four times. He hasn't even tried to touch me. He's just, like . . . a complete . . . gentleman.'

'You poor girl. Men are such beasts.'

'Four times, though, Bonnie. Doesn't it seem off to you?'

'You never got to know a guy before you jumped in the sack?'

Actually, Arlene thought, no, but she didn't care to say that. 'He hasn't so much as tried to hold my hand. What's that sound like to you?'

'Sounds like the guy's got more sense than you do, not like that's the hardest contest in the world to win. No offense. Look. You ain't got but sixty days sober. No time to be adding sex to more immediate problems, but if you're gonna do it anyway, and I know you are, for God's sake take it slow.'

'I guess.'

'Girl, you hear one word I say to you?'

'I'm just so damn sick and tired of sleeping alone, Bonnie. Damn tired of it. And I know he is, too. So, what's so terrible? I mean, what's his problem?'

'You're asking me?'

'Yeah. That's why I come all the way over here. I'm asking you.'

'Doesn't that strike you a little odd? To be asking me?'

'You're my sponsor.'

'So I'm supposed to know what this guy's thinking that I never even met.'

'You mean, ask *him*?'

Bonnie let out a big, indefinable noise and threw her hands up in a gesture of defeat. 'And she thinks she's ready to have a relationship. Lord help us all.' Then she walked Arlene to the door, since Arlene was going that way anyway, with or without help. 'Hey. This the guy you told me about with the scars?'

'Yeah.'

'You sure he knows you want him to?'

'Well, sure he knows. I mean, he must. What would I be going out with him for if I didn't want him to?'

'You better make sure he knows. Don't tell nobody I said that. You're supposed to get a year sober first.'

'Yeah, but you knew I wouldn't.'

Bonnie rolled her eyes and slammed the door shut.

★   ★   ★

It made her feel like a kid, the way she had to corner him at her own front door, as if her parents were waiting up inside.

Problem was, Reuben always paid for a baby-sitter. Well, it wasn't a problem, it was real nice, but it was part of the problem, because if she invited him in, well, there the girl would be, and she didn't have a car, so Reuben had to drop her home.

Arlene hadn't quite figured a way around that. So when he walked her to her door, which he always did, being a gentleman, she slid up to him and put her arms around his neck.

'I had a real nice time tonight,' she said quietly into his right ear. The muscles in his neck and shoulders felt tight. She waited for him to say the same. Or to say anything, or to relax, or put his hands on her back, but there they hung at his sides while he said nothing at all. 'How come you're so tense?'

'Do I seem tense?'

'Am I making you nervous? You want me to stop?'

'I guess I have mixed feelings about it.'

Discouraged as she'd been, that seemed like a good jumping-off place to Arlene, who figured mixed feelings to be better than no feelings at all. She took two steps to push up a little closer, but he yielded and ended up with his back against the door. Since he couldn't go anywhere from there, she kissed him. It didn't feel different from kissing anybody else.

It was a soft kiss. She didn't know why, since she seemed to be leading, and had never felt a soft kiss before. And it brought up all these soft feelings in her stomach, like little breaths trying to get out, only more fluttery.

She really hadn't expected to like it nearly that much.

She drew back to look at him, figuring this was the moment to find out one way or another if it bothered her. But he turned his head a little and she found herself looking mostly at the right side of his face, which was handsome and pleasant anyway – she'd always thought so.

'You finally coming in tonight?' It was a hard question to ask because she'd convinced herself she wouldn't have to sleep alone that night, even though she knew she might be wrong, and if she was wrong she preferred not to know it yet.

'I have to drive the baby-sitter home.'

'You could come back.'

'But Trevor's in the house.'

She still was mostly pressed against him while they discussed it, with her arms around his neck, listening to the change in his voice and watching opportunities to respond pass him by.

'That kid sleeps like the dead. You couldn't wake him up if you tried. Once, when we lived in Paso Robles, the house next door burned to the ground. Sirens in the middle of the night, people yelling. I had to take him out to the street in a fireman's carry, and he just hung there on my shoulder, sleeping. Don't you worry about Trevor. I'm talking too much, aren't I?' He smiled, which she found encouraging, so she kissed him again. 'So, you'll come back. Right?'

'Arlene. I'm not sure—'

She put a finger to his lips before she had to find out what he wasn't sure of. 'Don't you get tired of sleeping alone?'

'Of course I do.'

'Don't you feel that way about me?'

He slipped out of her grasp and slid around toward the stairs. 'Oh, God,' he said. 'Is that what you think?'

So he did feel that way about her, but had to get farther away to tell her so. 'You're like a saint, right, and that's how you got that name. Saint Reuben.'

'No. You have no idea how much of a saint I'm not. If you could spend one minute inside my skin, you'd know.'

'So, come back.'

She took his hand, afraid to lose him before he answered, and he said he would.

From *The Other Faces Behind the Movement*

I'm such a jerk. It was right there to see. It's only five minutes to the baby-sitter's and five back again, but, fool that I am, it took me an hour to figure out he wasn't coming back. It was a bad hour, too, because I minded a lot that he didn't. More than I wanted to or expected to.

Loretta said I'm so used to guys pawing all over me that the more he wouldn't, the more I wished he would. I don't know. I'm not big on psychology. She made it sound like a sickness, like I only wanted what I couldn't get. Maybe I just liked how he didn't treat me cheap. Maybe I just liked being around a gentleman for a change.

But then, sitting there, thinking about all the things I was starting to like about him, it just got harder and harder the more he didn't come back. I ended up sitting in the living room, watching for his car down the street. Every time I heard a motor I'd get this little flutter in my stomach, and every time it drove on by I'd feel a cry right behind my eyes. I had to work real hard not to let it have its way.

Funny how sometimes I'd get involved with a guy because I thought somehow, for some reason, with some particular guy it wouldn't hurt that much. Funny I still thought it'd work after all that time, because it never had before.

Finally I gave up and called his house. He answered the phone by saying, 'I'm sorry, Arlene. I really am.'

And I said, 'So that's it, then? It's just never gonna be that way?' I was almost crying, and I know he could hear it in my voice, because *I* could. I hate that.

He said, 'Couldn't you just give me a little more time?'

I said yeah, I guessed I probably could if that's what the situation required, but one thing for damn sure, I was getting a new baby-sitter, and this one had to have her own car.

He laughed when I said that. I was glad he did. It always helps to laugh at a time like that, and if he hadn't I might never have figured out that he was scared to death.

I guess I can be slow about these things.

So we're having this nice laugh together, and the next

129

thing I know I'm crying, full-on, no point trying to hide it. I know, I'm too emotional. Everybody tells me that. If Bonnie had been there she'd've told me that's the perfect example of how I wasn't ready, but thank God she was not.

'Arlene?' he said. 'Are you all right?'

And I said, 'Dammit, I just hate to sleep alone so much. You'd think I'd be good at it by now. I get scared and lonely at night, and I just never get no sleep. I quit my night job so I could sleep for a change, but that only made it worse. More time to lie there scared and lonely. Sometimes I think I'll get up and go on back there, just to make the night go by.' I don't know if he followed the half of that, though, because when I get to crying it's hard to understand most of what I say.

He was quiet for a minute. Well, not a minute, but it seemed that long. Then he said, 'Do you want me to come over to your house just to sleep?'

And I said, 'You know, that would be very nice, 'cause I sort of got it in my head you might be here tonight.'

'Give me ten minutes.' That was the last thing he said.

After I hung up the phone I crossed over to the window and looked out through the trees at this thin little crescent moon hanging yellow over the hill and smiled because it was nice of him to offer. Even though I knew he wouldn't show. Once bitten. You know. But that man was all full of surprises. I learned not to try to guess him out after a while.

*　　*　　*

She'd given up and put herself to bed when she heard his quiet knock. She put on a robe and let him in. Well, opened the door to let him in, but he seemed to get stuck there on the threshold. She had to take his hand and give a little pull.

She wanted to offer a hug, but it seemed if she went forward, he might go backward, since he always had before. She turned and walked into the bedroom, hoping he would follow, hardly daring to turn around to see if he did.

She dropped her robe on the floor, not really thinking in advance how he'd feel about that, the way she slept with nothing on even if it was just for sleeping. When she looked over her shoulder he was standing there in her bedroom doorway, watching.

The lights were all off, so it was dark, except for that little thin sliver of yellow moon, and she didn't figure he could see much more than just the smoky outline of her pulling back the covers, settling in way over to one side to give him plenty of room.

In time he came around to the other side of the bed and lay down on his back on top of the covers. He was wearing jeans and a white shirt, and she hadn't seen him in jeans since that day she went by his house. When he came by to take her out he always dressed nice, with a tie and everything.

She rolled a little closer and rested her head on his shoulder. After a few minutes more in silence she said, 'Do you want me to take off my earrings? Are they digging into you?' She had three pierces on that side and didn't want him to be uncomfortable, figuring he would never say if he was.

'No. I can't even feel them.' It was the first he'd spoken since coming into her house. His voice sounded low and careful.

'Thanks for coming back, Reuben.'

'Why are you doing this? And don't say because you hate to sleep alone. I'm sure there are plenty of men who'd like to be here with you tonight.'

'Got any of their phone numbers?'

'Is it because Trevor wanted us together?'

'Damn, Reuben. Just how far do you think I'll go to help that kid with his homework?'

'Why me, then?'

Arlene sat up. 'You know what your problem is?'

'No, but fortunately I have you to tell me.'

'Your problem is you worry too much about your looks. I don't care near as much as you do, I couldn't possibly. Even if I quit my day job, I just wouldn't have time. Did you ever consider that if you'd never gone and gotten hurt like you did, you'd be way too good for me? I mean, you'd be in such a whole different league you wouldn't even give me the time of day.'

'Nobody's out of your league, Arlene. You're too pretty.'

'There's more to this league thing than just looks.'

'Good thing for me if that's true.'

There was a bigger side to the story for her, but no words in which to frame it. It wouldn't make sense to him, probably, or even ring true if she said she liked him because

132

he picked her up, wearing a tie, paid for a baby-sitter, took her to a nice restaurant, and then walked her to her door. How do you explain to a guy that until you met him you didn't know you'd been getting a raw deal?

She set her cheek back down on his shoulder and threw one arm across his chest, a big, solid chest, she thought, the kind that wards off evil spirits in the dark. 'Don't take this the wrong way, but wouldn't you be more comfortable out of those clothes?'

He didn't answer straight off; in fact, she thought he probably never would. Then he said, 'Maybe next time. Maybe tomorrow.'

And she was so relieved to think he'd be there again tomorrow she didn't say another word, not wanting to say or do anything that might break that spell.

Chapter Eleven

MATT

The store closed at nine and he wasted no time breaking for the door. Three times when he checked the clock, he'd been sure it was broken, but another minute had eventually ticked away. Not for any special reason did the time go so slowly. Not much more than usual. Work always crawled by.

He'd parked his motorcycle behind the shop, on the hill. It made so much noise, and the owner always gave him a dirty look if he idled it too close to the store. It didn't have an electric starter, or rather, the one it had didn't work. So he had to kick it over. And it didn't have a neutral light, so he had to rock it back and forth a bit to make sure it wasn't in gear. Which was hard on the hill. Hard to coast it, hard to be sure.

Thinking it was in neutral, he straddled the bike, jumped on the kick lever, and the bike, still in first gear, rolled forward off the side stand and fell with him.

Now there'd be another three weeks of gas-tank-shaped bruise on the inside of his thigh, but that was not the worst of it. Straining to pick the bike up again, Matt saw he'd broken the front brake lever. Hit the handlebar and sheared it right off. And the back brake wasn't any too good. He closed his eyes and thought about screaming. But it was a quiet night, the houses in this neighborhood filled with quiet people. Nobody liked trouble.

Besides, he'd tried that once. Stood in the street and cussed out the bike, called it every name he could think of. Hadn't fixed a goddamned thing.

He turned the bike around, straddled it again, coasted it down the hill. Popped the clutch and roll-started it. If only he'd thought of that to begin with. If only.

He ran the stop sign on the Camino because he had to, and nobody noticed. No cops around. So he cruised the Camino at twenty-five, half pulled over to the curb. That way if he had to stop suddenly, he'd have a fighting chance. Five guys in a low-rider Chevy slowed beside him, rolled down their windows, called him a pussy. Asked if he needed training wheels. It was a worse day than most, but not in a whole different ball park.

Only thing Matt hated more than going to work was going home and listening to the fighting. He had a tent in the overgrown backyard for when things got really bad. At nineteen, he knew he needed a place of his own, but it was not that easy. Everybody wanted first and last month's rent, nobody wanted to pay more than $4.25 an hour for anybody who was anything-teen.

He pulled into his driveway, cut the engine. Put the bike up on the center stand. From out there he could already hear it, but he went inside all the same. Everybody's got to be somewhere, and Matt was home.

Then he saw the letter on the dining room table. He never got mail. And it was from someone he'd never heard of. Ida Greenberg. Weird. A big, thick envelope. Pages and pages mailed to him from Ida Greenberg.

Whoever she was.

From *The Other Faces Behind the Movement*

You know what's weird? What's weird is when you mean a lot more to somebody else than they ever meant to you. I mean, a whole lot more. Like life on two whole different planets.

I been on the wrong end of that, too. My freshman year in high school, I was like head over heels in love with this girl. Her name was Laura Furley. I used to lie in bed at night saying that name to myself, over and over in my head. I had this pencil in my drawer that she'd dropped in the hall. I had it in this little box with tissue paper. I mean, it was weird. It was like a goddamn shrine or something. And I cut three pictures of her out of the yearbook and put them in a frame. I never said a word to her. I mean, not even hello. I'm not even sure I ever looked her in the eye. But I wanted to spend my whole life with her. And if I couldn't, I thought I'd spend my whole life thinking about how I couldn't. And then sometimes I would think, if she knew all this, boy, would she be amazed.

Probably she would have said, Matt who?

I'm not saying I think Mrs Greenberg was in love with me, it's not that. It's just weird. I mean, I never noticed her any more than any other customer in that store. I just knew her name. I just said, 'Hello, Mrs Greenberg. How are you tonight?'

Man. She must've been awful lonely.

Dearest Matthew,

If you are reading this, I have passed away. I left this letter in with some personal things, with a note to my son, Richard, asking him to mail it after I'm gone.

This morning I made some phone calls. To my insurance company and to my lawyer. I had to make a very big decision, and I made it. I have a $25,000 life insurance policy, and I decided not to leave it to my son. I don't trust that he would use it the right way.

I have decided to split it three ways. $8,333 will go to you. The same amount to Terri, whom I also like very much, and the other third to that nice lady at the cat shelter, because she is selfless and does good work.

This leaves one dollar for Richard. He will kick and he will be very temperamental. I think you may have to attend the reading of the will, and it may not be pleasant. But I have worked it out carefully with my lawyer. Richard can contest it, and he probably will, but he won't win. We've sealed it all up carefully.

You may do what you want with this money, but I'm trusting you to use it well. Not selflessly, just well. Definitely spend it on yourself. But don't waste it.

If you want to know why I chose you, it's because you always had a nice smile, and you asked how I was feeling. And then you listened to the answer. You never made me feel like I didn't matter, or like I wasn't there.

Now. The money is not exactly free. I have done you a big favor. Well, the biggest favor it's in my power to do. I know $8,333 doesn't go as far as it used to. But it's all I have. The house is mortgaged up to the hilt and my Social Security payments expire when I do.

Here's what I want you to do. Do a very big favor for three people. It doesn't have to be money. Just give them something that is as big to you as $8,333 is to me. And when they try to pay you back, tell them instead to pay it forward.

Give your time, if you have to, or your compassion. Lots of people have money but not that.

You are a nice boy. Enjoy the money.

Best wishes,
Ida Greenberg

Just a little over six weeks later he had it in his hand. He'd already put a fifty-dollar deposit on the apartment so the guy wouldn't rent it to somebody else. He spent the night there, in a sleeping bag. He had a decent bed at his folks' house but no way to move it yet.

It was quiet. Real little place, but nice and quiet.

When he opened the window he was right out on the slanting roof, because this apartment used to be an attic once, before somebody divided up the house. And he sat out on the roof in the dark, in the cold, in sweatpants and no shirt, just liking the quiet. What he saw from that roof was trees and nothing else. Just the side of a hill covered with trees. And a sliver of yellow moon gleaming through. Which was more than enough.

So he sat there for a while, wondering where people go when they die and what he could possibly do for somebody else that would mean as much as this $8,333 had meant to him. And what to buy with the rest of the money. And whether Mrs Greenberg would know. He didn't figure she probably would; it seemed corny to think she was watching. But he'd never known anyone who died, never thought much about it before, and he wasn't all that completely positive that she wouldn't know. Unlike the $8,333, it wasn't something he could take to the bank.

Which made him think about decisions, and whether his were good ones, and how this would change them, not being completely sure if she would know. But it was a long subject to think through and a little unclear, and before he finished he got cold and sleepy, so he went inside and to bed.

The next morning he drove his old piece of crap motorcycle to the Honda dealer in San Luis Obispo. They said they'd give him $75 in trade. The first thing that caught his eye was a real pretty brand-new 750. With a windshield, and all space-age aerodynamic in red and white, with a custom paint job. He sat on it. He shouldn't have sat on it. It cost almost $7,000. Which was just damn close to all he had left after first and last month's rent and that big security deposit. But, damn. It was more than pretty. It was, like . . . power. But it was too much.

They also had a new 350, like his old one but seven model years newer and no miles. And a neutral light and an electric starter. And then, for $3,500, they had a 250. With a nice custom paint job. Brand new. 350, 250. The 250 would go fast enough to ride on the highway. Just barely. And if he could go faster, maybe that would just get him a ticket, which he could not afford. Insurance ate up too much of his check as it was.

Then he sat on the 750 again, feeling that power. Nobody was going to pull up beside him while he was on this bad boy to talk about training wheels. But it was too much. It was most of the old lady's money. That was all she had, that insurance, like someone cashed in her life and that's what it all added up to.

This was giving him a headache.

He rode his old piece of crap to the Taco Bell. Had a breakfast burrito, thought some more.

Then he went back and bought the 250.

And on the way home stopped at Cuesta College to get a catalogue of all their extension classes. And sat on his brand-new little bike in the parking lot and leafed through the catalogue, and it was so cool because there was no possible combination of classes that he could not afford.

He stuck it in his backpack, and the motor started up nice and clean when he hit the button. He took Highway 41, just to feel the curves.

So, there. If she could see, she'd know he made a good decision. And if not, well. If not, he could see. He would know he didn't waste it, whether or not Mrs Greenberg ever found out.

From *The Diary of Trevor*

Mary Anne and Arnie have never been very nice to me. Like when I told them I thought Clinton was gonna win the election. Arnie hooted and laughed at me. Bush, he said. George Bush. Bet on it. Mary Anne came to school the next day in a cap that said *Ross for Boss* on the front. That's how much you know, she said.

And I used to have this big ol' thing for Mary Anne, too. What was I thinking?

Anyway, my mom said to pay them no mind. She told me a story of when she was a kid, and she told her uncle Harry, who was this big football fan, that Joe Namath and the Jets were gonna beat the Colts in the Super Bowl. He laughed at her. Then, when the Jets won, he wouldn't talk about it with her. She said some people just can't handle being wrong.

I said, the Jets and the Colts in the Super Bowl? Man. That must've been like a century ago. Both those teams totally suck now.

Thanks, she said. Now I feel real old.

When I gotta get up and say my project flopped, Mary Anne and Arnie are gonna give me hell. I sure hope Clinton wins the election.

Chapter Twelve

REUBEN

He woke with a start, fully dressed, on a bed not his own. His eye patch was still on, so he must not have known he had been about to fall asleep. He'd just drifted off for an hour or two, but the sun seemed to be breaking through the east-facing window. He lay still, momentarily too sleepy to identify his surroundings immediately. Someone's fingers were touching the uneven, partly deadened skin on the wrong side of his face. His impulse was to bolt, then he remembered. Knowing the fingers belonged to Arlene didn't kill the urge to get away; it just took about ten percent off the top.

He opened his eye but could not see her. She was on his left, the reverse of where she'd been earlier that morning. He shifted slightly and felt her lips against his left cheek. His stomach went cold. 'What are you doing?'

'Kissing your face.'

'Why that side?'

'It's still your face. Right?'

'That's how much you know. That skin came from my thigh.' He hoped the reality of that unfortunate detail might create its own distance.

'If I was kissing your thigh, would I be getting these kinds of complaints?'

And then it happened again, a touch of lips brushing just underneath the patch, upsetting his stomach.

'Arlene? This is making me uncomfortable.'

'Is there anything I could do that *wouldn't* make you uncomfortable?' Indignation rose in her voice, oddly comfortable in its familiarity. The rest of this, though, was too strange and new.

'You could let me up.'

She had been leaning against his side, pinning his left arm, making him feel trapped, but she didn't stay that way for long.

She stood in her robe by the window while Reuben attempted to locate his shoes. 'You know what your problem is?' He met her eyes. 'I say that a lot, don't I?'

'Probably just to me. I have a lot of problems.'

'You sure make it hard to like you.'

He wanted to say, Then why don't you give up? But in some small part of himself he feared that if he asked her to, she might. He found his shoes and opened the bedroom door.

'Why are you mad at me, Reuben? Why are you leaving like you're mad? What the hell did I do wrong?'

He walked down the hall toward the front door and

bumped into Trevor, in his pajamas, headed for the bathroom. With a cowlick in the back of his hair where he'd slept on it funny. And there was nowhere to hide, no way not to be seen.

'Morning, Mr St Clair,' he said, and locked the bathroom door behind him, leaving Reuben to wonder what he'd expected and why the experience had come up missing.

Just as he touched the knob of the front door, Arlene caught him from behind with a hand on his shoulder.

'So, you still coming back tonight?'

'Arlene, this is a mistake.' He wouldn't turn around to say it, just stood facing the street as if he was breaking up with her front door. 'I don't know why we ever started with this.'

'You want to come back, I'll explain it to you.'

He shook his head without turning around.

He stood in front of his first class, stomach unsettled and eye grainy from lack of sleep. 'Today is the deadline for the extra credit assignment. I'd like to see a show of hands. How many of you chose to participate?'

Mary Anne Telmin's hand shot up first, closely followed by another girl, named Jamie, who wore muted colors and tended to sit in the back and blend in with the walls. Then a boy named Jason, who liked to express his difficult growth phase by hitting and who needed all the extra credit he could get. After a second or two Arnie Jenkins raised his hand cautiously, the big, awkward, brutish boy who'd asked Reuben if he was a pirate.

'Chose to?' Arnie asked. 'Or really did?'

'Did you participate, Arnie?'

'Well. I chose to. I could use the extra credit. But I couldn't think of anything. I really tried, though.'

'Hard to document trying, Arnie. I think you'd better put your hand down.'

Reuben glanced at Trevor, who was staring at the wall on his right at close range. 'Trevor?'

Trevor made a face and raised his hand.

'Is that it? Four? Out of a class of thirty-nine? Well, congratulations to the four of you for making the effort. Now. You documented your work on paper the way I asked you to? Would you pass those forward, please? Then we'll present the ideas to the class. Mary Anne, would you like to go first?'

Reuben knew she would.

She stood in front of the class as though she'd always known she belonged there and had never quite felt comfortable anywhere else. 'Well. The earth only has just so many resources. So recycling is very important. And we don't have curbside recycling here in Atascadero. So I gathered some recycling bins, not enough for everybody in the city, of course, but enough for probably everybody who cares enough to ask for one. We put little ads on the bulletin boards around town, at the Lucky and the Kmart, saying we had them for free.'

Reuben interrupted briefly. 'We?'

'Oh. My father sort of drove me around. And then I wrote a letter to the City Council encouraging curbside recycling. And I got it signed by forty of my neighbors. There's a copy of the letter in with my paper, Mr St Clair.'

'Thank you, Mary Anne. I'll take a look at that. What about you, Jason?'

Jason walked up the aisle slowly, pausing to kick another boy's foot. 'Uh. Some people think we don't have gangs in Atascadero, but they're wrong. I mean, look at the graffiti. That's called "tagging".' He turned toward Reuben as he said this, as though everyone else in the room would know. 'It's a kind of gang talk, like bragging. So I went to the store owners who got tagged and said if you pay for the paint, I'll paint over it. Some of it showed up again the next day, but I painted over it again. One store I did three times. But after a while, I guess the taggers just got tired of doing it over.'

'You wrote down all the businesses for me, Jason?'

'Yeah, it's all there, Mr St Clair.'

'That's good, Jason, I'm impressed. Thank you.'

Not that the project was unusually impressive; it was more a consider-the-source observation.

Mary Anne Telmin seemed to get her nose out of joint when he said that, but truthfully he had not been impressed by her project. Earlier in the semester it had come clear to Reuben that her father did most of the work. 'Gathered' recycling bins, she'd said. Interesting euphemism for what a parent provides.

Trevor sat staring at the wall again. Reuben knew it would be a bad moment for Trevor, so he saved him for last, the way he might postpone his own pain if he'd had that choice.

'Jamie?'

Jamie shifted on her feet and stammered. 'I went to the Oak Tree retirement home and talked to some of the people there. And a lot of what they told me, I wrote down. Like a story. Of their life. So the class could read about them. Because sometimes young people don't know that old people have a lot to say. If I could use the copy machine in the office, I could make one for everybody. I couldn't do it at the copy place, it would have been too expensive. It's almost twenty pages long.'

'Thank you, Jamie. Why don't you talk to Principal Morgan during lunch today? See if she'll let you.'

'Okay.' She hurried back to her seat.

Reuben looked at Trevor and Trevor looked at him. Reuben felt a pang of embarrassment, remembering bumping into him in the hall outside his bedroom earlier that morning, but Trevor hadn't mentioned that.

Trevor took a deep breath and trudged to the front of the classroom, moving slowly and warily, like he was walking a gangplank. Reuben felt his own face flush, as if the presentation, the pressure, were his own.

Trevor stood in front of the class and sighed. 'I put a lot of time and energy into my project,' he said. 'But it didn't turn out like I wanted.' Looking quiet and empty, he turned to the blackboard and sketched out a simple version of Paying Forward. He used Reuben's pointer to indicate the first circle.

'This was Jerry. I helped him get a job. But then he violated his parole. I don't know if you can pay it forward in prison. I guess you can, 'cause I guess the people in there need a favor more than anybody. But I don't know if he will. Then, this was Mrs Greenberg. I spent about three whole days fixing up her garden. Only, she died.'

Arnie spoke out of turn, shouted out, 'I wonder if you can pay it forward in heaven.'

The class laughed and hooted, and Trevor exchanged a look with Reuben as though begging him to make it stop.

Reuben slammed his right hand on the desktop, hard. Trevor jumped. 'Those of you who did not bother to participate will please stop making light of those who tried.' The class stared at Reuben in stony silence, most with their mouths open. It was the first break in his calm even-handedness, and Reuben knew by the looks on their faces that he'd just become the human equivalent of Lou's flying yardstick. 'Please go on, Trevor.'

'Oh. Okay. Well, there was a third one too. But. Well, I'm not quite sure how good an idea that was. Anyway, I'm gonna come up with three more people. You know. Start over.'

Mary Anne Telmin raised her hand. 'But Mr St Clair, the deadline is past. He can't do anything about it now.'

Trevor stiffened to her challenge. 'I'm not doing it for the credit, Mary Anne. I'm doing it to see if the world really changes.' He glanced at Reuben again for support, and Reuben gave him a subtle signal, pushing down with his hand as if to say, Settle down. Don't rise to this.

Arnie raised his hand and jumped in. 'But you can't change the world on the honor system. Shoot, anybody knows that. Leave people on the honor system, they don't do it. As soon as you look away, they just don't. I mean, look what happened.'

Trevor rushed to his own defense again, tight and bristly now, as if being attacked from every side. 'It's not Mrs Greenberg's fault that she died, Arnie.'

'Well, people die, or they go to jail, or they just goof off, what's the difference? They still don't do it.'

'All right. That's enough discussion. It's easy to stand here and criticize Trevor's idea because he had problems with the result, but it was still the best idea, especially since most of you didn't even have one. Now, I'll look these over tonight. The best effort earns an automatic A in this class. Everybody who participated will see a positive effect on his or her grade.'

But as Trevor returned to his desk and found his place in the textbook, the discussion continued in scattered whispers.

He ran into Anne Morgan in the hall at the end of the following Friday. She said she'd told Jamie she could copy the stories in the office, and if he had just a moment, could Reuben come into her office for a chat. It had that 'Let's talk' ring to it, two words never followed by anything joyous or good.

He sat in the chair across from her desk, the same hot seat

he'd occupied on his first day, feeling only slightly more comfortable now.

'Now, Reuben, I don't want you to think this is a problem in my eyes. I just need to pass this along to you. I got a very strong complaint from Mary Anne Telmin's parents today.'

'Don't tell me. Let me guess. They think their little princess should have gotten the winning grade.'

'Yes, but that's not the end of it. They're upset because Trevor McKinney did. They claim that's inappropriate in light of the fact that you and Arlene McKinney are . . . dating.' An awkward pause, during which neither spoke or met the other's eyes. 'Which I didn't even know you were. And I'm not questioning you on that. What you do with your personal life is none of my business, Reuben. I'm uncomfortable even talking to you about it, but you have to know the complaint was lodged.'

'What did you tell them?'

'That I would discuss it with you and determine whether any bias was involved in the grading. Which I already know there wasn't, because I know that's not the kind of teacher you are.'

'Where did they come by their information? I feel like I'm under some kind of surveillance.'

'You've never lived in a small town before, have you? Atascadero might not be so small that everybody literally knows everybody, but all the faces become commonplace. And a new one stands out.'

'Especially mine. Sorry. I'm doing it again. So, in other

words, I go to dinner or a movie with someone, and the next day people are discussing it amongst themselves.'

'I'm afraid so.'

Reuben's lack of sleep seemed to tackle him suddenly, a quick fade that left him feeling weak and slightly sick. But he breathed deeply, and filled Anne in on the basics of Paying Forward. She listened carefully and seemed impressed with the scope of Trevor's idea.

'The purpose of that assignment was to get the students thinking globally,' he said. 'Jamie came up with an idea to change the consciousness of the class. Mary Anne and Jason tried to change Atascadero. Trevor had the only idea that might have gotten bigger than this town. He was criticized because the results weren't good. But the Telmins can't swear that the city will adopt curbside recycling, either. That shouldn't negate the effort. Which, by the way, in Mary Anne's case, was more her father's effort than her own. So I'm supposed to kick Trevor while he's down, and punish him for the fact that old people die, and junkies don't stay clean, and you can't cure anyone else's loneliness?'

'You didn't tell me about that last one.'

'Oh. Well. I'm sketchy on the details. And also, for your information, Arlene McKinney and I dated a handful of times. Dated. And that's all we did. And that's over now, and ended uncomfortably, and I think more has been made of that situation than the facts warrant.'

'That part was never my business, Reuben, but I'll tell the Telmins I discussed the students' projects with you and that I approve of the priorities involved in your grading.'

'It's not even just the beauty of the idea, Anne. If you could have seen how hard he worked. He put over a hundred dollars of his own money into that homeless man, and more than thirty hours on the old woman's garden. He was so hurt and disappointed.'

Anne watched him carefully as he spoke, and he saw something forming in her eyes, something about him, as though he was looking in a mirror. Then she repeated the observation in words. 'You really care for that boy, don't you, Reuben?'

'Well, yes. I do. But that doesn't change the facts.'

But Anne was already convinced that no bias existed, so Reuben must have been talking to himself.

From *The Diary of Trevor*

Sometimes I still think about Jerry. I wonder if they let him out of jail by now. And if they did, I wonder why he didn't come back here and say hello.

Sometimes I think maybe it wasn't his fault. Maybe the police just expected something bad from him, so they looked real hard and found it. Maybe if he was cleaner they would've been looking at somebody else to arrest.

Or maybe he really blew it.

Sometimes I think maybe he wasn't my friend at all. That he just said he was, for the money. But I hate to think that. So I like to pretend that he couldn't get back here some-how, like they let him off real far from home. And so he's just out there somewhere, paying it forward.

I know he's probably not. I just like to think it.

Chapter Thirteen

CHARLOTTE

She left her car in the park on the Marin County side and walked down the off ramp. Walked out onto the bridge in the northbound traffic lane because the pedestrian gates were closed. It was after three in the morning, with traffic on the bridge sparse to nonexistent. Every now and then a car would come by, and she'd try to make herself small.

There's a trick, she thought. Me small. Apparently her therapist was right. She was so accustomed to making jokes, she couldn't stop if she tried. Even in her own head, even when everything was terribly unfunny. It would be just like her to think of a joke about falling on the way down.

She looked over the reddish bridge railing. Beneath her in the moonlight she could see land. She wasn't over water yet and there was no platform beneath this part of the bridge. It would be easier here, she thought, with no platform. But no. Not here. Something about that hard ground. Not here.

A van came by. She turned to assure herself that it would drive on in spite of her, convinced that anyone who saw her would understand her purpose. That's when she saw that she was being followed. He wasn't close behind her, but he was definitely following. She'd thought about this. Going out at night, even if it was for the last time. It wasn't safe in this city at night. Splattering herself against the icy surface of the bay, that was one thing, but life held worse surprises than death, and she of all people should know it. She glanced over her shoulder again. He hadn't gained any ground.

Little guy, she thought. What was she so worried about? At five ten, carrying forty extra pounds on her already considerable frame, maybe she could take him. Unless he had a knife. Or a gun. Last time the guy had a gun. Little guy, but well armed.

She glanced again. Maybe she'd been wrong. Maybe he was just walking over the bridge, oblivious to her. *Yeah, right. I should be so lucky.*

There was only one thing to do. And it was exactly what she'd planned to do all along. She leaped up to the railing and pulled herself over.

There was a platform under the edge of the bridge, that much she already knew. She'd staked out this spot in advance. It wasn't far down. But now, in the middle of the night, with a potential violent rapist's footsteps clicking on the pavement behind her, it looked a lot farther down than she'd remembered.

She tried to turn around, to climb down, but a great fear

of falling hamstrung her movements. *Good one, Charlotte. Fear of falling. The first fall is the easy one.*

He was getting closer. She could almost make out his face in the darkness now, his footsteps coming faster. Dirty and seedy. A real lowlife. Okay, think fast.

She pushed off the rail and jumped kamikaze style to the platform below. Remembering to bend her knees on impact was not enough. She landed too hard. Overbalanced forward, grabbed on to the edge, seized by that sickening feeling like falling. She felt a twist in her ankle, felt something give. Not bad enough to be a broken bone, she thought, but it smarted, and she sat rubbing it, wondering why it should matter now.

When she looked up he was leaning over the railing, looking down at her. Don't come near me, she thought. I know the perfect escape.

'You okay?'

'I think I hurt myself.' *Oh, smart, Charlotte. Good. I'm injured prey, come get me. Good thinking.*

'You think that's a bad fall, the next one's a killer.'

'Very funny. What makes you think I'm going to jump?'

'What the hell you come out here for?'

'Well, *you're* out here. Were *you* going to jump?'

'No, I was going to try to talk you out of it.'

'You were? Why?' He didn't answer, and Charlotte's insides leaped and froze to see him start over the railing after her. 'Don't come down here. I'll do it, I mean it. If you come down here, I'll jump.'

'I ain't gonna hurt you. I just want to talk about this.'

He didn't fit the pattern. His voice, his manner held none of the implied violence she'd learned to smell. Still, she didn't exactly trust him.

He did much better than she had, turning around and shinnying down to the bottom of the rail. Then he went limp and dropped lightly onto the platform beside her, not five feet away. Easy for him, she thought, skinny little guy. Probably didn't weigh more than 120 pounds.

He must have seen her panic. Too bad. She thought she had a damn good poker face. 'Hey, look, lady. I didn't come down here to give you no trouble. I just thought we could talk about this. I mean, what do you got to lose? I try to convince you life is worth living. If I don't do so good, you jump. Nothing ventured, right?'

'How did you know I was going to jump?'

'What else would you be doing out here in the middle of the night? A lady out here by herself, San Francisco in the middle of the night? I mean, that's suicide. One way or the other.'

'What were *you* doing out here?'

'Waiting for somebody like you to try something stupid. I been sleeping in that park over there. Mostly during the day. Sitting up at night, waiting for a jumper. Sooner or later there was gonna be a jumper. Tonight's my lucky night. I'm sorry. I didn't introduce myself. Jerry Busconi.'

He held one dirty hand out. She shook it anyway. 'Charlotte Renaldi.'

His face lit up. 'Oh. Italian, huh? See, we got something in common.'

159

'Why do you care if somebody jumps off the bridge?'

'That's a funny question. It's a life. A human life.'

'Not yours.'

'No, not mine. Gosh, it's pretty out here tonight, huh? Real clear night.'

It had never occurred to Charlotte to look, until he said that. He was right. It was beautiful. Clear and clean smelling from the recent rains, which had moved through, headed south, leaving the stars out in numbers. Enough moon to see Alcatraz. And the lights of the city pressed together, cluttering the hill. Moon on the water. Sausalito on the other side, the dark shape of landmasses in the night.

She looked straight down at the dark water, and something came out of nowhere. A huge something right underneath her, monstrous in its size and suddenness. It startled her and she stumbled backward.

Jerry laughed. 'Ain't that a kick when that happens? That's one of them Norwegian ones, I think. Freighter. Dutch, I forget. Wallenius Lines, I think. Big puppy, huh? Kind of scares you, popping out of nowhere like that.'

'Why are you trying to help me?' She didn't look at him as she asked this. She leaned forward to watch more and more of the deck of that monstrous freighter appear underneath. The platform felt terrifyingly narrow.

'Good thing you didn't jump right then. Make some deckhand mighty unhappy.'

'Very funny.'

'Sometimes you gotta joke. What else can you do?'

'That's what I always say. And people tell me I'm being

inappropriate. My therapist says I'm minimizing my own trauma.'

'You want to go get a cup of coffee and talk about it? On me.'

Charlotte shook her head. The freighter had moved forward now, and away, completely visible, leaving dark water just underneath.

'You know, that's the prettiest part of the view,' she said.

'What is?'

'That black water. Right down there. That is a very comfortable darkness.'

'Ah, now that's where you're wrong. Just wait'll you get down there. That's a very ugly darkness. Very cold. Unforgiving. You won't like it one bit.'

'Better than where I've been. But how would you know?'

'Hey, I been down. Don't I look to you like a guy who's been down? I mean, just about every bad thing could happen to a person has happened to me. My life is shit.'

'Well, thank you so much, Jerry. For coming down here to convince me that life is worth living.'

'See, that's just the point, though.' He pulled his dark, ratty coat tighter around himself against the cold. A piece of torn lining hung down onto his jeans. 'I mean, if *my* life is worth living, then yours has gotta be better than you think.'

'You don't know anything about my life, mister. You have no idea what I've been through.'

'No, that's true. But the offer still holds. We go get a cup of coffee, you can tell me all about it.'

Charlotte didn't answer. Tears began to flow now, running down her face, tickling slightly as they dripped off the end of her chin. They'd been away for as long as she could remember. She leaned forward, allowing them to drop into the dark water. So far down.

'I'm gonna tell you a little story, Charlotte Renaldi, whether you wanta hear it or not. A few months ago I was, like, at the lowest place I'd ever been in my life. Even though I been lower since. And somebody I didn't even know came along and tried to help me. Just outta nowhere. Gave me money to eat and buy new clothes, and get a job. Didn't want me to pay him back. I was supposed to do something that big for three more people. That's called Paying It Forward. Just think what could happen with that, if people really did it. Let's say you don't jump. You pay it forward to three people. And they do nine, and they do twenty-seven. And then two more people I might find to help, they do their bit. Think about it. After a while nobody could jump off a bridge anymore, because there'd be somebody there, just looking for the chance to do their bit, you know? Anyway, I screwed it all up. Took the help and made a mess. I was so ashamed I couldn't even look this kid in the face.'

'It was a kid?'

'Yeah, how 'bout that? A twelve-year-old kid. Out of the mouths of babes, right? But then I thought, well, so I screwed it up. I mean, I'm a junkie, Charlotte. I'm always gonna be a junkie. I ain't never gonna be no fine, up-standing citizen. But then I thought, hell. Just pay it forward anyway. Kid tried to help me. Okay, it didn't work. Still, I'm trying to help you. Maybe you'll jump. I don't know. But I tried, right? But let me tell you one thing. I woke up one morning and somebody gave me a chance. Just outta nowhere. It was like a miracle. Now, how do you know that won't happen to you tomorrow? How do you know? What if you jump into that icy cold water, and turns out this big miracle was coming your way tomorrow? You'd miss out. Wouldn't you just kick yourself?'

Charlotte wiped her nose on her sleeve inconspicuously. She sobbed one more time, then laughed out loud. 'No, I guess I wouldn't, Jerry. I'd be dead. I'd never have to kick myself again.'

'Up to you.' He rose to leave.

Charlotte looked up, wondering what she would do then. Could he really climb back up? Probably, but she knew she couldn't. It involved pulling up your full body weight with your arms. But why was she even thinking of that? she wondered. Was she changing her mind?

'Tell you what, Charlotte. Do this one thing, just for me. Flip a coin on it. Let chance tell you what to do. Heads, come get a cup of coffee with me. Tails, splat on the bay.'

It may have been a release of tension, but it seemed like the funniest idea to her. She couldn't stop laughing once she'd gotten started. It made her hiccup once.

'You know, you're pretty when you laugh.'

That killed it. She glared at him defensively.

'I didn't mean nothing by it. I just said you're pretty. You got a pretty face.'

Charlotte snorted. That's what they always say about a big, plump girl. She has a pretty face. 'You want me to decide living or dying on a flip of a coin.'

'Yes, I do.'

'That's the stupidest idea I ever heard in my life.'

'Why? Why is it stupid? At least my way you got a fifty-fifty chance.'

He held a coin out to her in the dark. Placed it in her hand. She stared closely at it. A quarter, head side up. What if it didn't come down that way? She'd really have to do it. Well, something had to break. One way or another. Something finally had to make up her mind.

'Okay. Here goes.' Her heart pounded, blood roared in her ears. She levered her thumb under the quarter, flipped the coin up into the air. It arced too far out, and she missed it. They both leaned over the edge of the steel platform as far as they dared and watched the coin fall, turning end over end to the water below. But it disappeared, because the water was too dark, too far down. She didn't hear the splash, because it was too far away. A shiver ran through her.

'You're right,' she said. 'That's a bad darkness.'

'Shoot. My quarter.'

'Christ, Jerry, it's just a quarter. Here, here's a dollar.' She pulled the bill out of her pocket and stuffed it in his hand, hoping that in the dark she hadn't just given him a ten.

'No, that was special. That was my two-headed quarter.'

But she noticed he pocketed the bill just the same.

'Two-headed quarter?'

164

'Yeah.'

'Where do you get a two-headed quarter?'

'I don't know. That's the whole problem. That was unreplaceable.'

'Well, where did you get that one?'

'Stole it off a guy in a bar.'

'Oh. Sorry.'

'Shoot. Well, it's okay, I guess. Only you better not jump now. If you do, and I lose you *and* my two-headed quarter, then I'd be pissed.'

Charlotte rubbed her ankle and they sat for a few minutes, and she looked around again. At Marin, and the city side, and the lights, like somebody was alive out there. Thinking it looked more inviting than that cold, dark chasm that had eaten Jerry's two-headed quarter.

'So, you know someplace you can get coffee at this hour?'

'Hell, yeah. This is the city.'

'I don't know if I can climb up from here.'

'It ain't so hard.'

'I hurt my ankle, though.'

'I'll help you.'

It took a while, but they ended up on the concrete walkway of the bridge again, though Charlotte never could have done it without him.

Chapter Fourteen

ARLENE

She stood on his front porch with one hand poised to knock and her heart beating so hard she could hear it in her ears. She hadn't done anything wrong, which was just exactly what she had stopped by to tell him, so why was she so afraid he'd tell her to go to hell? Exactly when had this thing taken a wrong turn again? Arlene decided she must have been in some other room when it all happened without her.

She rapped hard on his front door and immediately wanted to run away. In fact, she'd taken two steps back when he opened the door. He was wearing dark blue sweatpants and a snug, plain white T-shirt.

'Arlene.'

'Reuben, do you think I'm easy?'

'No. Actually I find you quite difficult.' Then he leaned back on the door frame and smiled. And she couldn't take offense at what he'd said, because it was a nice smile, even though the left corner of his mouth didn't go along, so he must have been teasing her in a nice way.

'There goes the pot calling the kettle black. Can I come in for just a minute?'

The smile dropped away. 'Oh. Uh. It's a mess.'

'Your place? Get serious. You're not the type to have a mess.'

He opened the door just a little wider to show her the inside of his living room, all stacked with cardboard moving cartons. 'I haven't quite unpacked yet.'

'Well, hell, Reuben. That ain't a mess. It's not your fault if all your stuff just got here, right?'

'Right,' he said, still not sounding too sure of himself; but he stepped back from the doorway and let her in. 'Why would I think you're easy?'

'Hell, I don't know. I never know what you're thinking anyway. Just wanted to make sure you didn't.' She found herself a place on the couch.

'*Are* you easy?'

'Well, no. I don't think so. Well, not by my standards. I mean, I get along fine with sex, it's not that. But if I'm with one guy, then he's the only guy. Ricky's been gone over a year and I still haven't been with anybody else. That doesn't exactly make me promiscuous. What about you?'

'No, I'm not exactly promiscuous, either. Can I get you something to drink? Would you like a beer?'

'Hell, I'd love one to pieces, but no. I'm a recovering alcoholic.'

'Oh, I'm sorry. That was stupid of me.'

'You didn't know.'

'I noticed you never ordered drinks, but I didn't think about it.'

'We still don't really know each other all that well.'

That was the other part of what she'd come to tell him. That he kept himself so shuttered off from her that he felt like a stranger, which might have been why she'd ended up feeling cheap.

'I've got orange juice and ginger ale.'

'Ginger ale'd be fine.'

He went off to get it and she sat chewing on the edge of her thumbnail, telling herself to stop it but not stopping. At least he hadn't told her to go to hell.

When he handed her the cold glass she said, 'What did I do wrong, Reuben? I have no idea. What was wrong with kissing that side of your face, anyway? It's all you. I was just sort of, you know, accepting it. As part of you.'

He sat down beside her, perched on the edge of his seat the way he did whenever something made him uncomfortable. Well, see, he wasn't a total stranger. She knew that much about him.

'I'm not sure I can explain it.'

'Know what Trevor told me? He said you told him that it's better not to pretend like you didn't notice, because that doesn't fool you one bit anyway. And you know, when he said that, it made total sense. I thought, shoot, I been doing it wrong all these years, I'm sure not going to make that mistake again. So I didn't treat that side of your face like it didn't exist. So you left in a huff and I ain't heard from you since.'

'I'm sorry.'

'You are?' She hadn't thought he would be, she'd thought somehow she'd come out sorry, the guilty one. That's the way it usually went. 'Oh. Well, that's okay. Just kind of hurt my feelings some at the time.'

He took a little slide over to her and gave her a hug. He'd never done that before. And she'd always wanted him to, and always noticed that missing, so why, now that it was here, did it seem to make her feel a little uneasy?

He didn't let go right away, either. Just held on for a minute, making Arlene think maybe she'd cry again, and if she did, he'd have to think she was some kind of emotional basket case, always crying at the drop of a hat.

'You're right,' he said, his mouth up close to her ear. 'I get angry when people pretend they don't notice and I get angry when I know they do. I'm not sure what I want from people. I think I want them not to jump a mile when they first see me, and I'm never going to get that.'

Then he let go, and sure enough by that time she was crying, because she felt so bad for him. Which, in a way – but a way she'd never try to explain – was the reason she'd kissed his face that morning. Feeling bad for him, like Trevor with a skinned knee, like she'd been a mommy too long and thought she could make it all better if she kissed it.

He didn't have any reaction to her tears, and she wondered if she wanted him to notice or if she wanted him to pretend not to. It was a hard problem, he was right about that.

Then he said, 'Arlene, I've got a confession to make. These boxes didn't just arrive. They've been here for months. I just can't bring myself to unpack them. I've moved three times in the past four years. I get so tired of it. Every time I try to unpack, I just get overwhelmed.'

She stared at him and wiped tears out from under her eyes, sideways and carefully so she wouldn't smear her mascara. 'That is so wonderful.'

'What is?'

'That you told me that. That's the first real thing you ever told me about yourself. And what's even better, I can totally relate to that. Not with moving, but hell, I feel that way about all kinds of things. I just get overwhelmed. Immobile, like.'

And Reuben said, 'Yeah, like that.' And they smiled at each other and got embarrassed again.

'Maybe it would be easier if you weren't doing it alone. I could help you unpack.'

'You'd do that?'

'Course I would. Hell, what're friends for? Just let me use your phone a minute, tell Trevor where I am.'

Of course, the first thing Trevor said was could he come over and help, too, so Arlene put her hand over the phone and asked Reuben if he could. Reuben said yes, of course, but additionally he got this sweet look on his face, like he really liked Trevor, which Arlene already knew, but every time she saw it she liked it better than the time

before. He had good taste in kids, there was that to be said
for him.

Trevor got deeply involved in a box of books. He arranged
them on Reuben's bookshelf alphabetically, according to
the name of the author. This seemed to impress Reuben,
and it amazed the hell out of Arlene, who knew he didn't
get his knack for organization from her side of the family.

She stood in Reuben's kitchen unpacking better-than-
everyday china, handing it up to Reuben, who arranged it
on the high shelves. She felt so short beside him, like he
was standing on a chair, which he was not. A little half-
Siamese cat with blue eyes came mewing around her feet
and Arlene bent down to pet her. The cat arched her
back and purred.

'I didn't know you had a cat.'

'That's Miss Liza.'

They hadn't said anything for a long time, and after
saying that they fell silent again.

The light through the windows went murky with a
coming rain.

Then she opened the box with the pictures. They were
all framed and laid flat, wrapped in newspapers. She un-
wrapped the top one. It was a photograph of a nice-looking
young couple, a handsome young black man, hardly more
than a boy, with his arm around a pretty girl. And the man
looked a little familiar. Almost like Reuben. When she

looked up, he was over near the closet, looking back at her, watching her look.

'Is this your brother, Reuben?'

'I don't have a brother. That's me.'

'Oh.' *Boy, what a stupid thing to say, Arlene. Oh.* But it was a shock, one she hadn't nearly adjusted to yet. She must have known, somewhere in the back of her mind, that he wasn't born with his face blown up. But she'd never thought about it, and certainly never expected to see what he'd looked like before, when he was still whole. So she just kept looking. And he just stood by the closet, watching her look. 'Who's this pretty lady?'

'Eleanor. She was my fiancée at the time.'

'But you never got married?'

'No. I've never been married.'

'No. Me neither.' She had to tell him that sooner or later, and it just sort of came out.

Eleanor seemed about two shades darker in skin color than Reuben, smooth, shiny black skin, and her hair all drawn back, looking stylish, like somebody with a world of class. Like somebody Arlene never was and never could be. Like somebody Reuben really should be with. Arlene couldn't seem to get a bead on which face hurt her more. 'I can't believe how handsome you were. Oh, God. I'm sorry, Reuben. Sometimes I say the stupidest things.'

She looked over at Trevor, preoccupied with his bookshelf, to see if he was taking in any of this very personal stuff. He was not. He was lost in his own little world.

'Wouldn't it be nice if I still looked like that?'

'No.'

She hadn't known she was going to say that. It just sort of said itself. And the funny thing was, he didn't ask her to explain. He just stuck his head in the closet and went on about his unpacking.

From *The Other Faces Behind the Movement*

Because, you know, a man like that one in the picture, he would never so much as give me the time of day. He would never have shown up in a little hick town like this one in the first place, and if he had, he'd be with that handsome, sophisticated woman, and I just know he would speak down to me.

It was real hard to stop staring at that picture. Hard to explain why. It felt like it had ahold of someplace in my gut and it wouldn't let me go. I mean, it just put a whole lot of things in a whole different light.

And then, when I got over that, there was the one of Reuben's parents. They were real good looking too. And they seemed to have that same something, that same thing Eleanor had, and I couldn't even say for sure what it was, but this much I did know: Reuben had it and I did not. He'd never lose it and I'd never learn it. Some things start out a certain way and never change.

I asked Reuben if they were still alive, his parents. He said they were, that they lived in Chicago. Oh, thank God, I thought. Now I would probably not have to meet them, and if I never met them, I would never read on their faces that I was not Eleanor material and never would be.

And then, even though I tried not to, after a while I set Reuben's parents down and picked up that first picture again. While I stared at it I thought about my mother, and the way she used to shop. We didn't have much money, see, when I was growing up. So she'd buy seconds, different types of damaged goods, rather than an item of clothing that was whole and unflawed but essentially poorer in quality.

'But Momma,' I'd complain, 'it's got a stain on it.'

And Momma would say, 'Good thing for you it does, little girl, or we'd a never been able to afford it.'

Then I looked up at Reuben again and he was still standing in the closet, and one more time I caught him looking back at me.

This hard rain started pounding on the roof.

She tucked her boy into bed at ten, since it was Saturday, and no school the following day. He asked if they could get a cat and she avoided answering. A few minutes into the eleven o'clock news came the knock.

The rain was really coming down now. She didn't even realize how much until she opened the door. It fell in sheets behind him, and he stood on her front porch soaking wet, his hair, his clothes saturated, water dripping off his chin.

'You're sopping wet. You better get in here.' He stepped inside and she closed the door behind him. 'I'll get a towel.'

She went through her bedroom into her own bathroom to get the big cushy one. When she came out with it he had followed her into the bedroom and was standing by the bed, dripping water onto the carpet. She sat him down on the edge of the bed and toweled his closely cropped hair.

'Don't take this wrong, but what are you doing here?'

'I got lonely. It was the funniest thing. Something about having you and Trevor in the house with me all day. After you left the house seemed so empty. I don't want to be alone anymore, Arlene.'

As he said this last thing he reached out for her and put his right hand around behind her back and pulled her up close. She set one knee on the bed beside him and held the back of his head, feeling the moisture from his wet clothes soak through her bathrobe. He didn't touch her in any intimate way, just held her close, but it *felt* intimate, very much so, the way his forehead pressed against her chest and his face just remained there between her breasts, his breath warm.

'Why didn't you take your umbrella, silly?' She knew he had one. She'd unpacked it herself.

'I couldn't find it.'

'I put it in your front closet.'

'Oh. I didn't think of that.' A gentle kiss in the open V of her bathrobe, on the bony part of her chest, made it hard to swallow.

'Doesn't everybody keep their umbrella in the closet?'

'No. I don't.'

'Where do you keep it?'

'In the umbrella stand.'

'What umbrella stand?'

'That tall wicker thing.'

'Oh, is that what that was? I thought that was some kind of big skinny planter. I put it on the back porch.'

She could feel him lean back, still holding her to him, and if he'd gone all the way over backward on the bed she'd have been on top of him, which she somehow could not manage on such short notice. So she resisted without meaning to.

He said, 'You seem tense.'

'Do I?'

'Last time you were so sure.'

'Yeah, well. Somebody had to be.'

He pulled his head back a little and she wiped his face with the towel. Even though it was mostly wiped dry on her robe. Maybe she'd be lucky and wouldn't have to explain it. Maybe he'd just know somehow.

If he asked, maybe she'd give the easy reason, not that it wasn't true. That it was hard, being stone cold sober and all, and used to having that painkiller to grease over the rough spots, which you cannot help but have when any two people are so new to each other. But most of it wasn't that. Most of it was, as far as she could tell, that she'd been wrong about what this could be. He was not an in-the-meantime kind of a man.

And then, listening to the rain on the roof and pulling his head against her again and holding it there, she was able, by virtue of his presence, to help smooth over the moment, to know what she should have known all along. What she had known all along in a very deep spot where she knew better than to allow herself to go. Alone, anyway.

That Ricky wasn't ever coming back.

And even if he ever did, which he wouldn't, what kind of woman would she be if she opened the door?

She leaned forward with him and he ended up on his back on the bed, with Arlene on top, and the handsome young man in the picture came back again, filling up her mind. She would never understand the forces that had brought him from there to here.

It took her back to that place again, the one she didn't like. The one where she knew that, by all rights, he was something she should never have been able to afford.

Chapter Fifteen

REUBEN

He woke up knowing full well where he was and remembering everything. Still, the night seemed distant, like something you'd do while drunk. Something harder to imagine in the sober morning. He opened his eye.

She was on his right side, where she was supposed to be. Wide awake and up on one elbow, watching him. He wanted to reach his hand out, to see if she would take it, but he didn't.

'Hey,' he said quietly.

'Hey.'

'You okay?'

'Sure. Why wouldn't I be?' They lay together for a time, silent, not touching in any way. 'You slept in that eye patch all night. Isn't that uncomfortable?'

'Actually, yes. It is.'

'Someday you'll have to take that off around me.'

'Someday.'

'Is it real bad?'

This was not something he could explain. That it was not grisly, as people expected; maybe they would have liked it better if it had been. Grisly or not, people liked some vestige of an eye, some evidence that it had at one time existed as nature intended.

'It's both better and worse than what you're expecting.'

She slid down under the covers a little farther and rested her head on his chest. 'Know what I was just lying here thinking?'

'No. What?'

'I was just thinking you're gonna have to pay it forward.'

'Me? Why me? Maybe he was doing this for you. You're his mother, after all.'

'Nope. I saw his notes. It said your name in one of those circles.'

'I think his idea was to get us married, though.'

She fell silent, pulled away, rose, and began to dress.

Before he could slip out of the house, he heard Trevor in the kitchen, pouring something that sounded like cereal. And there was no way out of the house that did not involve crossing by the kitchen doorway.

He stopped quickly in the hall and Arlene ran into his back.

'What happened?'

'Trevor's up.'

'Well, of course Trevor's up. He don't ever sleep past six, not even on a good day.'

'This is kind of embarrassing.'

'Why?'

'I'm his teacher.'

'So?'

'I'm not sure what to say to him.'

'How 'bout the truth?'

Oh. Right. The truth. Trevor already knew parts of this, yet somehow Reuben hadn't thought to discuss it outright. Now it seemed he had no choice. He stepped into the kitchen, where Trevor sat at the table in his pajamas, pouring milk onto a ridiculously large serving of Rice Krispies.

'Hi, Mr St Clair.'

Reuben sat down at the table with him. Arlene circled around to the stove and asked how Reuben liked his eggs.

Reuben looked up, confused. 'Who, me? Oh. I didn't know I was staying.'

'Got someplace you got to be?'

'Uh, no. Actually, no. Thank you. However you're going to make them for yourself is fine.'

'Scrambled it is.'

Reuben turned his attention back to the boy. 'You don't seemed surprised to see me here, Trevor.'

Trevor shrugged. 'Your car is out front.'

'Good point.'

'Were you here all night?'

Reuben shot a glance at Arlene, more a silent cry for

help, really, but she was busy blowing on a burner, trying to get it to light. Surely she could hear all this but was leaving Reuben on his own. 'Actually, Trevor, yes. I was.'

'Cool.' Trevor pulled the Sunday paper off the chair beside him and dug up the color comics.

'Is that a problem to you, Trevor?' It seemed like a stupid question even as he heard himself say it, because most kids don't use the word 'cool' to describe their problems. It was so far from the reaction he'd expected that it seemed he hadn't quite heard it yet.

'It was practically my idea.'

'Another good point.'

'Are you two going to get married?'

'It's a little soon to think about that. But your mother and I do like each other.'

'I just knew you would. I just knew it. I sure hope you get married. I don't have too many new ideas for my project.'

From *Those Who Knew Trevor Speak*

When I got home that night I called Lou, long distance.

'Wow,' Lou said. 'You're getting laid. That's amazing. Wish I could say that.'

I tried to explain that something felt dishonest about it. It wasn't easy to explain. The only examples I could find involved my shame in being seen by Trevor the following morning. The feeling that I was doing him wrong by being there. He asked if Trevor seemed to mind, and I had to tell the truth.

He pointed out that the only person who felt odd about it was me. I thought that meant I was worried about nothing. I'm used to that. It's a specialty of mine. That's what I wanted him to tell me, I think. That my anxiety was based on nothing, like a shadow with no mass behind it; then, once he'd told me so, I thought it would disappear like a shadow flooded with light.

That's not what he said. He said I was the only one who felt dishonest and I was the only one who knew my intentions. Maybe my intentions were dishonest.

I tried to dismiss his comment, but the minute he said it I felt this great sweep of shame. I admitted to Lou something I'd never said out loud to anyone. Arlene wasn't quite what I'd pictured for myself. She wasn't someone I'd usher into a room on my arm with great pride.

'In other words,' he said, 'you're ashamed of her.'

'I didn't say that.'

'Sure you did.'

All these thoughts started going around in my head at once, making it hard to breathe. I realized that this was her worst fear about me. That I looked down on her. Worst fears are always based on a grain of truth. That's what's so bad about them. I wondered if she had a friend she talked to like this. I wondered if she talked about my face and how hard it was to be physically close to me.

Lou said, 'If you really want somebody else, go find somebody else. You're not doing her any favors.'

I said, 'No. I want her.'

It surprised us both.

I just liked the way I felt around her. The way she made me feel. Which suddenly seemed so much more real and important than wearing a woman on your arm.

Lou told me a story about his most recent lover. A man who, like most men in his life, held him at arm's length until Lou couldn't take it anymore.

'I finally issued an ultimatum. Get the hell into my life, or get the hell out of it. If you want to stop feeling dishonest, Reub, try making an honest woman out of her.'

When I got off the phone things began to look clearer.

When he finally found it, the ring he knew was the right ring, he saw he would have to all but drain his savings, which he hated to do. Rainy-day money. It made him feel good just knowing it was there. But he knew it wouldn't be there for long.

The ring wasn't big enough to be flashy, but it was big enough, set in white gold with smaller diamonds half-way around the band. A little old-fashioned, but he liked that about it. A little like his mother's, but not enough to be significant. It was just the right one because he knew it was.

He left the ring sitting in the store, went home, and obsessed about it. Decided to sleep on it, but he didn't sleep well. In the morning he went by the jeweler's again, afraid it would be gone. When it wasn't, he put it on layaway, knowing he could still change his mind.

But on his next breakfast-table encounter with Trevor, he knew he had to do it. He looked at Trevor and knew. He couldn't buy a cheaper ring, or cheapen their relationship by buying none at all. To do right by Arlene was to do right by Trevor. And of course, himself.

He had it in his pocket the next night when he took her out to dinner.

She wore a rose-colored silk blouse and smiled openly, looking for all the world like someone he'd always known and always wanted, with no doubts in between. He stuck his hand in his jacket pocket and grasped the little velvet-covered box. He was sure. He almost brought it up but missed the moment. But he would. It was only a matter of timing. He was sure.

And she might not be.

He'd been so busy with his own doubts, he'd forgotten to consider the very real possibility that she might say no. He took his hand back from his pocket and tried to forget the box was there.

When he walked her to her door later that evening, they both claimed exhaustion. Reuben gave her a small, chaste kiss.

The moment made him nervous and reminded him of the night she'd come into his arms unexpectedly, with an offer of herself, right around the time he'd expected the kiss-off. He'd loved her for that. Even as he ran away. Everything else had been a game to avoid this very moment, when he knew damn well she was what he wanted, and knew also that something was wrong.

'You okay?' she said. Her voice sounded faint. Scared. Or he was scared enough himself to hear it that way.

'Sure. Why wouldn't I be?'

'I dunno. You seem kind of funny tonight.'

'Just tired.'

'Yeah. Me too.'

He called himself a coward on the way to the car.

Halfway home it hit him, like waking from a dream. He could not imagine what he had been thinking, or why. He could not believe he'd almost said it out loud. He thought about Arlene, tried to bring her picture to mind, but she looked like a stranger. When he got home he found the receipt for the ring in his drawer, right where he'd left it.

Miss Liza jumped on the bed with him and rubbed against his chin. He told her everything. Described the cliff from which he'd almost jumped. She agreed that humans were impulsive and strange. At best. He told her he'd return the ring in the morning, but he never quite got around to that.

Chapter Sixteen

SIDNEY G.

For their benefit, he injected a little swagger into his walk. He knew they were behind him, his senses said so. His simple good sense said so. He knew as he left the bar that they would follow. The beers had gone to his head, affecting his gait and balance, a dislocation that needed to be thoughtfully overcome.

He turned into the alley anyway. To do otherwise would have made him someone else entirely. Which he would never allow. Sidney G. until the end, but this was not the end. It would take a bigger army than this. Besides, he could feel the cold steel against his side. Consider things equal.

'Hey, big man.' A sharp call from behind him, in a voice he knew. A voice that had been in his face earlier tonight.

Hey, she'd been sitting at the bar alone; how was he to know she was with this guy? And also if it had worked, why should he have cared?

But this was a small town, nothing like the real world, and this big, stiff redneck behind him had some other big stiff rednecks on his small-town, small-time team. These fools thought fists would tell the final tale.

Toto, I don't think we're in Kansas anymore.

'I'm talking to you, stupid.'

Sidney G. stopped, wavered slightly, and turned around. There were four of them at the mouth of the alley, backlit by the streetlight, breathing clouds of steam into air left cold and clear by yesterday's rain.

They moved up, the lady's sorry boyfriend in front, with his three stooges standing just to the rear, smiling in a sickening chorus.

Gotcha now, trash-talking city boy.

That's what you think.

'So, big man. Tell me again what you said about my momma.'

Sidney G. smiled. Breathed deeply, expanding his belly against his waistband and its bulge of cold metal. 'Hey, you know, dude, that wasn't really true, what I said about your momma. I didn't really do her.'

The four men sneered, heavy with their own imagined power.

Got you on the run now, city boy.

That's what you think.

'I mean, big ugly lady like that? I don't care how much she begged. Just not into it.' Sidney smiled and pulled the gun out from under his coat. He was drunk, full-on drunk. Drunk enough to make a mistake. A really stupid mistake, like facing four men in an alley, never stopping to look behind his back.

He tried to clear his head too late.

A strong hand grabbed his right wrist from behind, another wrapped around his upper arm. A victim of his own slowed reflexes, Sidney G. sank to his knees under the pressure, felt the sickening, cracking give in his elbow. Thought he was going to throw up from the pain. Thank God he was oiled. Man, that would hurt like a son of a bitch in the morning. If there was a morning.

Bent double with the pain, gun skittering over the pavement out of his reach, he felt the heavy boot dig into his gut, lifting him slightly off the ground. But he didn't cry, or apologize, or beg for mercy; he just spit on the man's shoes. Sidney G. to the end, which this seemed to be.

When he first heard the sound, he was too drunk and in too much shock to know what it was. A bee buzzing near his ear, maybe. But the legs turned, all those legs he'd been staring through. And his head came up slightly and he saw it, like a mirage, haloed from behind in the night through all those legs, a little dude on a little scooter, revving the throttle like he thought he had a Harley underneath him.

The little guy popped the clutch, the bike jumped and almost sprang a wheelie, then tore down the alley into the fray. The legs jumped to safety.

Goddamn, Sidney. The cavalry.

The little dude stopped beside Sidney G. and reached a hand down, and he took it, almost pulling the kid off the bike, like a drowning swimmer who nearly pulls down the lifeguard.

Kid let go in order to pop the clutch again. Then, holding strong to the left hand Sidney gave him, he pulled Sidney to his feet. Sidney jumped for the seat, missed by a mile. Fell to the pavement and was being half dragged. Kid tore along out of reach of their pursuers, bouncing Sidney G. behind him. Sidney didn't take offense, though – worse stuff waiting in that alley.

Then the kid hit the brakes, spun the bike halfway around, nearly dumped it. Pulled hard, and Sidney got a leg over the back of the seat, grabbed a piece of the kid's jacket with his left, trailing his twisted right arm.

They sat that way for a protracted second, listening to the rev of the engine, noticing that the five men had positioned themselves on both sides, blocking the alley in each direction. Three on one side, two on the other. A no-brainer.

'Hold on,' the kid said.

Dammit, I'll try.

Kid shot the bike forward and whipped it around, hard to do in that little space, dabbing and correcting with his feet for balance, headed for the side that held only two.

Hit the gas and went right at them.

Sidney wondered how long it would take them to get smart and pick up the gun.

One of the men caught the kid's sleeve and yanked. Pulled him over sideways, trying to lay the bike down. Hit him in the eye, Sidney told himself, but he had only one hand and he needed it to stay with the crusader. The bike

189

lurched over to the left. Sidney G. put his foot down and so did the kid, fighting against the weight and crazy angle of the bike.

It'll never work, he thought. We're going over.

But then, Sidney G. rode bigger bikes. This one was light.

One good push from each of them brought the machine half upright. The kid hit the gas and the bike lurched forward, wrenching his sleeve loose from the last redneck's grasp.

They tore out of the alley, cornering right, toward the freeway. Sidney heard a popping sound behind him, which he recognized as gunfire from his own weapon. But no impact or pain to go with it, other than the pain of leaving that gun behind; he'd miss it.

'What the hell did I ever do for you?' he screamed into the kid's ear, but the wind and the engine roar took his words away.

A wave of sickness and pain washed over him. They skidded onto the freeway ramp, Sidney G. having enough to do just holding on. Just trying not to pass out.

He flickered in and out of the space just underneath consciousness. The pain was there, waiting patiently for him. He'd go up and face it in a minute. He always had before.

There was something clean and victorious about waking

up feeling that bad. It meant he was alive still. That he'd survived again.

He opened his eyes.

The ceiling spun slightly. He looked down at his right arm, the source of the worst pain. It was clearly broken at the elbow, swollen to two or three times its normal size, and pointing in an unnatural direction.

He dug his pill container out of his jacket pocket with his left hand. Spilled the contents out into his lap. Found two Percodans and swallowed them without water.

Then he lay there with his eyes closed, tallying up the damage. The tops of his knees felt bruised and abraded, but he didn't want to look down. Not yet. No significant movements until the pills kicked in. And he sensed a place in his gut that might even involve a cracked rib or two. Drawing a full, deep breath was somewhere between inadvisable and impossible.

He drifted half asleep for a few minutes and then it washed over him, the relief, like the throwing of a switch. Gradually muting the pain, pushing it so far into the background that it was practically not there at all.

He moved to stand. Well, the pain was there, actually, but it almost felt like someone else was having it. He pulled to his feet and stood, wobbly and nauseous. Looked around, found himself in a small, barely furnished apartment. No one else around. He walked to the open window, hoping fresh air would help.

He found the kid outside the window, sitting on the roof. He looked skinny and pale and no more than twenty, and like somebody Sidney G. would never hang with, never in a million years.

'Hey,' the kid said.

'Hey.' Sidney G. breathed a sigh of relief, now consciously accepting that he was alive, and doped well enough on the Percs to consider that a good thing. 'You must be the guy pulled me outta there last night.'

'Yeah. I would've taken you to the hospital but you passed out. I could barely keep you on the bike. I had to hold on with your left arm over my shoulder. I couldn't work the clutch. Had to come all the way home in second. Didn't dare try to go any further.'

See? Sidney thought. Life had this way of being good to him. Just what he didn't need was a trip to the hospital. Start there, end up in jail. Wouldn't even be in this backward little whistle-stop if he could afford for his whereabouts to be a matter of record. Stupid kid wouldn't have thought of that, but it worked out without a problem. He'd go back to L.A., quiet like, and see that doctor who kept good secrets. Then he'd slip out of town again before anyone was the wiser.

'You know, kid. Good thing you're not like me. Good thing for me, that is. I woulda just sat at the end of that alley and laughed. Figured that son of a bitch brought it on hisself.'

The kid turned his eyes up to Sidney G., a dark, cold look on his face. No sense of humor, no style. A good haircut but nothing to go with it. Nothing of substance inside.

'Funny way to say thank you.'

Sidney G. sat on the edge of the window. He didn't say thank you, not unless he damn well got it in his head to. Sure as hell didn't say it on cue. He looked through the trees, down to the street, where a little snip of white from the kid's scooter showed through. Made him feel good to see it. Somewhere down deep it made him feel good. Like it had last night.

'Cute little scooter you got there. Ever ride a real bike?' Sidney G. took a cigarette out of his pocket. Tried to light it with his left hand. Kid grabbed the smoke and the lighter away and threw them down to the street. 'Hey.'

'Not in my place.'

'Yeah, hell of a nice place you got here. A real palace.'

'Bite me.'

'Excuse me?'

'You heard me. I said bite me.'

The kid came in through the window. Sidney backed up, groggy from the pills. How could he have backed up? He never did, not even in the face of death. But that arm. He didn't even want it touched, jostled, plus he couldn't think straight. So he ended up with his back against a bare wall and this hopeless little punk right in his face.

'It *is* a real bike, and it's a damn good thing for you it's small, or we'd both be dead. That guy who was trying to kill you had it almost over on its side. If I couldn't have held it up with one leg we'd both be dead now. Why did I even do that? Why did I risk my life to help you? You're such an asshole.'

'Excuse me?'

'You heard me.'

'I could take you with one hand tied behind my back.'

'Go for it.'

But then again, it was his good right that was tied, and besides, the stupid little brat had helped him, even if he was being a snot about it now.

'Why did you, anyway?'

'I didn't know you yet. Didn't know what an asshole you are.'

'Why would you help somebody you don't even know?'

'You wouldn't understand.'

The kid backed up out of Sidney's face, and Sidney, who agreed that he probably wouldn't understand, went downstairs and found his cigarette and lighter on the front lawn. He sat smoking for a while, wondering what to do next.

From an interview by Chris Chandler for
Tracking the Movement (1998)

SIDNEY: *I'm not such a bad guy. Am I such a bad guy? Just like everybody else, I guess, only they're dead and I'm still here. Do you think I'm such a bad guy?*

CHRIS: *I don't even know you, Sidney.*

SIDNEY: *Kinda hurt my feelings that he took a disliking to me. Not that I care. I mean, what a jerk. But you sorta think, somebody saves your life, it'll be special from that point on.*

Only thing special was when he told me about the Movement.

I didn't know yet. Had to wonder if it'd hit L.A., or if I'd be the one get to bring it in. But that's a bad way to hear it, anyway. Somebody tells you you're not even good enough to sit on their front grass. But I'm still trying to get it, you know, why somebody'd take the time to do what he did. So he tells me about the Movement, but then he says I'm not allowed to touch it. Do you believe that shit?

CHRIS: *He was angry.*

SIDNEY: *He tell you that?*

CHRIS: *Yeah. He did.*

SIDNEY: *I don't believe that shit. Why? 'Cause I talked down his little scooter? Why would he take that dislike to me? Like I got some kinda disease, I'll just destroy the whole thing. Movements are for the people. They belong to the people. I'm the people just as much as blondie with the teeny-tiny scooter.*

CHRIS: *Matt. His name is Matt.*

SIDNEY: *Yeah, whatever. Nobody tells me what I can and can't touch.*

Later, back in the city, in a run-down duplex in South Central, Sidney G. lay in bed beside her and told her he'd missed her, which was pretty much true. His right arm had been encased in a Fiberglas cast, almost from wrist to shoulder. It itched slightly in the heat, and the painkillers buzzed in his head.

She asked how long he would stay this time.

'Long as you want me to,' he said, even though it was

nowhere close to the truth. 'Stella, you don't think I'm an asshole. Do you?'

She snorted and rolled to face the wall. 'You got your moments. Since when do you care what anybody thinks?'

'I don't, I guess. Ever heard of Pay It Forward?'

'No, what the hell is it?'

He tried to stroke her hair with his left hand but she jerked her head away. She was mad again. Still. Over something long over and done, something as basic as who and what he was, had always been to her.

'A new movement.'

'What kinda movement?'

He lay on his back with his left hand behind his head and told her as much as he knew about it. As much as the kid had told him – before kicking him out without so much as a ride to the train station. He even told her that the kid only explained it as an example of something Sidney could never be trusted to do. He wasn't sure why, maybe because it was Stella and he had missed her some, but he explained that the kid had told him to go away and have no part of it, that he'd start over with somebody else, somebody who could be counted on to pay it forward. That he didn't even want Sidney's fingerprints on his precious living chain letter.

'Kinda hurt my feelings.'

'You got no feelings.'

'Hey.'

'It's true.'

'So, you do think I'm an asshole.'

'What the hell you even tell me about this Pay It Forward

thing, anyway? Why you even still thinking about it? What a stupid idea. Think how long that'd last in L.A.'

'I guess.'

'You gonna leave money for the kids this time?'

'If I can do some business today.'

But the only business Sidney had on the books for that day was heading out of town again. He'd already stayed too long.

From *The Diary of Trevor*

I have no idea what happened between Reuben and Mom. Must've been really weird, though. Because now every time I see Reuben he says, 'So. Trevor. How's your mom?'

And then he says, 'So. Does she ever ask about me?'

Ask what? I'm always thinking. But it's usually better not to mix into these things.

Then I get home and Mom says, 'Ever see Reuben?' And I say yeah, I see him all the time. And she says, 'So. Does he ever talk about me?'

Sometimes I want to yell at them both. I want to say, 'Just talk to each other! It's not that hard! I mean, this is not brain surgery, guys.'

But grown-ups hate it when you talk to them like that.

So, I have this system. I never tell either one of them what they really want to know. Then, sooner or later, they're going to have to break down and talk to each other.

Sometimes I worry that I'll be this weird about a girl when I grow up. I hate to think that.

Chapter Seventeen

ARLENE

Loretta stirred milk into her coffee cup with that little *clink-clink* sound that grated on Arlene's nerves. Loretta's Mr Coffee machine was broken again, and since she had never been any too fond of instant, she had shown up at Arlene's house for coffee this morning. Arlene's Mr Coffee machine never broke, so she was forced to conclude that Loretta used hers too hard.

Arlene decided that when she had two years sober like Loretta, she would not drink twenty-two cups of coffee a day. Then, realizing the uppity sound of that sentiment, she mentally changed the wording: *if* she ever had two years sober.

It wasn't as easy as it looked in the directions.

Usually she liked having Loretta around, the more the better, but she'd been out of sorts the past week, so much so that she hadn't phoned her sponsor once, a detail not lost on Bonnie.

Loretta's voice broke the stillness. 'You don't talk much about him anymore.'

'Who?'

'What do you mean, who? That guy you was all fired up about.'

'Oh.' Somehow she thought Loretta meant Ricky, a fact she couldn't explain and chose not to mention. 'I guess I been sort of avoiding him.'

'Didn't go so good, huh?'

'What?'

'You know. Sleeping with him.'

'No. It went fine.'

'I'll bet.'

'It was nice. Really.'

'Has he got a lot more scars when he gets his clothes off? I mean, are you, like, touching them, everywhere you touch?'

Arlene combed her hair back with her fingers and wished she still smoked. Or that there was a pack around here somewhere so she could fall off that wagon. There were more scars when he took off his clothes. Around his ribs on the left, and that arm looked real funny. But she hadn't noticed until morning, and it wasn't that big of a deal. 'No, Loretta. It's not that.'

'He doesn't have scars, like . . .'

'What?'

'Down there?'

'No.' Arlene stood up and walked to the stove. This was going to get girl-talk personal, and soon she'd end up spilling the part she didn't even want to know herself. Arriving at the stove, she saw her cup was full, and couldn't find another good reason to be there. 'No, down there he is just about what I'd expect him to be, only more so.'

'So, what's the problem?'

'I wish I knew.' She sat back down. Head in hands. This could not be delayed any longer. 'Last time we went out he didn't stay over. He was acting kinda funny. You know how people act.'

'No. I thought lots of different people acted lots of different ways.'

'I mean how people act when they're trying to say something. Didn't you ever do that? Practice in the mirror, something you gotta say? And then, when you see them, it just sorta hangs there. Like everybody can hear it. I kept thinking the waiter could hear it.'

'So, what did he say?'

'He never did. But I know anyway. He was trying to break up with me. I could tell.'

'You don't know that until you ask him.'

'I know now.'

'You should ask him.'

'Then he might tell me.' She could see Trevor out the window, playing on the garage roof with his friend Joe. She'd never exactly told him not to, but he must have known she wouldn't like it all that well. When she stuck her head out the kitchen window, he climbed back onto the plum tree and waved.

'So, you gotta talk to him sometime.'

'I thought maybe I'd go over to his house with Trevor.' That had worked out unexpectedly well last time, but it seemed a tenuous thread, a little tricky to explain, so she didn't try.

'So, now it's a big deal that he not break up with you.'

'Why does that seem so strange?'

'Last I heard he was just for sex till Ricky come home.'

Arlene rocked back in her chair and fixed Loretta with that look she reserved for the immature, the rude, and the plain stupid. 'Ricky ain't comin' back. Don't you know that, Loretta?'

Loretta's eyebrows arched. 'Don't *I* know that? Don't *I* know? Honey, on last count the only living soul on the face of the planet to not know that was you.'

Arlene sighed and threw the last of her coffee down the sink drain. 'Well, I demanded a recount,' she said.

When Trevor bounced through the kitchen door, she told Loretta to get lost. She said it in a kind of sign language – the kind that works only when you've known somebody a long time.

'I was just gonna have one more cup, Arlene.'

Arlene picked up the Mr Coffee machine, pulling the plug out of the wall as she carried it away from the counter. Three more cups' worth sloshed in the pot. 'Be my guest,' she said and handed the whole mess to Loretta.

'Well. A brick wall don't have to fall on me.' But damned if she didn't take the machine with her.

'Hi, Mom. How come you gave Loretta the coffee machine?'

'Oh. No special reason, honey. Listen. You ever see Mr St Clair now that school's out?'

'Sure, Mom. I see him all the time.'

'Where, exactly?'

'I go over to his house.'

'Oh. We should do that. Sometime. Together.'

'Okay. Now?'

'Well. Maybe not now.'

'Why not now?'

'I didn't call or anything.'

'I never call. I just ride my bike over.'

'Well, that's different, though, honey. With you.'

'Why is it different?'

'Um. Give me a minute to think.'

On their way over in the car, which had been making a troublesome noise lately, she asked yet again, 'When you go over there, Trevor . . . and talk to him . . . does he ever . . . like . . . ask about me?'

'Yeah.'

'How many times?'

'Every time.'

'Really?'

'Yeah. Really.'

'What does he ask?'

'Well, he always says, "How's your mother, Trevor?" and then I say, "Oh, fine, she's fine," and then he says, "So. Trevor. Does she ever ask about me?"' A long silence. 'If he asked you to marry him, would you?'

'He ain't gonna ask me that.'

'If he did.'

'He won't. Can we talk about something else?' It was time to change the subject anyway. It wasn't a very long drive.

When he answered the door, Trevor just bounced right in like he lived there. 'Hi, Reuben,' he called on his way by.

'Hi, Trevor. Arlene. This is a surprise.'

He was in sweat clothes and unshaven, which looked kind of funny, the way the hairs grew only on one side. And he looked sad. Not that any of that mattered to Arlene, who was busy noticing how much she'd missed him. It was a big, heavy feeling, suddenly almost more than her insides could hold.

'Sorry I didn't call first, but—' *But what, Arlene? How you gonna finish that sentence? But I didn't want to give you a chance to say no. Don't bother.* Or worse yet, to hear him say her name in that awful way, the way someone does when they start a sentence that's going to hurt like all hell.

'It's okay. Come in.'

She did, and stood feeling awkward, aware of Trevor

watching, not sure what to say. It wouldn't be like the last time, when they were unpacking, and Trevor was all lost in another world. She wouldn't be able to really talk. But then again, she consoled herself, neither would he.

'Trevor, where do you get off calling Mr St Clair by his first name? I didn't raise you up like that.'

'He said I could. Just for the summer. When I get back in his class in the fall I gotta switch back.'

'It's true, I said he could.'

'Oh. Okay.'

Somewhere in the world, Arlene knew, there was something more to say. If she could only find it. She perched on his couch and he brought her a ginger ale. The silence felt bigger than anything the house could contain.

Trevor said, 'Where's Miss Liza?'

'I haven't seen her for a while. I think she's out in the backyard, stalking birds.'

'I'll go see.' He thundered off, leaving Arlene with room to speak, which she now no longer wanted.

'Arlene, I—'

She jumped in fast, before he could say what she knew he would say if she wasn't careful. 'I really missed you.'

'You did?' He sounded surprised.

'Oh, yeah. Little things. I got used to having you around.'

'What kind of little things?'

'Oh, just, you know.' She knew he didn't. 'Like the funny messages you used to leave on my machine. I don't remember any word for word, but they were funny. I miss things like that.'

'I'm sorry I didn't call. I've had a lot on my mind.'

'Yeah. Me, too.' *Yeah. That's what they all say.*

She reached out and touched his right cheek. The stubbly one. She was making a fool of herself, she knew, but she didn't care. She was almost ready to beg. Everybody regards that as so unthinkable, but somewhere in the back of her mind she figured people do it all the time. Just listen to popular music and you'll hear it. I'd get down on my knees for you. Ain't too proud to beg. Baby, please don't go.

She was just getting ready to tell him it was the sex, more than anything, that she missed. Well, not even the sex itself, though that too, but the frightening closeness that came along. She was just getting ready to tell him that she couldn't give it up again, not so soon. Even though later wouldn't be any better.

Before she could, Trevor came back in with the cat draped over his shoulder.

They stayed for an hour or so, during which Arlene spent most of the time marveling at the ease with which Reuben and Trevor talked to each other. She watched closely, like it was something she could learn.

The following night he called and asked her to dinner at his house. He said he was all settled in and felt ready to cook.

'I was hoping to get your machine,' he said. 'I was going to leave a funny message.'

'Want me to hang up so you can call back?'

'No, that's okay. I'll try to be funny when I see you.'

That's when she first realized that he never had been funny before. Not face-to-face. Only as a voice on a tape.

'Reuben?'

'Yes?' She hated the way she said his name. That big, awful, weighty way that people do before bad news. She knew it came through that way, too. Heard it in his voice. Everybody hates to hear their name spoken that way.

'The last time we went out?'

'Yes.'

'I know what it was you were gonna say to me.'

'You do?'

'Yeah. I do. But don't say it, okay? Please. Just don't.'

'Okay. I won't.' He sounded – she couldn't put her finger on it. Hurt? Relieved?

'You won't?'

'Not if you don't want me to.'

Wow, she thought as she hung up the phone. Who'd have thought it would be that easy?

She'd never been in Reuben's bed before, which was huge and comfortable. The sheets felt new and crisp. She lay on his right side with one leg thrown over him, running her fingers through the hair on his chest. Then stroking over his ribs, feeling the scars under her fingers like a topographical map, just to remind herself where she was. They felt good to her touch because if they hadn't been there, this wouldn't have been Reuben.

She wasn't sure if he was asleep. She allowed herself to drift into a feeling, a sense, that she somehow watched all this from above. Not so much physically, but more in a sense of perspective. She'd been so sure it was over, but if she could have gotten up a little higher, seen a little further, she might have been able to see this. She wondered if she would remember this feeling next time something seemed, in the short run, to be going wrong. She knew she probably would not. She knew people transcended that line of knowledge all the time, but damned if they didn't tend to cross right back again.

She whispered quietly, hoping to plant words in his head without waking him, without really calling attention to herself. 'I'm so glad you decided not to break up with me.'

His eye opened and he blinked and swallowed as though he'd been half asleep. 'Break up with you?'

'Yeah. But let's not even talk about that now.'

'I was never going to break up with you.'

'You weren't?' She propped herself up on one elbow, as if staring more closely might help. 'Well, what were you gonna say to me, then?'

'Is that what you thought I was trying to say last time?'

'Yeah. It wasn't?'

'So that's what you asked me to please not say?'

'Yeah. What was it, then?'

She watched his chest rise with an intake of breath. Having had guys ask her some pretty weird things, usually

208

things that tested her moral flexibility, the waiting wasn't to her liking.

'Never mind. You wouldn't have liked it.'

'Maybe not, but you damn well know I gotta hear it now.'

'Don't laugh, okay? I was going to ask you to marry me.'

Arlene's throat felt tight. Even if she had known what to say, which she did not, she probably couldn't have said it. He braved the silence for a remarkable length of time.

Then he said, 'Not right away. I just thought we could be engaged. For as long as it takes to get to know each other well enough. To take that step. I thought it might be better for Trevor. If I was his mother's fiancé. Instead of just a guy who sleeps over. And better for you. Not in that order, though. I thought of you first. I thought you'd feel better wearing an engagement ring. Even if we didn't set a date right away. It was meant as a symbol of my intentions. Which are honorable. Are you ever going to say something?'

'You bought a ring?' That was something, probably as good a something as any other.

'I guess I did.'

'Where exactly is this ring right now?'

'In my dresser drawer.'

She rolled away and lay on her back with her head on her own pillow. Reuben had a textured ceiling. That was most of what she remembered from the pursuant silence. She wanted to ask which drawer, but she never did.

'Just think about it,' he said. 'Don't answer now. Just think about it.'

She said she would. She didn't say she wouldn't think about anything else, that she'd be up all night thinking about it, but that's the way it turned out to be.

Chapter Eighteen

REUBEN

Arlene had fixed chicken fajitas, Trevor's favorite, to honor the special occasion. Reuben ate too many, the way he had that first night in this house. The same house felt warmer now. Now and then he glanced over at her, expecting a sign.

She had her hair done up, and she was wearing the ring on her left hand, but if Trevor had noticed, he'd failed to comment. Reuben figured he hadn't noticed. It wasn't like Trevor to fail to comment.

'Want me to clear the table, Mom?' he said at last, breaking the quiet.

'In a minute, honey. Reuben and I have something we want to tell you.'

'Okay, what?'

'I think Reuben wants to tell you.'

'Okay. What?'

'Trevor? Your mother and I have made a big decision. That affects you.'

'Okay. What?'

'We've decided to be . . . engaged.'

'Engaged? Like, to be married?'

'That's right.' He glanced over at Arlene, still holding her fork tightly, her eyes closed, as if the words might hurt.

'Yes!' Trevor shouted, startling Arlene's eyes open. 'Yes! I knew it! I told you! This is so completely cool.'

He jumped up from the table and launched into a little dance, which Arlene said made him look just like Deion Sanders.

Reuben said, 'Who's Deion Sanders?'

He looked up to see both Arlene and Trevor staring with their mouths open. 'Who's Deion Sanders?' Trevor asked, a study in astonishment. 'You're kidding, right?'

Arlene rose to collect the dinner dishes, obviously more comfortable now that the tension had been broken. 'Trevor, honey, not everybody follows football.'

'Even so. Deion Sanders.' He sat back down, elbows on the table. 'Don't you *ever* watch football, Reuben? Hey. I just thought of something. Can I call you Dad now? Am I supposed to call you Dad?'

Reuben felt a little warm spot grow behind his ribs, a place that for so long had known only pain. 'That would be fine, Trevor. If you're comfortable with that. And if your mother is.' Arlene looked at them both and nodded. 'So, this Deion Sanders. Does he play for the 49ers?'

Trevor rolled his eyes. 'Boy. We got a lot of work to do on you.'

★   ★   ★

'I thought Trevor was a 49ers fan,' Reuben said when she came back from tucking Trevor into bed.

She slid under the covers, igniting that spot of warmth again. Not even so much sexual, though it could easily enough cross that line. Just comfort, a sort only barely familiar.

'He is. But Deion Sanders plays for Atlanta. So he's sort of an Atlanta fan, too. When Atlanta plays San Francisco, he just can't handle it. He gets so upset, he can't even watch.'

'I love you, Arlene.'

The words seem to reverberate in a suddenly empty room. Reuben wondered who was more amazed to hear them.

'We're gonna make a great family,' she said after a time. 'He sure loves you.'

And then it dawned on Reuben, a thought he'd never had before. It was a sweet thought, but at the same time it stung somehow. He'd never quite known, or let himself know, how much he'd been missing by sealing himself so completely away from others. 'I should go kiss him good night.'

'Yeah. I think he'd like that.'

Yeah. I think we both would.

From the chin down, Trevor lay covered in a Teenage Mutant Ninja Turtles bedspread. The light from the street lamp showed the left side of the boy's face in a soft glow.

'Hey,' Reuben said, and sat down on the edge of his bed.

'Hey.' And then, as a pleasant afterthought, 'Dad.' A

smile broke on his face and came all the way out of hiding. 'Doesn't that sound cool?'

Reuben felt the contagion of the smile sneak onto his own face. 'Very cool.' They sat quietly for a minute. 'Maybe we can watch some games together.'

'Cool.'

'I warn you, I don't know the first thing about football.'

'I could teach you. You know what? This means something went right with my project after all.'

'I was thinking about that. About Paying It Forward. I was wondering how I'm going to do that. How do you do that, Trevor?'

'What do you mean? It's not a how, exactly. You just do.'

'How do you think of things to do for people? I'm afraid I don't have your imagination.'

'You don't think it up with imagination. You just look around. Until you see somebody who needs something.'

'That sounds easy.' *Everybody needs something. How far would you have to look?*

'It *is* easy.'

If you're a child, Reuben thought. 'Good night, Trevor.'

'Night, Dad. Is Mom happy?'

'I think so. I think we both are.'

From *Those Who Knew Trevor Speak*

Actually, I think she was scared to death. But isn't everybody at a time like that, faced with such a big decision? I was scared to death too, but I had every intention of going through with it. But there was also . . . I mean, to complicate things for her . . . I mean, his name came up. Here and there. Which seemed normal to me. I still expected it would work out.

Until that day.

October 19, 1992. It's one of those dates you don't forget. In fact, you don't forget anything about it. You remember the jingle that was playing on the television. You remember the thought that was spinning around in your head a split second beforehand, when everything was still in order. It's trite to say, but your life divides up into before and after, and you don't have trouble placing things in time anymore. You can almost date them, something like B.C. and A.D. I guess it sounds like I'm wasting a lot of time feeling sorry for myself. I won't lie. I haven't completely let go of it. In some ways I have. Not all ways. I'm probably being too sensitive. Maybe other people's wounds heal in a reasonable space of time.

No, I take that back. They don't.

Chapter Nineteen

OCTOBER 19, 1992

Reuben sat on the couch sharing a bag of microwave popcorn with Trevor. Now and then a piece fell, only to be retrieved by Miss Liza, who spent most of her time at Arlene's now, with the rest of the family. Every time she ate a kernel, Trevor told her that cats aren't supposed to like popcorn. She seemed unconcerned.

They watched Buffalo play the Raiders, a good game for Trevor to use as a teaching tool, since he wasn't overly concerned about the outcome. He cheered for Buffalo, but not so much that he couldn't breathe.

Just as the game had gone to commercial, Trevor had been attempting to teach Reuben the difference between a touchback and a safety. Also between a touchback after an end-zone interception and a touchback after a kickoff. Reuben figured he had most of the basics by now, but might have been unclear on these few details.

A Coca-Cola commercial came on, the jingle familiar,

destined to become too familiar, because now Reuben always thinks about it in connection with everything else. Not on purpose. He just hears it in his head every time the whole ordeal plays through again. Which it still does from time to time.

Trevor was feeding Miss Liza a piece of popcorn on purpose. She stood up on her hind legs to take it, one paw braced on Trevor's jeans, one poised in the air as if she might need to bat the prize away.

It should have been a good moment, a good day. A good life. By all rights it should have been.

Reuben heard a knock on the door.

Arlene called in from the kitchen. Said she would get it.

She swung the door open. Reuben looked up. Waited for her to say something. He couldn't see her face, just the back of her head, but he wanted to see her face for some reason.

A man stood in the doorway, saying nothing. A wiry, rather small man, with dark curly hair. The silence seemed to twist into Reuben's stomach somehow, as if stomachs can know things without needing to be taught. Reuben glanced over at Trevor, who stared at the doorway, his eyes fixed and expressionless. That cola jingle kept going against the back of Reuben's brain.

Somebody had to say something, and it was the stranger who finally spoke. 'You don't seem too happy to see me.'

Arlene stomped into the bedroom and slammed the door. Alone in the empty, open doorway, the wiry little man turned his attention to Trevor. 'Aren't you even going to say hello?'

'Hello.' Trevor's voice sounded hollow and cold. It never had before. That was the moment, really, that Reuben knew something had happened – something irrevocable. Trevor never talked that way to anybody.

'You don't call me Daddy no more?'

Reuben felt Trevor cast him a sideways glance. This was all building up to hurt, but he couldn't feel it yet. Just a numbness, a shock, the kind that allows almost anybody to survive almost anything, against their own bets.

'You said never call you Daddy in front of people.'

'Well, that was before, boy. That was then, this is now. You don't even sound like you're happy I'm back. Whatsa matter, boy, cat got your tongue?'

Trevor launched himself off the couch and ran for his bedroom, slamming the door hard enough to make Reuben wince.

The man crossed the living room to the couch and stood over Reuben. Towered over him. Just stand up, Reuben thought, because he would surely be a full head taller and outweigh this little man by half again. But his body didn't do anything he told it to do. The man looked him over the way people who haven't seen his face tend to do, but openly, as though Reuben wasn't looking.

'Who the hell are you?' he said.

Chapter Twenty

GORDIE

Gordie had a date with a man he'd 'met' on the Internet. Gordie loved the Internet, the one thing that, two thousand miles from his old home, his real father, his old familiar life, hadn't changed. Gordie loved things that never changed. The man called himself Wolf, though surely it was not his name. On the screen, you can become whatever you've always wanted to be, and Gordie had become Sheila. Until later that night, how was Wolf to know?

Wolf suggested they meet on Pennsylvania Avenue, right in front of the White House. Right against the White House fence. This was fine with Gordie; in fact, he wondered why he hadn't thought of it before. The street would be crawling with Secret Service and D.C. city cops. Maybe Gordie wouldn't get beat up this time. Maybe that's the one place he'd be safe.

He spent an hour on his makeup.

Ralph, his stepfather, watched TV in his recliner in the

living room. Standing quietly in the kitchen doorway, Gordie could hear the slight click of his breathing, almost a snore. He slipped by Ralph's chair with his head turned away, and Ralph did not wake up.

Gordie stepped out into the city night.

In his pocket he held enough money for bus fare to get there. He jingled it through his fingers. It was not enough to get back. Maybe Wolf would drive him. Maybe Wolf would be different and wouldn't want to send him home at all.

Or maybe he'd have to walk. He should have brought something to wash the makeup off his face, in case that happened, cold cream or something. But he hadn't. He'd chosen to believe that this night he would not be making his way home alone.

He climbed the shallow stairs of the city bus, blinking in the glare of the light. The driver handed him a transfer as if he wished he were wearing rubber gloves, flinging the piece of paper forward so their hands would not touch. It fell into the aisle. Gordie bent down to pick it up and heard a snicker behind him. He should have worn a longer coat over his tight satin pants, the ones with the zipper in the back. Should have done all kinds of things. Should have admitted that the world he stepped into that night was the real one.

He sat right behind the driver, his eyes on the filthy aisle floor, careful not to meet the eyes of the snickerers. It was a trick he'd learned from a movie about gorillas – exaggeratedly averting your gaze to avoid aggression. It only worked about half the time. Gordie figured it probably worked better on the gorillas. Probably they were more civilized.

Gordie paced up and down in front of the iron fence that surrounded the White House. Tourist couples walked by hand in hand, tugging on the arms of their children to bring them in close. Uniformed cops strolled by, stared into Gordie's face, shook their heads or clicked their tongues in judgment. Everybody felt free to judge. It never occurred to anyone to hold their opinion in silence.

Their breath clouded steamy in the biting October air.

He glanced at his watch. Nearly ten o'clock.

At ten o'clock, Wolf would officially be two hours late. Gordie would be left to wonder if he had failed to show at all, or if he had arrived, seen the perfect-cliché white carnation and the young male who wore it, and gone home again. Or maybe gone out and picked up a prostitute, a woman. Anything to keep from going home alone. That was the one part of all this that Gordie truly understood. After a glimmer of hope that there would be company for the evening, almost anything would be better now than going home alone.

If Wolf had shown up and beaten the hell out of him for being Gordie rather than Sheila, that would almost have been better. Then in the morning he could go to school with his tongue gently exploring a swollen lip or a cracked tooth. He would know at least that something had happened. He would bet he was alive. Nobody would beat him up at school, because the bruises would satisfy them that he had received his due already.

He glanced at his watch again. It was after ten now. He would have to walk home.

A uniformed cop cruised by on foot, straining to look into Gordie's face, like a rubberneck at a tragic accident. The cop had dark oily hair slicked back under his cap, and a broad nose. Handsome in a macho sort of way, Gordie thought. He seemed to find Gordie predictably disgusting, but Gordie knew he wouldn't use his fists to say so. He just knew. After all these years, he could tell danger before it struck. He couldn't stop it, though. Just see it coming.

'Excuse me? Sir?'

'What?' The cop stopped suddenly, rocking forward slightly on his toes.

'I seem to have gotten stuck out here with no bus fare.'

'Get your pocket picked or something?'

'Yeah.' *Okay.*

'What the hell you pacing out here for? I been watching you for two hours. Is this, like, a solicitation thing?'

'No sir. I was supposed to meet a friend.'

''Cause if I thought you were out here peddling your services, I'd run you in so fast. Hey, how old are you, kid?'

'Eighteen.'

'Yeah. Sure you are. What's it to me if you got bus fare?'

That's when Gordie knew the cop would give him money to get home.

'I just thought, well, it's a long walk. I could get hurt, you know?'

The cop moved his head as if to study Gordie's face from additional angles. 'You sure as hell could. Why don't you wash that crap off your face if you don't want to get hurt? Here.' He handed Gordie a clean, folded white handkerchief from his shirt pocket.

Gordie took it obediently and wiped his face, feeling a sense of loss. It had been a damn near perfect makeup job. It had looked smashing. He hated himself already, felt ugly without it. Dark flesh-colored smears and streaks of black mascara marred the perfect white cloth now. He tried to go easy around the eyes. Maybe some of the green shadow would survive.

He tried to hand the handkerchief back, but the cop threw his hands up in disgust. Gordie folded the smeary mess to the inside and stuck it in his pocket. He liked that he could keep it. Nobody ever gave him anything.

'Is that better?'

'Shoot, kid, not much. Still looks like hell. Look.' He dug in his uniform pants pocket and handed Gordie three one-dollar bills. 'Go home. Wash your face. Don't let me see you around here again.'

'Thank you, sir,' Gordie said, and took off at a half trot, feeling somehow warmed.

★   ★   ★

Gordie clutched his bus transfer in one hand, fingernails digging through the paper. *Halfway home, don't blow it now.* He stared through the window into the lighted chamber of the bar. It looked welcoming. He had a fake ID, out-of-state though it was. If they wanted to believe it they might.

No women inside that he could see, but he could be wrong. Could be a bunch of good old boys on a night out from the wives. He could learn that too late.

No money for a drink, but someone might buy him one. Gordie just hated like hell to go home alone. Hated to go home at all. He could wash his face for real in the men's room, save himself a hell of a beating if his stepfather was awake and caught him coming in.

Three men appeared in the doorway. Stepped out toward him onto the street. My God, what had he been thinking? He'd really done it now.

'What the hell are you?' one of the men called out, louder than necessary.

Gordie turned quickly and headed for the bus stop. He could hear the click of his own heels in his head; in fact, for a moment, he couldn't hear anything else.

Then, from behind him, 'Got a nice little swish to her walk. Hey. You hear me talkin' to you, boy?'

'You sure that's a boy?'

Two voices. Maybe there were only two of them now. He glanced over his shoulder and saw all three, gaining ground on him.

He broke into a sprint.

A light, powdery snow began to fall.

A split second later something caught him around his legs. His feet came out from under him and he pitched forward. It seemed to take a long time to fall. On the way down he thought about the cop who gave him the handkerchief and the three dollars. If he was here now, watching, would he help? Or laugh?

His chin struck hard on the concrete, and he felt the wind go out of him. He saw some kind of color explode inside his head, behind his eyes. Felt a big male body on top of him, pinning him. Couldn't breathe.

'You wish, huh, boy?'

A slight downward pressure, like a simulation of anal sex. Why was sex always the insult of choice? Gordie felt blessedly removed from this thought, from his body, a gentle sense of shock that always kicked in to help him survive.

Then the great weight lifted and a hand pulled him up to his knees by the back of his hair. He wavered there for an instant, free and unrestrained. A hard shoe in the middle of his back knocked him forward again. He fell loosely, like a sock doll, struck his nose on the concrete. Felt the blood flow down his lip and tasted its metallic flavor at the back of his throat. Something personal and familiar.

A third voice sounded, hollow in his ears. Distant, as if from the end of a long tunnel. His ears felt plugged, and they rang. 'Shit, he just a little boy. I'm goin' back to the bar.'

'Maybe he don't know he's not a little girl.' It was the voice of the man who'd pinned him.

'Leave 'im be, Jack. Come on.'

Gordie lay motionless on the cold sidewalk, playing dead. Nothing touched him. He thought he heard their footsteps walk away, but there were other footsteps. People walking up and down this street. They had been there all along, he realized. He'd been too busy to notice. His senses acutely alive now, he heard the click of their shoes as they cut a wide circle around him.

Blood from his nose pooled around his fingers as he pushed to his feet.

From *The Other Faces Behind the Movement*

You know I got death threats after it first happened? Can you explain to me how it was my fault? Enough people say it is, though, you start to wonder. Like, if I hadn't been out that night. If I'd gone out the next night. The Kid would have made it to the airport by then. He'd be back in his hometown. I guess everybody's thinking it should have been me. I'm just so damned expendable. I'm sorry. I don't mean to sound bitter.

I think if there's a message in all this, it's that things happen the way they're supposed to. The way they have to. I couldn't have gone out on a different night, and the Kid couldn't have made it out of the city that night. Look how much good came in the long run.

It's not my fault. People just like to put a name and a face on their hatred. My face goes real well with hatred. I've noticed that.

It's better, now, though. It was hard for the first few months. But now. Everything's better now.

His mother was home from work – the good news. Ralph was still awake – the bad.

Gordie held the smeary handkerchief to his nose and tried to slip by. If only his mother would let him slip by. But she wanted to see his face, so Ralph saw it, too.

'Oh, honey,' she said, grabbing Gordie's arm. He tried to pull away, but he felt so weak and shaky. 'Oh, Gordie. Honey. What happened to you?' She turned him around and tried to move the handkerchief away. His only cover.

'Nothing, Ma. I'm fine. I fell down, is all.'

She disappeared suddenly, pushed out of the way by her new husband. Ralph loomed in his face, holding Gordie's wrist to keep him from running. Gordie longed suddenly for the familiar company of the three men from the bar. They seemed safer in comparison. At least they were not in his home.

'What the hell's all over your face, boy?'

He felt the back of Ralph's hand, hard. He heard his mother scream. Gordie fell easily, steadied himself on hands and knees, tried to keep his head down. *No more. Not tonight. Please no more tonight.* He wiggled a loose molar with his tongue.

'Stand up to me, boy. You hear?' A roar, a bellow, like the roar of a forest fire out of control. He did not stand up.

Out of the corner of his eye he saw his mother grab Ralph from behind, grab him with her arms around his neck. They yelled at each other, but Gordie couldn't make out the words. Ralph shook her off, turned back to Gordie. But Gordie had seen that brief window of opportunity and used it. He launched from his crouched position like a runner at the gun.

He locked the door of his room before Ralph could catch him.

The door shuddered when Ralph hit it. Gordie wedged a chair under the knob. His hands trembled, a feeling that ran all the way to a place inside his gut. A second strike came, followed by the sound of wood splintering, but the door held.

Then relative quiet.

Gordie could hear his mother's voice, the steady, comforting litany of it. Couldn't make out all the words, though. Something about how Ralph should take some nice deep breaths and she would fix him a nice drink.

Their footsteps moved off down the hall.

Gordie washed his face in his bathroom sink. The comfort of warm water, the sting of soap. Leftover blood and makeup swirled down the drain.

Then he lay on his back on the bed, wondering what Wolf might have looked like. Wishing he had aspirin, but they were in the kitchen.

In time he heard a shy, gentle knock that he knew was his mother. He rose painfully and unlocked the door, then lay down again.

'Lock it behind you, Ma.'

'He's asleep, sweetie.'

'Passed out, you mean.'

She didn't answer. She sat on the edge of his bed and handed him three aspirin and a half glass of water. He swallowed the aspirin. She gave him an ice bag for his face. He wanted to put it everywhere at once. His head pounded with pain, his chin and nose felt painfully swollen. His jaw ached at the spot of the loose teeth. He put the bag over his nose and eyes. The world disappeared.

'He's not a bad man, honey. It just makes him mad. If you could just wash your face before you come home. Maybe change your clothes. Just don't rub his nose in it, you know?'

'Sure, Ma. Okay, I will.'

'He's not a bad man.'

'Ma? I just want to go to sleep. I don't really want to talk tonight, okay? I just want to go to sleep.'

He heard her slip out and close the door gently behind her.

He woke hours later from a bad dream, with melted ice soaking the sheets and pillow around his head. The pain wouldn't let him get back to sleep. He'd been dreaming of the cop who gave him the handkerchief. In the dream, he didn't help. He laughed.

Chapter Twenty-One

CHRIS

The call came in at 7 a.m.; hard to think of it as a good thing. His girlfriend, Sally, groaned, rolled over, and wrapped a pillow around her ears.

Even through a fog of sleep, Chris recognized the voice immediately. Roger Meagan, a friend of sorts. A cop. An unlikely friend. Overall, Chris didn't think highly of cops. He'd met some he liked quite well – Roger, for example – but it discouraged him that the only honest, idealistic, unjaded cops tended to be the brand-new ones. He didn't figure he blamed them for callousing up, not in a world like this one. He fought the tendency himself. Maybe if he could fight it, so could they.

'Sorry, Chris. I forgot you like to sleep in.'

What he liked had nothing to do with it. He rarely got to bed until three. 'What's up?'

'I'm not sure, really. I don't know. Maybe nothing. Maybe a story. I don't know. I guess that sounds stupid.

Wake you out of a sound sleep, then say maybe it's nothing. But if it is something, it's something big. Real big. I just thought it might be a good thing for you to hear it first. I mean, it's known, but – one little angle of it. If you could break some pattern . . . if there is a pattern . . . oh, hell. I'm not making much sense, am I?'

'You're sure as hell not, Roger, slow down. Let me get my brain cells back in line. One fact at a time.' Were there facts involved? He hadn't heard any yet.

'You know gang killings have taken a real drop lately.'

'I heard that. But it's just a fluke, right? I mean, what else could it be?'

'I don't know, Chris. I figure that's where a good investigative reporter comes in.'

'So you want the name of a good one?'

'Shut up, man. You're good. You know you are. Look. Two months ago, the number of shootings drops eighty percent.'

'Drops *to* eighty percent?'

'No. *By* eighty percent.'

'I didn't know it was that much.'

'Well, everybody kind of wants to lay low about it. Like, you just know it can't last. Everybody acts like it's magic or something. We just stay real quiet, like we think we'll . . . I don't know, scare it away or something. Then last month, one gang death in all five city boroughs. One, Chris. Do you realize how remarkable that is? I mean, in a good weekend sometimes we'd get two dozen. I mean, not a good weekend, but . . . you know.'

'And this month?'

'Everybody's alive so far. So far as we know.'

Chris felt his brain pull away into the intricate strain he associated with contemplating infinity. Hard enough trying to figure out how things happen. Why things happen. But why they *don't* happen? Like doing a story on the wind. What would he do, interview people on a street corner in the South Bronx? Excuse me, ma'am, what's your theory on why you weren't hit by a stray bullet last month?

'You think there's a reason?'

'Man, everything has a reason.'

'Want to put your next paycheck on that?'

'There are no accidents in this world, Chris.'

He almost scoffed, but caught himself. Imagine taking the jaded side in an argument with a cop. 'Roger. Where in God's name do you think I'd begin with something like this?'

'Start with a guy named Mitchell Scoggins. He knows something about something. We picked him up on an illegal weapons charge. Went out to settle a score with some rival banger, but nobody got hurt. He said it was a point of honor. But – what honor? Whose honor? Since when is it a point of honor to go after your enemy with a gun and then not kill him? It's like a new gang law or something. But he won't tell me anything about it. I'm "the man", you know? He's not going to talk to me.'

'Where's Mitchell right now?'

'Doing thirty days at County.'

1993 interview by Chris Chandler,
from *Tracking the Movement*

MITCHELL: It's not a New York thing. I mean, now it is. But it didn't start here. It started in L.A. I mean, way I hear it. I mean, word on the street. They sayin' that.

CHRIS: I hear you know all about it. I hear the whole thing started with you.

MITCHELL: Not even close. Nice try, man. You think I got a ego, huh? I tell you what the word is. Guy named Sidney G. He take credit for the whole thing. Tell you he the guy thought the whole thing up. Not that I ever met him. Hell, Sidney tell you all kinda shit. That's the word on the street. Others say no. Sidney G. mighta got it started in L.A., but it's not his. Just picked it up somewheres. Brought it back.

CHRIS: What? Brought what back?

MITCHELL: The Movement.

CHRIS: This is all part of a movement?

MITCHELL: It moves, don't it?

CHRIS: Tell me about it.

MITCHELL: I don't know. I don't see how you one of us. I mean, who the hell are you? Know when I'd tell you? If you crossed me. Then I'd come after you. But I wouldn't kill you, not unless I'm all paid back. Forward, I mean. Then I'd say, I come to kill you, but man, did you luck out. Then I would tell you. It'd be, like, part of my job.

CHRIS: What did you mean, 'forward'? You said something about being all paid back, but you changed it to 'forward'.

MITCHELL: You need to go see Sidney G. He like to talk.

233

CHRIS: *Know where I can find him?*
MITCHELL: *Shit, no. Never even met the man myself.*

He direct–dialed the West Coast after five, New York time, to save a little money, since this probably wouldn't work anyway.

'Parker Center.'

'Detective Harris, please.'

'One moment.'

She clicked him onto a silent hold. He sat for several minutes, fidgeting, jiggling his leg. This was such a waste of time. Then there was ringing on the line.

'Harris.'

'Harris. Chris Chandler here.'

'Right, buddy. What can I do for you? Kind of a zoo here. Gotta talk fast.'

'Thought maybe I could call in a favor.'

'If it's legal and it doesn't have to be right this second.'

'No, whenever. Tomorrow. Monday. Whenever. Thought you might go through your computer. See if you can find me a banger named Sidney G.'

'Last name?'

'Don't have it. I know that doesn't help.'

'What do you need on him?'

'Anything that might tell me where he is. Like, if he had a parole officer, say. Then I'd know how to get in touch.'

'This'll take me a few days.'

'Whatever.'

'There'll be dozens of Sidney G.'s.'

'I'll just have to track them all down, I guess. Just get me a list.'

'Your life, man. Give me three working days.'

Harris faxed him a list two days later: Sidney Greenaway. Sidney Gerard. Sidney Garcia. Sidney Gilliam. Sidney Guzman. Sidney Guerrera. Sidney Galleglia. Sidney Garris. Sidney Gant. Sidney Gonzales. All gang-involved. Three out on parole. Five with only last-known addresses. Two currently incarcerated.

Chris took two months tracking them all down. He thought it made him feel alive. Sally said he'd become totally obsessed, and moved out, maybe temporarily, maybe permanently. Depending on when he came to his senses. He never found Sidney Gerard. The other nine Sidneys had no idea what the hell he was talking about.

He lost two other writing assignments in the meantime, and eight pounds. And started drinking again, though not all that much at first. It bothered him, thinking he would always know it was Sidney Gerard, because it's always the one you can't find.

Looking for a man named Sidney G. Originator of the Movement. Want to make him famous. No personal ques-

tions asked. Or anybody else with info on Sidney G. or the Movement. Something about being 'Paid Forward' or 'Paying Forward'.

Write to C. Chandler at P.O. box below.
Cash reward for right info.

He placed the ad to run for a month in the *L.A. Times*, then decided he'd wasted his money. Homeboys don't read the *Times*. And he had no money to waste, because he'd done no real work for too long.

He visited his brother and borrowed another grand, which was loaned with no guilt or bad feelings. He'd done it before and had always been good for it.

Then he placed the same ad in the *Valley News* and the *L.A. Weekly*.

He opened a P.O. box and tried to work on another story. Every day he checked the box. Every day it was empty. Not even crank letters from impostors out for reward money. Where would he get more money if something broke?

Dear C. Chandler,

Somebody I know see your ad in the Weekly *and show it to me. Sidney G. didn't invent nothin. Not in his whole life. He left me with two bastard kids. He don't care. He is such a asshole. He got that thing from somebody he meet in Atascadero. He hide out there when things get hot. But it don't work forever.*

Last I hear his sorry butt in jail. I don't know where or

care. But his name ain't Sidney nor G. that just what he call himself. His name Ronald Pollack Jr. No wonder you can't find him. I hope you got more trouble for him. I hope it's a trick. That's why I write this. Not for money. But I need money real bad, with these two kids. If you want to send some.

Yours Truly,
Stella Brown

1993 interview by Chris Chandler in Soledad State Prison, from *Tracking the Movement*

CHRIS: *You could be a famous man. Right here in prison.*

SIDNEY: *See how much you know. I'm already famous in this prison. Legendary.*

CHRIS: *I mean famous all over the world. Could help your situation.*

SIDNEY: *In what way?*

CHRIS: *You know, go up before a parole board, and there it is on your record that you made this huge contribution to society.*

SIDNEY: *I don't even come up for parole till ninety-seven.*

CHRIS: *That could change too.*

SIDNEY: *What I gotta do?*

CHRIS: *Tell me how this Movement started.*

SIDNEY: *I tol' you. Started in my head.*

CHRIS: *You must be a really smart guy.*

SIDNEY: *I am.*

CHRIS: *How did you think of something this big?*

SIDNEY: *Just kinda come to me. I just saw the way things kept going all around me. I thought, Somebody's gotta do something different. Change this mess. Then I thought it up.*

CHRIS: *Wow. I'm impressed. You didn't even hear or see something similar? You know, to put the idea in your head?*

SIDNEY: *Nobody put ideas in my head but me. So, how you gonna make me famous? I mean, even more than I already am.*

CHRIS: *Well, I produce freelance stories. I'll have to get a video camera in here. I'll have to go through channels for permission. Then, when we have a spot together, I can sell it to* Weekly News in Review. *They take almost everything I do.*

SIDNEY: *Think the fools that run this place'll do it?*

CHRIS: *When they find out they have a star in their midst.*

SIDNEY: *Maybe the governor'll pardon me. When he see it.*

CHRIS: *You're not exactly on death row, Sidney. I wouldn't count on a pardon. Maybe early parole.*

SIDNEY: *Yeah. Well. You do what you can for me, white boy. I'm sure you can see I don't belong here. Big contributions I could be makin' on the outside. The world need me out there.*

CHRIS: *Yeah. Absolutely, Sidney. I can see that.*

Chris arrived back in his apartment in New York about 7:00 a.m. Right away he called his cop friend, Roger Meagan, woke him up. That's justice.

'You did me a good one, buddy. I owe you. I think this is going to be big. I don't know why I think that. No, I don't even think it. I know it. I just know somehow. Maybe it isn't big yet, but it will be. And by then it'll be my story. Not that I'm at the bottom of it yet. But I will be.'

'Who the hell is this?'

'It's Chris. Did I wake you?' He knew damn well he had.

'Chris, what the hell are you talking about?'

'That story you put me onto.'

'You got to the bottom of that?'

'I told you, not yet. But I will. Tracked it to this small-time banger calls himself Sidney G. He says he thought the whole thing up. He's full of shit, of course.'

'Thought *what* whole thing up?'

'The Movement.'

'This is all part of a movement?'

'It moves, doesn't it?'

Roger groaned. 'I don't know what the hell it does, Chris. I haven't even had my morning coffee. Want to loan me some of your energy?'

I wish I could, he thought. He pulled off his shoes while he talked, and fixed himself a drink with the cordless phone clamped under his chin.

'It's like this, buddy. So far as I can tell. Somebody got it in their head to pass this thing along. It's like a pyramid scheme, only it never goes back to the originators. People just keep doing amazingly nice things for people, and it just keeps going forward. It never goes back.'

'So, what's the angle?'

'There doesn't seem to be one. That's why I'm so excited about this, Roger. Thing is, it's a bitch to track down, because apparently there are no names involved. People go around saving lives, sparing lives, giving money away, and most of them never know who it was that helped them. No records kept.'

He'd learned more about this last part from his visit to Stella than his Sidney G. interview. Sidney remained sketchy on details. Stella had looked at the five one-hundred-dollar bills in his hand and opened right up.

'That's weird, Chris. This is weird.'

'Damn right it's weird. That's why I love it.'

'But, Chris. I mean . . . if somebody saved your life, wouldn't you get their name? So you could pay them back? You know, what goes around comes around?'

'But that's what this is about. You never pay it back. You always *pay it forward*. Like, what goes around goes around even faster.'

'That makes no sense.'

'Why doesn't it?'

'What good is it to the person who started it?'

'Well, this is the world they have to live in. Right?'

A long silence on the line. 'So this gang banger is real altruistic?'

'No. Hell, no. I told you. He's full of shit.'

'So, who started it?'

'I don't know. But I'm going to find out. I'm going to do a major puff piece on this jerk. On *Weekly News in Review*. Make him out to be a total hero. Then I'll put out some kind of eight-hundred number or P.O. box or something, for people with more information. This thing must have touched a lot of people's lives by now.'

'Chris. If the guy's full of shit, why do you want to make him out a hero?'

'Because he's a liar, Roger. And somebody out there knows it. Somebody out there might take offense when they get a whiff of his attitude. Might want to set the record straight.'

'Sounds like career suicide. You'll come out the fool.'

'Anybody can be taken in, Roger. My career'll survive it.'

'It's a long shot, Chris.'

'Life is a long shot, Roger.'

He hung up the phone. It would work. It had to work.

From *The Diary of Trevor*

It feels like there's something wrong with not liking your own father. Like I should be ashamed about that. But it's true, and I don't know what I'm supposed to do about it.

Yesterday I said that to my mom. That I just don't like him. I thought I might feel better to say it out loud.

I thought she would yell at me or hit me or send me to my room.

Instead she just looked tired.

Chapter Twenty-Two

ARLENE

She bumped into Reuben one Saturday morning at a gas station on the Camino. She hadn't seen him in months.

She didn't see his white Volkswagen until after she'd gotten out of her car, and when she did, she almost got back in and drove away. She'd left the engine running because the old Dart didn't always start again after you turned it off. The sign said not to do that, but Ricky, who always smoked while he filled his tank, told her that almost never goes wrong.

Knowing he was there, her heart got to pounding so bad she could hear it in her ears. She felt dizzy and strange and couldn't decide what to do.

And then he came walking out of the convenience store and he saw her. He turned his gaze down to the asphalt and headed toward her, toward his car. She could tell he wanted to walk the other way – that showed – but she was parked close to his car, so there was no way out for either one of them.

'Reuben,' she said, thinking her voice sounded scared. He didn't look up. He didn't say anything. She could still hear her heart. 'Reuben, say something, okay? Yell at me or swear or something. Please?'

He looked up. She met his eye. It made her dizzy again. He looked away.

'Reuben, I just had to try, you know? I had to. Thirteen years, Reuben. He's the boy's daddy and all. Scream at me and tell me I hurt you and I'm not even fit to live, 'cause I know it's all true. Don't just stand there and say nothing.'

He walked around the pump island, right up to where she stood. The toes of their shoes almost touched. He looked deadly calm and she figured he was going to hit her. It would almost have been better if he had. She looked at his face, so close up like that, and it struck her that she'd missed him. Struck her so hard it almost knocked her down.

'He impregnated you,' Reuben said. She'd never heard his voice like that before. Deep. Scary, almost. 'In what other way has he been a daddy to that boy?'

'Well, that's just it, don't you see? He wants to make up for that now. He wants to pay back what he took from me.'

She winced, sure she was about to be struck. Reuben turned away. He walked to his car and drove off without looking back. That was a lot worse.

★　　★　　★

244

When she got home Ricky was lying on the couch, watching TV. 'You moved any muscle at all since I left you?'

'I don't need a lecture today,' he said. He barely moved a muscle to say it.

'Thought you was gonna look for work.'

'On Saturday?'

'Any old day would do. And if you ain't gonna do that, at least pick up your clothes and do your own damn dishes.'

He swung around and sat up slowly, like it hurt him to do it. 'What the hell got into you this morning? I ain't never heard so many complaints come out of you all at one time.'

'I been saving 'em up.'

'I will look for work,' he said slowly, 'when I have me a little more time sober. Ain't easy, just cold turkey like that.' He lit a cigarette, a little unsteady at it. 'When the shaking stops, say. Right now I'm taking on about all I can.'

'Yeah, well if you'd kept it up you'd have almost four months sober instead of just a handful of days. When I had me just a week or two sober I had to work two jobs to keep up the payments on that goddamned truck you ditched me with. And take care of a kid on top of that. I didn't have no goddamn choice.'

'Thought I told you I didn't need no goddamn lecture.' It came out so loud, so strong and angry, she wouldn't dare say anything else. Which she guessed was probably the point. 'What the hell got into you? Huh, Arlene? You hear me talkin' to you? Can't I do anything right anymore?'

'I dunno, Ricky. Can you?'

'Even in the sack now, where we always got on good before, I just can't do nothing right with you. Not that we ever do now.'

'We do, sometimes.'

'Lady, what you give me ain't hardly enough to starve a man.' He crossed the room and stood close, which felt vaguely threatening. 'Used to you'd say I was the best you ever had.'

She stood up to him anyway. Kind of quiet, but she said what she needed to say. 'Sad commentary though it may be, Ricky, I suppose that was true at the time.'

Then she stood, without backing off, and blinked too much, waiting to see what he would do. He didn't explode the way she expected. Just brought his hand up to his face and rubbed his eyes, like the whole thing made him feel tired. She watched his face and wondered why she used to think he was so handsome. He wasn't, really – at least, not taken one feature at a time.

'I just wish to God you hadn't said that. This is about that colored man, right? I hate to even talk about that. How could you let that man in your bed? For God's sake, Arlene. First time I saw him sitting there on the couch I thought, well, at least I know she ain't sleeping with him. Every time I think about it I just—'

She looked up to see Trevor standing in the kitchen doorway. 'I thought you were playing outside.'

'No, I was in my room.'

He turned and slipped away again. She followed him down the hall and into his bedroom.

'Trevor, honey? I'm sorry you had to hear that.' She waited for him to say something back, but the waiting hurt, so she couldn't do it for very long. 'I ran into Reuben this morning.'

'Oh, yeah?' But said with little emotion.

'I thought you'd be interested in that.'

'I see him at school all the time.'

'Oh. Right. Does he ever ask about me?'

'No.' That's all he said, just no. Kind of flat and cold. He didn't go on to say, Why should he? But Arlene could hear it anyway; she could feel that place in the air between them that those words didn't fill.

'Honey, I know I made a mistake.'

'So, fix it.'

'I don't think you understand, Trevor.' Tears took hold against her will. They felt hot and angry. She could think of all kinds of things he wouldn't understand, including some she didn't understand herself. Like why she wasn't ready to give Ricky the boot, even as bad as things were going. She chose to state the one reason that lay completely out of her hands, the part she could not change if she tried.

'Reuben's real upset, honey. He got hurt. No matter what I said to him, he wouldn't take me back now. No way. You didn't see him this morning, honey. He's real upset. He ain't never gonna forgive me.'

'You don't know that he wouldn't.'

'I know.'

'You don't know until you ask him.'

'I know now.'

'You should ask him.'

'I can't, Trevor.'

'Why not?'

'He'd say no.'

'So? You could ask.'

'See, honey. You don't understand. Like I said. I guess it's a grown-up thing.'

She looked over her shoulder on the way out of his room. Trevor looked down, picking nervously at the bedspread.

'Maybe I don't want to be a grown-up, then.'

'Well, honey, nobody really does. God knows it got shoved on me against my will.'

She closed the door quietly behind her.

When she got out to the living room, the TV was still blaring, but no Ricky. His GTO was missing from the driveway. The dirty dishes and clothes were all still there.

She was halfway through the dishes when she heard a knock on her kitchen door. She opened it and Bonnie came through like a freight train. Might have mowed her right down if she hadn't jumped out of the way.

'Girl, are you actually *trying* to be the stupidest woman on the planet, or did it just happen that way by accident? My God, girl. You had that honest, decent man who loved you and wanted to marry you. What's the matter, afraid you might get happy?'

'It's been going on for months, Bonnie. Why get on me now?'

'I just now heard it. You conveniently forgot to tell me. Just so happens you haven't called your sponsor since October. What a coincidence. I got news for you, girl. You don't call your sponsor for more'n four months, you don't have a sponsor.'

Arlene took a deep breath, bent on remaining calm. Her blood pressure had been an issue lately. She poured two cups of coffee and set them on the kitchen table.

'Then why is it I got a lady in my kitchen yelling at me?'

'You don't want me here, I could go just as easy.'

'I want you here, Bonnie.' She sat down in front of her own cup and put her hands over her face. Life kept taking too much out of her. She was going to run out any minute. She could feel it. 'I just want you to say you're still my sponsor.' The tears wanted to come back. Probably she'd be too tired to stop them.

Bonnie sat down in front of her coffee. 'If you're still halfway interested in taking my advice.'

'Tell me how to undo all the mistakes I been making.'

'That's a good start. Okay. Number one. Pack up all his stuff and put it out on the lawn.'

'He's trying though, Bonnie. He really is. He's sober, and going to meetings. It takes a while to change, you know that.'

'Girl. Unlike you, I go to every meeting they hold in this town, every day. If he was going to meetings, don't you think I'd know it?'

'He says he's going.'

'And you're just stupid enough to believe it. Want to know where he's been?'

Something about the way Bonnie said that told her that she held some kind of card. Arlene didn't want to see the face on that card. She tried to answer, but nothing came out.

'Hanging out over at Stanley's.'

'Who's Stanley?'

'Wake up, girl. Stanley's, the bar. On the Camino.'

'He's been drinking?'

'With his ex-wife. Cheryl what's-her-name.'

'You're making that up.' There was a buzzing in her ears like a mild shock, and a numb feeling to go with it. Lots of lies in a small town; this was just one more. 'How the hell would you know anyway? You never go to bars.'

'Me'n Loretta had to go by, make us a twelve-step call. I didn't know the guy from Adam, 'cause it's not like I seen him at any meetings or anything. Loretta, she told me who he was. She didn't want to tell you. Now, you ready to put that fool's clothes out on the front lawn?'

Arlene took a breath and tried to know what she felt. She knew she *should* be ready now. They'd hit low enough. 'If it's true.'

'Would I tell you if it wasn't true?'

'I'll just ask him right to his face.'

'Oh, right. And he'll tell you the whole truth.'

'I'll see what he says.'

'And if he says one thing and I say another? Then who you gonna believe?'

Arlene folded her arms onto the table and let her head fall into that dark cradle. It wasn't nearly comfort enough. 'I didn't think he'd do this to me, Bonnie.'

'Why not? He always did before. And you know what I always say—'

'Yeah, yeah, sure, Bonnie. If nothing changes, nothing changes. If you always do what you always did, then you'll always get what you always got. Insanity is doing the same thing over and over, and every time expecting a different result. I'm up to my ears in little slogans, Bonnie. It ain't doing me no good. I really screwed up everything, didn't I?'

Silence, then she felt Bonnie's hand on her back. 'I'll just leave you to hold that good thought for a while.'

Arlene heard the kitchen door close. She didn't bother to raise her head.

That same evening, Arlene was sitting on the couch watching TV with Trevor. Watching that program called *Weekly News in Review* – which she never found all that fascinating anyway – and her thoughts ran elsewhere.

She knew pretty much what Ricky would say when she mentioned Cheryl Wilcox. He'd say Arlene had given him no choice. That if she wanted him at home she should have given him a little more to stay home for.

She was thinking she should have talked to Bonnie about the sex. Tried to explain that she couldn't make it work with him now. They had, of course, they did, but it didn't really work for her. There was something about it. Something . . . heartless, maybe. Yeah. Maybe that was just the word.

And Bonnie would have said, Yeah, well, everything changes. But it wasn't a change. It was just how it had always been with them. The only thing that had changed was her.

Anyway, none of that mattered now.

She pulled her attention back to the program.

Trevor said, 'This might be interesting.'

'What might? I missed what he said.'

'Next story coming up is about how gang violence might be about to become a thing of the past. Because, like, one person came up with an idea to change everything.'

'I'm sorry. I forgot to pay attention.'

'That's like what I was trying to do. Only not with gangs. Just, you know. One person changing everything.'

By now the program had gone to commercial.

She heard the loud, unmuffled motor of Ricky's GTO in the driveway. Her heart jumped.

She reached for the remote control and shut off the TV. 'Go on into your room now, honey.'

'I wanted to watch this program.'

'I'm sorry, honey. This is important. I gotta have a private talk with your daddy.'

He left the room like he'd been told.

When Ricky swung the door open, she could tell he'd been drinking. He was trying to hide it. Maybe that's how she could tell. He was trying too hard to hide it.

'We need to talk, Ricky.'

'Not now, hon. I'm gonna take a hot shower.'

'That's good. You do that.'

While he did, she packed up all his belongings, which really wasn't much, and loaded them into his GTO. She left him one pair of jeans, one shirt, and one pair of socks, which she laid out on the bathroom sink.

'Don't need those, hon, I'm going right to bed.'

'Fine. I'll call Cheryl and tell her you'll be right there. I'll tell her to turn down the bed.'

And she did.

Ricky dressed and left with no words spoken, and remarkably, no trouble.

Chapter Twenty-Three

CHRIS

The 800 number rang directly into his home. And rang and rang. It rang intermittently in the middle of the night, jarring him out of sleep. The callers seemed surprised, at least as surprised as Chris. They mumbled that they'd expected an answering service or voice mail or something. Most wanted more information about the show they'd seen earlier that night. Nobody seemed to have information. Everybody seemed to want it.

At six in the morning he gave up, drank a pot of coffee, and watched the phone. It didn't ring for hours. He fixed himself a small glass of brandy, feeling he deserved it somehow in lieu of sleep. And peace – he wanted peace. He thought of it as artificial peace. But he needed more than a small dose of peace, so he poured another.

At ten after nine the phone rang again.

The caller said, 'I want to talk to someone who's responsible for that stupid news program last night.'

'Well,' Chris said, 'the thing is, you *are*.'

He listened to a silence on the line.

'Oh. I am?'

'Yes. You are. My name is Chris Chandler and I wrote, produced, researched, and otherwise put that story together.'

'Well, it was a piece of crap, man.'

'Everybody's a critic.' He took a long pull on his brandy. It was helping him feel more relaxed.

'I can't believe you bought that crap about that guy. Sidney G. Man. He is such an asshole. He is a total liar. Totally. How could you have bought all that crap?'

'Actually, I didn't.'

'You didn't?'

'No.'

'You didn't believe he thought up that whole thing?'

'No.'

'Then why did you make that stupid story?'

'Well, it's like this. I know he's a liar, but what good does it do to say so? I got nothing to go by. I don't really know. I was hoping somebody who actually knows something would help me call him a liar.'

Chris did not feel inclined to believe he had such a person on the line or, suddenly, that he likely ever would.

'Well, I know something, and I say he's a liar.'

'You know where he got this idea?'

'Yeah. He got it from me.'

Oh, right, kid. I see. It's not all Sidney G.'s idea. He's just a lying asshole. You thought the whole thing up. You deserve all the

255

credit. 'Okay. So you're the real hero, and I should do a show about you?'

'No, I didn't think it up. I just paid it forward. I just found that asshole getting beaten half to death behind a bar in Atascadero and I saved his butt. I told him about the Movement.'

Chris felt a little tingle behind his ears. Atascadero. Stella said Sidney hid out in Atascadero when things got too hot. But he hadn't mentioned that in the story, he quite purposely hadn't, because he didn't want Sidney to know he'd ever talked to Stella.

'Uh. You know, uh . . . what's your name?'

'Matt.'

'Matt. I'm sorry, Matt, if I was being a little rude. All night I've been up talking to people who know less than I do about all this. So, listen, you don't happen to know how this thing got started, do you?'

'Only that it didn't start with that asshole Sidney G.'

'And you don't know who it was that paid it forward to you?'

'Well, yeah. Of course I know that. Her name was Ida Greenberg.'

'Wait. Wait just a second, okay, Matt? I have to get a pen. I have to get a whole lot of information before you hang up. Don't hang up, okay?'

★   ★   ★

Chris sat baking for a moment at the curb. Atascadero was hot, unbelievably hot. The guy who rented him the Ford said this was unseasonable, like that should somehow help. Chris had rented the Fairmont at the San Luis Obispo airport. It felt boxy and strange, like something his father would drive. It did not have air-conditioning.

He checked the address again, the one that Mrs Greenberg's neighbor had given him. Supposedly the address of a son, the sole surviving heir. He shut down the engine and walked up to the door.

He knocked. Waited. Knocked.

He heard the sound of a small, high-revving engine, like a power mower. He couldn't tell if it was coming from the backyard of this house or the house next door.

He walked around to the back and looked over the ancient wood fence. A man in his forties was cutting the grass. He wore a sleeveless white T-shirt and tight jeans that made his gut and love handles stand out in sickening relief. Dark hair jutted out at the collar and sleeve lines.

Chris already didn't like him.

He didn't seem like a man who would keep an obsessively neat garden, but that's what Chris saw. Flower beds covered in chips, roses trimmed and tied back. Not one blade of crabgrass on the lawn. Seemed this guy could tend his yard but not himself.

He called hello a few times but couldn't make himself heard over the roar. He leaned on the fence and waited, feeling sweat creep down the nape of his neck and run down his back.

When the man finally saw Chris out of the corner of his eye and looked up, Chris waved his arms. The man stopped and cut the motor, leaving just a humming echo in Chris's ears and a welcome silence.

'I'm looking for Richard Greenberg. Would you happen to be him?'

The man wiped his forehead with the back of his hand and ambled over to the fence. He didn't seem to be in much hurry.

'My name is Richard Green.'

'Oh. Maybe I got my information wrong. I'm looking for Ida Greenberg's son, Richard.'

'Yeah. Okay. You got him. Whadaya want?'

'I just wanted to ask you a few questions.'

'About what?'

'About your late mother.'

Richard snorted. 'Not exactly my favorite topic.'

'Why's that?'

'I got my reasons.'

'Because she didn't leave you anything?'

'What the hell do you know about that? Hey, who are you, anyway? You some kind of friend of hers? Yeah, all right. She stiffed me when she died. You know that much. Left me one dollar. Left the rest of her life insurance to these people she hardly knew. That's what kind of swell lady my mother was. What the hell do you want to know and why?'

'That's what I wanted to talk about. Her will. What about her house? Did she own it?'

'Her and the bank. She left me in the cold, I'll tell you.

258

One lousy friggin' dollar. Now I gotta live over this guy's garage and do his garden so's he'll gimme a break on the rent. Which is kind of ironic. Because I think the reason she stiffed me was that she got mad at me 'cause I didn't do her garden. I figure this is, like, Ida's revenge. What the hell is your stake in this?'

'I'm just a reporter looking into a story. It seems she was passing on some kind of . . . I'm not sure how to explain it. Like a chain letter, but with deeds instead of letters.'

'I don't know nothing about that. I got no idea why she did it.' He turned quickly and started back to his mower.

Chris reached into his pocket and pulled out the photocopy Matt had made for him and given to him on his arrival. The letter. 'I'll tell you why she *said* she did it.'

Richard turned back. 'Said to who?'

'One of the people she left the money to. In this letter.'

He moved closer again. 'That crazy cat lady?'

'No. The kid from the grocery store.'

'Oh, right. That was so rich. What a slap in the face. I been her son for over forty years. These two little teenage slobs bag her groceries and they get my money.'

He ripped the photocopy out of Chris's hand. Chris watched him read silently for a few seconds.

'"I don't trust that he would use it the right way." That's a good one. Christ. I would have invested it in eating. That's such a lie. She was pissed about the garden.' He threw the letter up into the air. The pages fluttered onto the still-uncut grass. 'I said I'd do it. She finally paid some kid to. Said she didn't pay him, he did it for free. Yeah, right.

Kids love to do that. She was obsessed with that garden. She never loved *me* that much. I gotta finish here.' He walked away from the fence again.

'Excuse me. Can I have my letter back?'

Richard ignored him and pulled the string on the lawn mower; the noisy engine jumped to life. Chris pulled himself up to the top of the fence and scrambled over, rescuing the letter just before Richard could run it through the shredder.

'Did you talk to the lady at the cat shelter?'

'Yeah. She really didn't know Mrs Greenberg at all.'

'I didn't really, either. I just ran her groceries over the scanner.' Terri stood in the alley behind the grocery store, lighting an already half-smoked cigarette with a disposable lighter. 'I know. I shouldn't smoke. I'm trying to quit. Really. That's why I only smoke half at a time.'

Chris sat on his haunches with his back up against the brick of the building, his eyes closed against the heat and glare. A light breeze had come up, and even the breeze felt hot.

He shrugged slightly. 'I didn't say anything.'

'No. I know you didn't. I don't know. I wish I could help you.'

'Did you talk at all when she came in?'

'Barely. She usually complained about her arthritis. She was nice, though. I make her sound like she wasn't. But she was. Nobody likes to listen to someone complain about aches and pains. But I figured she had to tell somebody. You know? She was lonely. Her husband died. So I listened. Now I'm glad I did. I mean, for eight thousand dollars she could have told me about every ache she ever had.'

'Do you remember the last time you saw her?'

'Kind of. She was in a good mood.'

'What did she say?'

Terri let her head drop back and closed her eyes. Blew smoke up into the heavy heat. She shook her head. 'It was such a long time ago. You know?'

'Okay. I understand. Look, I'm staying at the Motel Six. Maybe another day, maybe two. I don't know. Maybe I'm wasting my time and I should go home. But if you think of anything. If anything comes back to you. Give me a call, okay?'

'Sure, okay.'

'And if you think of something later . . .' He handed her one of his cards.

She read it, slipped it into her shirt pocket, and ground the cigarette under the toe of her shoe. 'I guess my break's over. Sorry I wasn't much help.'

'You were as much help as anyone else,' he said, and walked back to his rented oven.

He found her house. That was easy. The tricky part was explaining to himself why he even bothered. A dead woman's house wasn't likely to tell much of a story.

The sun had dipped to a slant, the day's heat broken, but barely. He stood in front of the little blue-gray house and admired the garden. Perfectly tended. Someone new must be living here now.

He knocked on the door; no reply.

He sank onto the top porch step and began to feel stuck. His motivation to leave drained away. He could go get dinner, but he wasn't hungry. Why go back to the motel when he wouldn't sleep?

A boy rode down the street on a heavy old bike, delivering the afternoon paper. He didn't throw one at Mrs Greenberg's house. Maybe the bank still owned it.

But banks don't keep up the yard work. Do they? Maybe whoever lived here didn't take the afternoon paper.

He took his MasterCard out of his shirt pocket and stared at it. Tapped it on his knee. He'd maxed it out, then transferred the balance to a Visa with a better rate. And sworn he'd cut this one in half, so as not to double his debt. But he hadn't cut it in half. He'd used it for a plane ticket, and a motel, and a rental car. And for what?

A woman came out of the house across the street to fetch her paper. Chris sprang to his feet.

'Excuse me,' he called and sprinted over. It seemed to alarm her. 'Excuse me, can I just ask you a question about this house across the street?'

'Old Mrs Greenberg's house?'

'Right. Did you know her very well?'

'Not very.' She crossed her arms, uncrossed them, tugged

at her housedress nervously. 'My husband doesn't think we should get too friendly with the neighbors.'

'Is someone living in the house now?'

'No, it hasn't been sold yet. The bank owns it.'

'Who's keeping it up so nicely?'

'I really couldn't say. If you'll excuse me.'

She backed through her door and closed it quickly. Chris took a deep breath and walked back to Mrs Greenberg's front porch. He stood looking through the front windows. Sheets covered the furniture. Everything seemed coated with a fine layer of dust. He collapsed on her steps again.

He should just go home. He knew that now. He couldn't interview a dead woman, and even if he could, where would it lead him? Someone paid it forward to her. Maybe she didn't know that person's name. Maybe she was part of the twelfth generation, or the hundred-and-twelfth. If he was the best investigative reporter on the whole goddamned planet, and he wasn't, he would never trace it all the way back to its roots. Not without some kind of written record.

The paperboy came back and dropped his bike on Mrs Greenberg's perfect lawn. He came up the walk toward Chris. Chris waited, figuring the kid was heading for him or had something to say to him, but he took a detour around to the side yard. As he walked by, Chris saw he was carrying a bag of dry cat food.

When he came back, he had a pair of hedge clippers.

'Hi,' Chris said as he walked by.

'Hi.' The boy began trimming the hedge that ran like a

fence against the neighboring property. It wasn't looking too seedy to begin with.

When he'd worked his way closer, Chris said, 'You're the one keeping this place up.'

'Yeah.'

'Who pays you to do it?'

'Nobody.'

'Why do you do it, then?'

'I don't know. Just because.' He furrowed his brow and concentrated on his work for a moment. Then he looked up and said, 'I don't think she would like to see it get all ratty again. I don't know if she can see. What do you think?'

'About what?'

'Do you think that when somebody's dead they can still look down like that?'

Chris wrestled with the question for a moment, then shook his head. He'd never really pinned down what he believed in that respect. 'I guess not. But I'm not sure.'

'No, I'm not sure either. I figured it's better to be safe.'

'So, you knew her.'

'Yeah.'

'Did you know her well?'

The boy stopped his work, let the clippers hang straight down from his hand, and scratched his nose. 'Not real well, I guess. We used to talk.'

'About what?'

'Oh, I don't know. Stuff. Football. This project I was doing for school. She was gonna help me with this project. But then she died.'

Chris rose to leave. He could talk to every living human in this city and not stumble on anyone who really knew. But he had to try one more time, because in the morning, he now knew, he'd be flying home.

'You wouldn't happen to know anything about her will?'

'Her what?'

'Her will. Why she left money to certain people.'

'Oh. That kind of will. No. I didn't even know she had a will.'

'Yeah. I didn't figure you would. Well, good-bye.'

'See ya.'

He sat in the car for a few minutes, watching the boy work. Thinking it was odd for a boy that age to work when he had death as the perfect excuse to get out of it.

Then he wondered if Mrs Greenberg *was* looking down.

If you are, he thought, how about a clue? How about letting me see something here?

But all he saw was a boy cutting a hedge.

He started the motor and drove away.

From *The Diary of Trevor*

I still don't think even one single person has paid it forward.

I guess it was a stupid idea.

Only, I think Mrs Greenberg would have. If she could.

And Reuben wants to. I know he does. But he just can't think of anything that big.

Here's the part nobody seems to get. It doesn't even have to be that big. I mean, not really. I mean, it might just seem big. Depending on who you do it for.

Chapter Twenty-Four

REUBEN

Reuben arrived home from school at four-fifteen. Trevor knocked on his door at four-thirty.

'Where's Miss Liza?'

'In the kitchen eating. I just fed her. Is that why you came by, Trevor? To see the cat? Or did you want to discuss something?'

'That second thing.' Reuben stepped back and swung the door wide. Trevor came in and perched on the couch. 'If you don't mind.'

Of course he minded, considering the possible topics. 'Of course not, Trevor. You know you're always welcome here.'

Miss Liza came running in from the kitchen and jumped on Trevor's lap. 'Wow. She must've heard my voice. Huh?'

'You should be flattered, Trevor. You're more important to her than food.'

While he small-talked, Reuben nursed a sinking feeling

inside his chest, familiar but more pronounced than usual. He'd thought he would still have Trevor, could always be friends with Trevor, but it hadn't worked out quite that way. It hurt to have the boy around, and Trevor seemed to notice. Trevor's once-daily trips to Reuben's house had dwindled. The last time he'd claimed he'd only come to visit the cat, and he hadn't stayed long.

'What's on your mind, Trevor?'

'I was just wondering if you were still going to pay it forward. I guess you don't exactly have to. The way it worked out. I just thought maybe. I just wondered.'

Reuben took a deep breath and sank into his chair. Sometimes, when the urge to cry came around, and it did, it seemed to come behind both eyes, like an ancient trace memory.

'I've thought about that, Trevor. I guess I still would, if I could. I just don't know yet, what I could do for anybody. I'm having a hard time with that.'

'I know somebody who needs something.'

'Is it someone I know?'

'Yeah. My mom.'

'I'm sure your dad can help her, whatever it is.'

'She threw him out. Besides, he couldn't have helped her with this. This is something nobody else could do except you.'

Reuben's chest burned. She'd thrown him out. Did that make everything better, or worse? 'Look. Trevor. I really respect the work you did on that project. And I'm going to do my part to keep it going. Sometime. With somebody. But the way things stand between your mother and me . . .'

'Yeah, that's what she said. She said you were upset. But I thought, that makes it really good, you know? Because it's supposed to be a big something. You know. A big help. And if you help somebody you really want to help, then that's not very big. You know? But if you're all mad at my mom, and you helped her. That would be a big thing.'

His fingers scratched behind both of Miss Liza's ears, and she leaned in closer and purred, her eyes half closed.

Reuben stood and walked to the window, needing to be as close as possible to somewhere else. His good ear rang, and he couldn't imagine why it should. As if through a long tunnel, he heard himself say, 'I'm sorry, Trevor. I'm not sure I'm a big enough man to do something like that.'

Trevor's face twisted with disappointment. The cat jumped off his lap and ran back to the kitchen.

'Don't you even wanta know what it is that she needs?'

Better taste in men, he thought, but of course he didn't say it. 'Maybe it would be better if we just talked about something else.'

Trevor shrugged. 'I got nothing else I was gonna say.'

'Tell me more about what you said earlier. You said she threw him out.'

He shrugged again. 'Not much to tell. They kept fighting. Couple days ago she told him to get out. And he did. I guess I'll go home now.'

'I'll give you a ride.'

'Nah. I got my bike out there.'

'I don't mind. We'll put it on my bike rack.'

'I guess. I gotta go say good-bye to Miss Liza.'

They rode back to Arlene's house in silence.

Why had he suggested driving the boy home? He asked himself that question all the way there. If he really didn't want to see her, and he really didn't, why hadn't he just let Trevor pedal home the way he always had?

He wanted to ask Trevor if his mother was home or at work, just to prepare himself somewhat, but he couldn't quite bring himself to say the words.

He pulled up across the street. Her car wasn't parked out front. A wash of relief and disappointment struck, warring, with Reuben as the unfortunate battleground.

He cut the motor and they sat quietly for a minute, listening to an odd, intermittent crashing sound, like a series of small car accidents. It seemed to be coming from nearby.

'I wonder what that is,' Reuben said absently. He didn't feel particularly motivated to drive away again.

'I'll see.' Trevor got out of the car, leaving the passenger door open, and walked a few paces. He stopped opposite his own driveway with his hands in his pockets. Then he came back and sat down in the car beside Reuben.

'It's my mom. She's pounding the heck out of that truck with a baseball bat.'

A wave of cold numbness struck deep in Reuben's gut. His ear began to ring again, and this time he could hear his own blood rushing around in his head, like the ocean in a conch shell.

'I thought she wasn't home.'

'No. She's home.'

'Her car's not here.'

'It broke down. Now she has to take a bus to work. I think that's why she's all mad at the truck. She still has to pay for it. And now she's gotta take a bus to two jobs. She had to go back to the Laser Lounge nights.'

'Since she threw your dad out?'

'No. All along. He never really made much money or anything.' The ugly metallic sounds of her pounding punctuated their words and their silences. 'That's my baseball bat, too. Man. That thing's never gonna be the same.'

I wish I could do that, Reuben thought. It made him feel itchy and explosive, feeling how much he had to vent.

'Did you want me to get her a new car, is that it?'

'No. That wasn't it.'

'You wanted me to give her rides home from work at three in the morning? I guess that is a dangerous time to ride the bus.'

'I don't think the buses even run that late. No, Harry the bartender drives her home.'

Pound. Pound. Always the give of metal. No breaking glass. Reuben tried to remember if the truck still even had glass. 'What, then?'

'What, what?' Trevor seemed distracted by the noise, too.

'What does your mother need that only I can do?'

'For you to give her another chance. She knows she really screwed up. She knows that now. She does that a lot. Screws up. You know, like, sees a good thing and a bad thing and takes the bad one. She's not dumb. She knows. I don't know why she does it if she knows. It's just this thing she does. She says you'll never forgive her. But I figured, well, you could. It would be a really big thing. But you could. If you wanted to do a really big thing. For somebody. I mean, I remember you asked me once how you do something really big like that. Remember? And I said, well, you just look around. And find somebody who needs something. So, she does. Need something. I just thought you'd want to know.'

The interior of the car rang with the absence of words. The pounding continued outside. Reuben could hear Trevor's breathing. He wanted to hug the boy because he missed him, but nothing moved. 'I'm sorry, Trevor. I can't.'

'Okay.'

'I'm sorry.'

'Okay. She said you'd say that.'

'You talked about this with her?'

'Not exactly. She just said you were upset and you wouldn't ever forgive her. But I said she should ask. But she won't, 'cause she knows you'll just say no. So I asked.'

'I'm sorry, Trevor.'

'Okay. Whatever.'

The pounding stopped suddenly. The unfamiliar silence felt strange and stunning.

Trevor got out of the car without saying good-bye. He took his bike down and walked it across the street. Reuben waited and watched until Trevor closed the front door behind him. He started up the engine.

As he cruised by the mouth of the driveway he braked slightly. He didn't tell his foot to do that, but it did.

Arlene stood with the bat on her shoulder, panting and sweaty. She looked up and saw him immediately. The bat clattered onto the driveway.

Reuben pushed the accelerator to the floor. The little engine sagged, then picked up. In his rearview mirror he saw her standing in the middle of the street. He heard her shout his name.

'Reuben. Reuben, wait.'

He swung around a corner, though it would have been more direct to go straight.

From *Those Who Knew Trevor Speak*

She told me later that she tried to call me. She said she called me every day after that and I didn't answer. And I thought, How did she know I was home and not answering? Why couldn't I have been out? Nobody ever thought of me as someone who could just have been out. Well. I wouldn't say I was going out a lot at that time. But I didn't

just sit there and let the phone ring. I never did that. I don't
know why she thinks I did, particularly.

Maybe it was during that time I was having trouble with
my phone.

He lay on his back in bed, pretending to watch the eleven
o'clock news. The cat lay curled on his chest, making it hard
to breathe deeply, but he didn't move her.

The phone rang, and as he reached for it the cat stepped
off him and onto the bed. As he picked up the receiver,
he already knew who it would be. He didn't even say hello.
Just held it near his ear as though it might be dangerous.

'Reuben, please don't hang up.'

He hung up.

When it rang again he lifted the receiver and set it on the
bedside table. He got up and walked into the living room,
just to be sure he wouldn't hear anything, if anything was
said.

He paced around a little, but it made him feel awkward
to be naked and exposed, even in the privacy of his house.
He walked back into the bedroom and found Miss Liza
sniffing the receiver. He picked it up and heard Arlene
talking, a long string of breathless sentences, none of which
he made out.

He yanked the cord out of the wall and threw the phone
through the bedroom window.

He thought it might make him feel better, like beating a

wrecked truck with a baseball bat. It proved disappointing, though. Now, instead of an awkward naked man standing in his room alone, in his life alone, he was all that with a broken window. And a warm wind on his naked body. And no telephone.

He should have known he wasn't the venting type.

Chapter Twenty-Five

ARLENE

Trevor had gone to Joe's on an overnight. Arlene sat home alone, thinking how she'd drive by Reuben's if she had a car. Maybe she'd get her courage up, even knock on the door. If she had a car. Which she didn't. And the fact that she didn't made her mad. But her arms ached and trembled from her last attack on the carcass of that old beast in her driveway. How much more could either of them take? And it wasn't really the truck's fault, she had to admit. What the hell had she been thinking, cosigning that shiny new thing while she drove that awful old Dodge Dart? No wonder she was so sure Ricky would come home sooner or later. What a sweetheart deal.

Then she got madder thinking of that nice collector's item GTO he drove. All rebuilt from the ground up with shiny chrome headers and a new front end and differential and those big, brand-new monster tires. How did he dare drive off with that thing and leave her with the payments on that truck he totaled?

Here it was her one night off from the Laser Lounge and she couldn't even go anywhere. With no strength left in her arms to beat or break anything, all that anger was getting to be a problem. There was a bar on the Camino, just a short walk away. But she must not have wanted to take that route, because she called Bonnie at home.

'Now what?'

'Geez, Bonnie. Get in trouble if I don't call you, then you don't seem glad when I do.'

'I didn't say I wasn't glad. Just waiting to hear what trouble you got in now.'

'Nothing, really. Just my car died.'

'So now you're thinking about taking a drink.'

'Yeah. But that ain't why.'

Bonnie let the silence fall, gave Arlene the time she needed to sum it all up. But it seemed a little harder now. She was mad at Ricky. Right. Bonnie'd probably say, Duh. You and everybody else whose path he ever crossed.

But she really did her best to explain it. How mad it made her to think about him running around with Cheryl in that nice car, leaving her with that old hulk to pay off. Coming home and saying he'd go sober and be what he always should have been for her, then going right back to the same old crap, and now it was too late to ever get Reuben back.

Bonnie listened quietly, until the part about Reuben. Then she said, 'Bingo.'

'Did I say something smart?'

'I think you just said what's really eating you. But I can

understand. You're mad at Ricky. So mad you want to hurt him bad. So you're going to walk down to the bar and throw away a clean year of sobriety. Boy, that'll teach him. Every time you throw a punch, girl, you break your own jaw.'

Arlene sighed. Waited for the tears to come, but they didn't. They just came up missing somehow. She breathed again and decided she felt a lot clearer.

'Naw, I won't, Bonnie. You know that. If I was gonna do that I wouldn't have called you.'

'I know. You just needed to talk.'

'I feel a little better now.'

'Call again if you want.'

'Maybe tomorrow. Tonight I think I'll hike over to Cheryl's and bend Ricky's ear. Give him a taste of what I'm mad about.'

'If it'll help you, go ahead. You know damn well it ain't gonna help him.'

Just as she was leaving the house, she realized she hadn't packed up Ricky's shotgun. She had begun to feel a little quieter and more centered, so she took it along. It was a longer walk than she remembered. It didn't feel right, her having to go on foot, her having to be the one with two jobs, walking, but she had to follow this thought through.

Cheryl answered the door in her bathrobe, then almost closed it again; Arlene could see that little reflex.

'Too late to change your mind now,' Cheryl said.

'Oh, I didn't. Just that Ricky's got something of mine and I got something of his. I just want to trade up. Then we'll be all settled and done.'

A familiar voice, faint, calling out from the bedroom. 'Who is it, hon?'

'Never mind,' Arlene said, pushing past. 'I'll tell him who it is.'

She stepped into the bedroom with Cheryl dogging close behind, and found him in bed, the sheets pulled up to his waist. It was a hot night, and no cooler in Cheryl's bedroom.

'Arlene, what the hell?'

'You folks turn in early, huh? Well, I won't stay and chat. Where's the keys to the GTO?'

'Why? Why do you ask? I don't like nobody driving my car, you know that.'

'Well, that don't matter now, Ricky, because it's not your car. You're giving it to me.'

'Hell I am. I built that car from the ground up. It's my baby. No goddamn way, Arlene. Where the hell do you get off?'

Cheryl gave Arlene's shoulder a little pull and said, 'Get the hell out of here or I'm calling the police.'

Arlene opened the shotgun case. She was able to do it quickly, because she'd left the lock at home. It was her lock, after all. She turned around, not so much to point the gun at Cheryl, but of course it pointed where Arlene did.

'Go on and do that then, Cheryl. They're pretty damn slow and this won't take long.'

She turned back to Ricky, who'd managed to plaster himself to the headboard. 'Here's where I get off, Ricky. You sweet-talked me into cosigning that truck. You swore on your honor you'd never let me down. Then you totaled it, left me to work two jobs to pay it, and got something else real nice. Now you got two choices. Pay me every cent I'm out for that truck, or give me the damn GTO.'

He held up his hands in calm, slow gestures, as if to hypnotize the violence out of her. But really she wasn't feeling violent. Just set on clearing things up. 'Put the gun down, baby, we can talk.'

'I think we'll have a better talk this way. You know, Ricky, I used to feel so bad for you, 'cause you told me them stories about all the women in your life tried to kill you. How your first wife held a loaded gun in your face and Cheryl threw that blanket over you and beat you with a skillet, and that one in between took that knife to you. I thought to myself, poor Ricky. Getting mixed up with all these crazy women. But you know, I really understand now. Get a piece of paper, you can write me out a bill of sale.'

He scrambled for a little message pad in the drawer of the bedside table. Cheryl threw him a pen.

Arlene hadn't heard her call the police, and didn't much care if she had. This was just a nice calm business transaction.

'So, I'm selling you my GTO.'

'Damn straight.'

'Make it out for how much?'

'One dollar and other valuable considerations. Don't try putting the wrong license number. I'm not too dumb to check.'

'What are the other considerations I get?'

'I think it would be very considerate of me not to shoot you. Don't you think so?'

He put his head down and concentrated on a flurry of scribbling, then handed the slip over, reaching out carefully, ready to jump back.

She read his scribbling. 'You forgot to sign it.'

'Oh, yeah.'

He signed it and handed it back.

'Where're the keys?'

He balked a moment, sulked almost, like a little boy, then he said, 'Better get her the keys, Cheryl.'

Arlene took them on her way out the door.

'Thanks. Here's Ricky's shotgun. Now we're all even. Oh, wait. I forgot.' She dug a dollar out of her pocket and threw it on the living room floor.

She left the gun in Cheryl's arms and walked to her new car. She liked it. It was kind of slick. Nice new race-car paint job, though maybe orange was not ideal. Pretty under the hood. She'd have to replace those old glass-pack mufflers, of course, so the whole goddamned world didn't have to hear her coming.

At her back she heard Ricky say, 'Damn. I really loved that car.'

She sat in the driver's seat and started it up. It rumbled underneath her while she adjusted the seat to fit her legs.

Before she could shift it into drive Ricky arrived at the window with the shotgun and stood spraddle legged and angry, aiming through the window at her head.

'Get out right now, Arlene, I mean it. Gimme that bill of sale back and nobody gets hurt.'

She rolled the window halfway down. 'Oh, I forgot to tell you. I don't keep it loaded. And I didn't bring back any shells. *I* bought those, remember?'

In the red glow of her taillights she enjoyed the look on his face for an instant; then he faded into the night, the dark. The past.

She stopped at the auto parts store on the Camino, which was open until nine, and bought one of those club things for the steering wheel. Then she took it out for a ride, just for the joy of riding. It had a lot of power. It would get her around.

She was beginning to feel a little better.

She had no special place to drive, so she drove by Reuben's house. A light burned in the bedroom, and his car was parked out front. She circled the block and drove by again.

On the third trip she stopped and cut the engine, and just sat awhile. Looking. Thinking about a time when she was welcome there and could have knocked and gone right in. Thinking about how the cat used to rub under her chin to wake her up, and how they would have been married by now and could have pooled their financial resources to get her a new car. He would have helped, she knew he would. That was just the kind of man he was.

Something big and heavy sat in her chest. It felt harder and harder to breathe around it.

After a while she drove home. She put the club thing on the steering wheel and locked it up for the night.

He might come back for it. But she'd report it stolen if he did. She had a bill of sale, all nice and legal.

She'd tell the cop, 'I demanded my money for the truck, but he couldn't pay it, so I said I'd take the GTO. He signed it over to me. He didn't have to, you know. Nobody held a gun to his head.'

Then she remembered that Ricky had two outstanding warrants in this state, and felt much better about her chances of finding the car in her driveway in the morning.

She tried calling Reuben, but he didn't answer the phone. It wasn't very late. How did he even know it was her? She tried to lie down and sleep, but nothing happened. Other than the thoughts that rolled around in her head, like all the things she'd said to Reuben on the phone last night, and whether he'd even been listening or not.

She got up and dressed again, and checked the car, which was still there. She drove over to Reuben's again and sat outside for an hour. When she saw the lights go out, she knew it must be time to move, one way or another. Go in or go home. No point to just sit there all night.

Her heart pounding in her ears, she walked around to his back door and knocked. The bedroom light came on again.

The back door opened and Reuben stood in the doorway in his bathrobe. He didn't look angry. Big and imposing, that he looked. And yet at the same time vulnerable somehow, like he couldn't really make her go away, even if she were to physically drive home.

'I thought you were just going to sit out there all night,' he said.

'You knew I was out there?'

'Of course I did.'

'How'd you know that?'

'Your muffler made me look out the window. Or lack of muffler. Where did you get that car?'

'It's kind of a long story.'

'You left Trevor home alone?' She smelled a hint of judgment, as if he'd accused her of losing whatever manners and sense he'd helped her to find.

'He's spending the night at a friend's.'

'Oh.' He slid his hands into the pockets of his robe and they stood a moment, both looking down at the stoop. 'Why the back door?' he said after a time.

But that was a question she couldn't quite answer. If called upon to guess, she might say it had something to do with shame, but she wasn't anxious to learn exactly what. So she changed the subject as best she could.

'I love you, Reuben.' She allowed the words to echo between them until their sting wore off. She hoped he would say something, maybe even something nice. But she could only wait just so long. 'I guess that's all I came by to say. I know it doesn't really change what happened. But I wanted you to know. I don't guess I ever said that before. Even though it was true enough. Anyway. I just had to say it now.'

His hands came out of his pockets to hang at his sides, and his chin rose slightly. He said, 'I notice you didn't feel compelled to say that until it was over with him.' His hand came up to the edge of the door, leading her to believe she'd better talk fast, before it slammed shut.

'That's not why, though, Reuben. I know it looks that way but it's not. Know why? It's because of that time you drove Trevor home. And you went by the driveway and slowed down. Almost stopped. Until then I thought you just flat out wouldn't talk to me. After that I knew part of you wanted to talk to me and part of you didn't.' She winced slightly, waiting for the door to slam, but his hand found its way down to his side again. 'I know you don't forgive me, Reuben. I don't expect you to. But some little part of you must miss me, right? God knows I miss you.'

She reached for his dangling right hand and he allowed it to be held. He looked into her face for a minute, even though it seemed to hurt him. The light wasn't good, coming mostly from behind him, and she wasn't sure of her ability to read his face. She smiled, hoping he could see, hoping she was not about to cry. Holding her hand firmly, he stepped back and pulled her inside.

★　　　★　　　★

In the morning the sun came in strong across the head of his bed, just the way she remembered. She opened her eyes to see him awake and watching her. When she smiled he rolled away.

'Hey. You okay?'

He didn't answer.

'Talk to me, Reuben.'

'This was probably a mistake.'

'Yeah, well, that's just your opinion.' He rose and began to dress. His scars seemed sadder somehow, in bright daylight, and in a moment when he insisted upon distance between them. He might have known this, because he dressed quickly.

'Fine,' he said. 'You caught me in the middle of the night. I let you in. Things got carried away. Now I guess you think everything that happened is water under the bridge. Well, it isn't.'

He perched on the edge of the bed, faced away, as if this was the only thing he still remembered how to do. She moved over to his side of the bed, sat up. Draped herself across his back and tried to hold him. His body felt stiff and resistant.

'Don't, okay? Just go home now, Arlene.'

She could hear in his voice that he was crying, and it startled her. He never had done that before, so far as she knew. It was a weakness she attributed only to herself. And she knew he would want no witness to the moment. So she did as she had been asked.

Chapter Twenty-Six

CHRIS

Until Sally called, he didn't realize, consciously, how much he had missed her. He hadn't let himself realize. He had allowed it to hover, little bats at the edges of his day's work, shadows in his periphery, but he had ways to keep things at a proper distance. Obsession with work, obsessive exercise, too much sleep, too little sleep. Drinking himself to sleep.

But then she called, and there it was, all that feeling, and he knew in some part it had been there all along.

She asked how he'd been and he said fine, which was a lie.

She asked how the story was going and he said it wasn't going, it was gone, dead-ended, a cold trail, which was true.

Then nobody said anything for a painful few seconds, and he asked her out to dinner. She said she'd had dinner out every night this week, but if he'd come over to her new apartment she'd cook.

He said he loved her, which was true, but it caused her to fumble a bit, and make it clear she would still hold on to the right to reserve judgment.

It was after dinner when the phone rang. He was sitting close to her on the couch, thinking how familiar it was, the smell of her. Maybe partly perfume, partly just her skin, or maybe her skin smelled like perfume. He wasn't sure. He was thinking a drink would be nice, but not saying that.

Then the phone rang, and he prayed it would not be for him.

She picked it up, and her face went dark. She covered the mouthpiece with her hand. 'You gave out this number?'

He shook his head. 'Call forward.'

Whatever moment they had been close to achieving, it disappeared from his horizon. He knew that. It cracked in the air between them and he felt it.

'It's a young lady, for you.'

'It's not what you're thinking.'

She handed him the phone and left the room. He sat breathing, holding the receiver for a moment. He could hear her in the kitchen, moving dishes in the sink, a bit harder and louder than necessary. He always ended up being himself in front of her, with his real life all too visible, and then it all fell down.

'Hello?'

288

'Chris Chandler?'

'Yeah. Who's this?' He tried not to sound irritated but it might not have worked.

'Terri, from the grocery store. You know. From Atascadero? Am I catching you at a bad time?'

'Uh, no, it's fine, Terri. What's up?'

'Well, you said to call you if I thought of anything. Only this probably isn't much. It's probably nothing. But I did think of something. That last time I saw her? I remember what she was in such a good mood about. I remember I said her garden looked really nice. And her face just kind of lit up. And she said, "Oh, isn't it wonderful?" or something like that. She said, "The neighbor boy did all that." She told me his name but I forget it now.'

Chris waited in silence a moment, hoping for, expecting, something more. Her garden had been important to her. That much he already knew.

'Well, I said it was probably nothing.'

'No, I'm glad you called, Terri. Really. If you think of anything else . . .'

'Well, that's it, I guess. For now. Just that she was all happy about the garden.'

'I appreciate your calling, Terri. I really do.'

'Well, I don't want to run up my phone bill. Bye.'

He hung up the phone, blinking slowly, and saw her standing in the kitchen doorway. 'Oh, God, Sally, it's not what you're thinking. I'm not seeing anyone. It was just one of those people I interviewed about that story.'

She didn't move out of the doorway. He wondered if she

believed him, if she ever did, if she ever had. If she really
should.

'I'm trying to decide if that's better, or worse,' she said.

But then she smiled and came back and sat close. He
picked up the phone and left it off the hook.

It was just as he was moving onto the bed. That's when it
began to hit him. Shirt off, pants unzipped, following her
naked body as if tethered to it. Not trying to think about
anything else, not realizing there could be anything else to
think about.

It came in through the back of his mind, in the
unwelcome voice of Richard Greenberg, or Green, or
whatever the hell his name was. Three sentences, echoing
when least wanted.

'Said she didn't pay him, he did it for free. Yeah, right.
Kids love to do that.'

He pushed the words away again. She pulled him down,
her mouth on his neck. Hands exploring his bare back. So
familiar, so sorely missed.

'What's wrong?' she said.

'Nothing. Nothing's wrong. Why?'

'You seem distant.'

'No. I'm right here. God, I missed you.'

He kissed her. Richard was right. She paid a kid to do her
garden. She must have. Which had no bearing on this
situation whatever. Useless. So she was happy because her

garden had just been done. It meant nothing. One of his legs, sliding between hers. How had he lived without this so long? Said she didn't pay him, he did it for free. Big favor, for a kid. For anybody. What kind of kid would do that for free?

'You are not right here, Chris.'

'Oh. I'm not?'

He rolled over onto his back, and knew. Something religious in the revelation, because he'd asked Mrs Greenberg for a sign. Let me see something. And all the while he'd been looking right at it. What kind of kid would do that for free? Same kind of kid would keep doing it for free long after the lady was dead.

He'd been looking at the next link back, and he'd driven away.

He shouldn't have asked the kid if he knew about her will. What a stupid way to go at it. Why would the kid know about her will? Why should he? Nobody knows how someone else is going to pay it forward. He should have asked the paperboy if he knew anything about the Movement.

'The paperboy,' he said out loud.

Sally got up and began to dress. 'Go home now, Chris.'

'I'm sorry.'

'That makes two of us.'

He sat on Mrs Greenberg's front porch. The weather hadn't changed, or if it had, it had changed back to hot in his

291

honor. The neighbor lady across the street glanced out her kitchen window now and then, as though she'd do well to keep an eye on him. Imagine how crazy she'd think I am, he thought, if she knew I'd come three thousand miles to sit here. Twice.

A paperboy came by, on foot, walking the route with a cloth bag over his shoulder. A red-haired boy with freckles. He lobbed a paper at the house next door.

'Hey, kid.'

The kid froze, looked panicked. Didn't answer.

'I don't bite.'

'I'm not supposed to talk to strangers.'

'I just want to know what happened to the other kid.'

'What other kid?'

'The paperboy who was here last month.'

'He won the prize.'

'What prize?'

'Best paperboy of the year.'

'So, where is he?'

'He won the week off with pay.'

Oh. Crap. Chris thought of the nearly maxed MasterCard in his shirt pocket. It wouldn't keep him here another week. The red-haired boy was trying to hurry past. 'What's his name, do you know?'

'Trevor.'

'Trevor what?'

'I forget.' Level with Mrs Greenberg's walkway, the boy broke into a run and disappeared down the street.

Chris began walking in the opposite direction. Passing the

next-door neighbor's lawn, he briefly picked up their paper. The *Atascadero News-Press*. He memorized the street number of their office, on the main drag. El Camino Real.

A wave of heat hit him as he opened the rental car door. By the time he found the office it was closed for the day.

He slept fitfully, after much trying, and woke after eight to the day's heat, already gearing up to punish him. He could feel it gather strength. He couldn't remember when he'd last eaten. He had breakfast at Denny's, found the newspaper office again. Sold them a song and dance about a national award for enterprising young people. They gave him a name and address without question. He got lost twice trying to find it, finally had to stop for gas and a map.

When he knocked on the door it was after nine. It wasn't until the sound of his knock faded that Chris felt awake enough to realize that the kid would not be home. Kids go to school on weekdays.

A small, pretty, dark-haired woman flew out the door.

'I'm twenty minutes late for work. Whatever the hell you're selling, I ain't buying it.' She pushed past him into the driveway and stood beside an orange GTO from the sixties, fumbled in her purse, for keys, he assumed. The car was parked behind a late-model truck, stripped, and damaged as though it had been through a meteor shower.

'Shit,' the woman said. 'Left my keys in the house.'

'What happened to that truck? Looks like somebody took a lead pipe to it.'

The woman turned the knob on her front door, then ran into it, as though amazed that it didn't open.

'Shit. I locked myself out.' She turned to consider him, as if for the first time. 'Who the hell are you and why aren't you going away?'

'My name is Chris Chandler. I'm a reporter. I'm looking for Trevor McKinney.'

'He's at school. Where the hell you think he'd be? And I'm late for work, and locked out, and standing here talking to you ain't puttin' me in no better mood.'

'Did you leave any windows open?'

'Just that high one.'

'Come on. I'll give you a leg up.'

He laced his fingers and offered his hands like a stirrup, poised under what he assumed to be the bathroom window. She stepped up onto his hands, surprisingly light. She reached up to the window, put her fingers under the screen, and pulled hard, bending the frame. The screen shot across the driveway, mangled, he presumed, beyond repair. It landed beside the truck, looking only lightly used in comparison.

She leaned the top half of her body through the window, and he hoisted her up higher. She disappeared.

A moment later she came barreling out the front door again.

'So, where's Trevor's school?'

'I'm late for work.'

'You'd have been a lot later if I wasn't here.'

'I wouldn't have locked myself out if you hadn't distracted me at the last minute.'

'Where's that school again?'

'What the hell you want with my son?'

'Just want to ask him a couple of questions. About a Mrs Greenberg.'

'I don't know no Mrs Greenberg.'

'He does.'

'For all I know you could be a kidnapper or a pervert. I gotta go.'

She dropped into the low bucket seat, struggled briefly with a club on the steering wheel, fired and revved the engine. The old glass-pack mufflers roared. She drove off without so much as a wave good-bye, cutting a little close to his legs on the way out of the driveway.

As it turned out, there was only one junior high school in town anyway.

Chris stopped at the office, where he was given a visitor's pass and instructions to room 203, where Trevor McKinney was apparently scheduled to arrive for social studies class.

When he stepped into the classroom, only the teacher was present. Chris stared at the teacher's face for a protracted moment, then glanced away. He felt he needed to look more closely but didn't dare.

'Chris Chandler,' he said, and stepped forward to shake

the teacher's hand, focusing awkwardly on his tie. 'I'm looking for a Trevor McKinney. I was told he'd be here next period.' He flashed his visitor's pass.

'Yes. Take a seat, Mr Chandler.'

The teacher seemed curious but asked no questions.

Chris didn't want to sit at a small desk but, in a kind of regression, felt compelled to do as he'd been told. The room looked small to him. He wondered if his own junior high had been bigger, or if it was all a matter of perspective.

He glanced at the teacher's face again and the man looked up, as if he could tell. Chris turned his eyes to the blackboard as though he'd planned to all along. The board was blank, freshly erased, except for a sentence in neat block lettering.

THINK OF AN IDEA FOR WORLD CHANGE, AND PUT IT INTO ACTION.

'Is that an assignment?'

'Yes.'

'Interesting assignment.'

'It can be.'

'Any of the students change the world yet?'

'Not yet. Some of them have had good ideas. Trevor had a particularly good one.'

Three students walked in and slapped books down on desktops. Chris recognized the paperboy immediately. The boy looked back at him.

'Remember me?' Chris said.

'I think so.'

'From Mrs Greenberg's house.'

'Oh, yeah.'

The boy walked over and stood by his desk. 'I think I asked you the wrong question,' Chris said. 'So now what I'm going to ask is this: did somebody do a big favor for you, and is that why you take care of Mrs Greenberg's garden for free?'

'No. Nobody did a big favor for me.'

'You don't know anything about the Movement?'

The boy's face looked blank. 'The what?'

Chris felt something sink in his gut. Another expensive trip to nowhere. Another dead end. What good would it have done, anyway? So the boy might have taken him one link back. Then it all falls down again. His girlfriend was right. It was all obsession with him, no thought or sense, and all too often it added up to nothing.

He stood to leave.

'Well, bye,' Trevor said.

Chris shifted his weight from one foot to the other and back again. 'Your teacher told me you had an interesting idea for that assignment.' He pointed to the blackboard. The room was filling up with children now, a claustrophobic feeling.

'Yeah, I invented this thing called Paying It Forward. It was for last year's class. I got the best grade. But you know what? It was a total bust.'

That tingle hit behind Chris's ears, a hot feeling, slightly dizzy.

He smiled.

'Maybe it didn't work out as bad as you thought,' he said.

From *The Diary of Trevor*

There are absolutely no words for how cool this is.

First off, everybody's telling my mom what a great mom she is. And everybody's telling Reuben what a great teacher he is.

And then they're saying I'm a great kid, and I say, Nah. Not really.

I mean, anybody could have thought of this. It's so simple. Sometimes I think, How could it work? That's so amazing. And other times I think, How could it not work? It's so simple.

The part about believing people might really do it. I bet that's the part nobody could get right before now.

But you know what? If they want to tell me I'm brilliant and special, let 'em.

It makes Mom and Reuben happy.

Chapter Twenty-Seven

ARLENE

'You taping this, Mom?'

Arlene was not only taping but counting the number of times he asked. 'Yes, Trevor, like I told you the last six times.' But there was no anger or genuine impatience in her words. She understood.

'I think we need more chips, Mom.'

Arlene sighed. Normally, she'd have told him to get up and get more chips himself, his hands weren't broken. But his grandma was here, having driven all the way from Redlands to share this moment. And Joe and Loretta and Bonnie and Ricky's sister Evelyn, the boy's aunt, were here. And Reuben was a maybe, though he hadn't shown yet. And it was an irreplaceable, special moment for the boy, Trevor's very own moment, so Arlene supposed she could understand how he didn't want to miss even a minute of the program. Even though it was going on tape. Even though Chris had promised him a professionally taped version of the segment. Even though the segment hadn't begun yet and everybody was staring in endless, nervous fascination at a story about welfare reform that would have bored them to tears on any other night.

She brought a fresh bag of chips out from the kitchen, and the show went to commercial. Arlene pushed the long ribbony hanging strings of a few helium balloons out of her way to wade through bodies to the VCR.

'Don't turn it off!' Trevor shouted, and everyone jumped.

'You want the commercials?'

'Maybe they'll come back and say something about the next story.'

'Okay, fine. I ain't touching it.' She raised her hands in an exaggerated surrender.

She went back to the kitchen for another beer for her momma, and a 7UP for Loretta. She pulled back the kitchen curtain, staring down the empty street as if she might see him drive up. Maybe he was just running a little late, she thought. Even though he'd never been late to anything in his life, so far as Arlene knew.

Then she heard it from the living room. A narrator talking about Sidney G. and the story they'd done before. How a bit more information had come to light. How pleased they thought the viewers would be to see the real thinker behind this wave of kindness that threatened to take over the country with sudden goodwill.

And then they said Trevor's name. It made her stomach tingle. Trevor's name on national TV. My son, she thought, and her knees felt a little too wobbly to move back into the living room. Just for a moment she wondered if it was really fair to call him her son, even though he was, because it felt like taking credit for his sudden fame. Really she did not feel the least bit accountable. By all rights any son of hers should have been an average kid, and she supposed in most ways Trevor was. Which is what made all this so odd and amazing.

'Mom, get in here, quick! It's on!'

She wobbled into the living room with little help from those knees. On the small screen, Trevor was riding his bike down Mrs Greenberg's street, throwing newspapers onto the lawns. Trevor. Her boy. The same one who sat on the couch in twitching silence, watching. Arlene tried to remember if she had ever known anyone who had been on television, but no one came to mind.

That old bike looked so crappy. She'd have to get him a new one. Why hadn't she already? My God, what would people think?

She leaned both hands on the back of the couch, and her momma reached back to put a hand on Arlene's. Gave it a squeeze and then left it there. It was such a strange moment, she almost forgot to watch the show. But it was on tape, anyway, and she'd probably have to watch it four or five times before it all sank in properly. Her momma's hand on hers. For once in Arlene's whole goddamned life she must've done something worthy.

Now Trevor was standing in the yard beside Mrs Greenberg's house, showing where he keeps the dry cat food that he buys with his own money, because he knows Mrs Greenberg wouldn't want any of those strays to miss a meal in her absence. And the power lawn mower he uses to keep her grass neat, even though it isn't really hers anymore. And the plastic gas can he has to tie to the handlebars of his bike when the mower runs out of gas. And most of this was unfamiliar to her. She was learning, along with much of the country, what her son did while out of the house. He had a life, and it hadn't struck her before, at least not in such an obvious way, that he existed on his own, apart from her.

Now the inside of a classroom. Her gut constricted at the image of Reuben in front of his blackboard. In front of that sentence. The one that started it all.

She reached across the couch and gave Trevor a little nudge on the shoulder. 'Did he say he'd come?'

'Huh?'

'Reuben.'

'He said he'd try.'

Suddenly Arlene felt the need to drive by his house, to see if he was sitting home, watching in bed alone, to avoid her company. But it didn't seem right to duck out of the festivities. Not on Trevor's big night. In a few minutes, when the segment ended, she had to be here to break out the chilled champagne for the grown-ups. Well, not for her or Loretta or Bonnie, but for the other grown-ups. And the sparkling apple juice for Trevor. Only, if he asked, maybe he could have just a couple of sips of champagne. In honor of his big night.

Maybe Reuben would arrive in time for the postprogram celebration.

Reuben did not arrive, though. And Arlene did not drink champagne. She brought out more dip and waited for a moment alone with Trevor, so she could tell him how damned proud she was. But the company stayed, and the program got shown three more times, with Trevor fastforwarding through the commercials. Between the excitement and the half glass of champagne, Trevor was asleep long before that moment could present itself for real.

Arlene woke up sick. Which wouldn't have been so bad if Momma had not been in the house.

Momma had been sleeping on the Hide-A-Bed sofa in the living room, yet the sound of Arlene running to the bathroom first thing seemed to bring her out of hiding. That radar of hers. When Arlene came back through the bed-room, with the blood all drained out of her face, there was Momma sitting on the side of Arlene's bed. A vision in polyester. But Arlene got back into bed anyway. That's how bad she felt.

'Been drinking?'

'Momma, I ain't had a drink in over a year. You know that.'

'Big celebration last night. All that excitement.'

'You were right there. You saw me drinking apple juice.'

'Don't know what you did after we went to bed.'

'My God, Momma. Can't you never cut me no slack?'

'Okay, okay. Just asking.' A long, ringing silence.

Arlene wondered if she should ask Momma to call her in sick to work. No, she wasn't a kid anymore. She should do it herself.

'Stomach flu?'

'How the hell should I know, Momma? I just woke up sick.'

'Been happening a lot?'

'This is the first I seen of it.'

'Just thought you might be pregnant.'

'Don't even think it.'

'Just asking.'

'Do me a favor, Momma. Go make breakfast for Trevor. I got to call in sick to work. I got to get some rest here.'

When she left the room, Arlene felt breath drain out of her in relief. If Momma didn't volunteer to drive back to Redlands today, Arlene might have to suggest it.

After the call she drifted back to sleep, but the nausea woke her again. As she climbed back into bed, Trevor came in to kiss her good-bye. His grandma was ready to drive him to school.

'You too big a celebrity to ride your bike now?'

'Aw, Mom. She just wants to.'

'We'll get you a better bike real soon.'

He sat on the edge of the bed and she parted his hair with her fingers and brushed it aside.

'One I got's okay.'

'Nah, you deserve better. Just blow me a kiss, okay? I don't want you gettin' sick.'

'Love you, Mom.'

'I'm real proud of you, Trevor. Just so proud I could split. Know that thing about how everybody gets fifteen minutes of fame? That's just about how much time they gave you on that show, huh?'

'School today's gonna be real fun. I bet Mary Anne Telmin won't even talk to me.' His face twisted into a satisfied smile. 'Mom?' he said on his way out the bedroom door. 'I like my bike okay. Really.'

Then he blew her a kiss.

She woke up later that morning feeling better. So she called work and said she'd be in for the afternoon. Only just so much work she could afford to miss.

But the next morning she felt bad again, only she dragged in to work anyway. Low-grade bug, she figured, though the boss said maybe stress.

Arlene couldn't imagine what she had to stress about when everything in life seemed so amazingly good. She spent the morning half working, half wondering if she should call Reuben to see if he'd caught the show. How could he have missed it? Or for that matter, how could he have missed seeing it with them?

When she got home from work Momma was finally

gone. But she'd left a note by the phone in that distressingly perfect penmanship of hers.

That reporter fella called. Really needs to talk to you. He wants to fly out and see you in person. Something concerning Trevor, and some mail and something I didn't quite get, only that it was about the White House in some regard. Call him collect if you want. As soon as you can. Maybe you should see a doctor. Could be an ulcer. Maybe you inherit that from your old man.

Love, Momma

Arlene took a deep breath and picked up the phone. Thank God this was Friday, so she could wake up feeling like hell for two more days and it wouldn't matter on payday. She didn't feel right calling Chris collect. It would have made her feel poor, like a beggar. The phone rang five times, then his answering machine picked up.

'This is Chris Chandler,' the machine said. 'If this is Arlene McKinney, I'm on my way to the airport to grab a red-eye to California. I'm sorry to catch you off guard, but we really need to talk in person. All kinds of stuff going on. I promised you I wouldn't give out your address and phone number, but now I've got all these important messages for you. They want me to start the interviews for the Citizen of the Month spot right away. You have no idea how much timing is involved with this. This story may not stay hot for long. See you in the morning. If it's anybody else, please leave a message.' Beep.

Arlene glanced at the clock and wondered if she could stomach food. Wondered how long Trevor's fifteen minutes of fame was destined to last.

The knock came before 8 a.m. Arlene lay very still and listened to Trevor's footsteps running to answer the door. She swung her legs over the side of the bed, half thinking she would not throw up this time. Her thinking proved too optimistic.

By the time she'd managed to dress herself and get out to the living room, Trevor had nearly buried himself in a mountain of envelopes, tearing them open like a kid unwrapping Christmas presents.

Chris stood when she entered the room, but she waved him down again.

'You don't look too good,' he said.

'No, I'm fine. Just stress.'

'Look, Mom. I got four hundred and nineteen letters. And that's just the first two days. And not only that, but Chris says the network wants to tape an interview with me for Citizen of the Month. You know that thing they do on the six o'clock news? Well, next month it's me. I'm going to be the Citizen of the Month! Cool, huh? Chris'll tell you all about it. And that's not even the best part. I get to go to the White House! The president invited me. To meet him. Me!'

Trevor stopped and gasped for breath. Arlene wanted to

shake herself more fully awake. Probably some parts of this were happening and other, less likely parts were not.

'The White House?'

'Yeah! Cool, huh?'

'*The* White House?'

'Yeah, the president wants to meet me. And Chris says it's gonna be on all the news shows and in all the papers. Me shaking hands with the president!'

Arlene looked away from Trevor's breathless expression to Chris. 'All by himself?' she asked Chris, who opened his mouth to respond, but never got a word in edgewise.

'No, Mom, you get to go too, on account of you're my mother, and Reuben's invited too, because he was the teacher who got us to do that assignment in the first place. All expenses paid. We get to stay at the Washington Arms Hotel. Chris says they've got a *doorman*. And he says somebody from the White House is going to come get us at the airport in a big car and tour us around the city. Isn't that just totally cool?'

'You and me and Reuben?'

'Yeah, isn't that just totally cool?'

Out of the corner of her eye Arlene saw Chris smile shyly. A trip to Washington with Reuben. Who she couldn't even call to ask if he'd seen himself on TV. She felt a slight wave of nausea again and wondered if she should get closer to the bathroom.

'That's pretty cool, all right, Trevor.' She tried to sound sincere. Because it *was* cool, unbelievably so, to the point that it hadn't all quite settled in yet. But with Reuben . . .

'Remember when you said we're all supposed to get fifteen minutes to be famous? Chris says I'm gonna get, like, hours. Boy, I better start answering some of this mail.'

Arlene excused herself to the bathroom, silently noting that even the coolest things can cause a sickening amount of stress.

From *The Diary of Trevor*

Well, this is the last I'll get to write in this diary for a while. 'Cause I am leaving it home. Shoot, I got a president to meet. I won't have time to write in a silly diary.

But, boy. When I get back. Watch out.

Reuben says I have the rest of my life to write down everything that's about to happen to me.

I just hope that's enough time.

Chapter Twenty-Eight

REUBEN

They took the train to Santa Barbara, then a shuttle bus to LAX, the only part of the trip to come out of their own pockets.

On the train Trevor wanted to sit by the window, and it only seemed right to seat Arlene beside him. Reuben ended up alone one seat back. He couldn't read on a moving vehicle, it made him queasy, so he sat quietly, watching the backs of their heads.

He could hear the endless litany of Trevor's tapping foot. The boy was wired for sound. As Reuben supposed he should be, on his way to the White House.

He couldn't help but notice that Arlene, by herself, looked a relative stranger, or at least somewhat estranged, while Arlene and Trevor together still looked like his family. An odd sensation, one that left his discomfort no room to breathe.

In the airport Trevor talked to him. And talked and

talked. Endless strings of breathy speculation. What the president would be like, what sights they would get to see. Would they have to go through a metal detector or show ID to get in?

He asked Reuben several times, in several different ways, if Reuben thought his Citizen of the Month interviews had gone okay. Then he showcased his knowledge of White House history.

'Did you know there was a fire there?'

'I think I might have heard that.'

'That's why they painted it white.'

Reuben thought Arlene was not listening, but she broke in on that comment. 'You're making that up.'

'No, really. The War of 1812. And in 1929. I think they painted it that first time. Is it okay to call him Bill?'

'Who?' Arlene asked absently.

'The president.'

'Oh, God, no! Oh, my God, Trevor, don't you dare. Don't even think about it. You call him Mr Clinton, or President Clinton, or Mr President, or just plain "sir."'

'What if I get to meet Chelsea?'

'Cross that bridge when we come to it.'

'I hope I get to meet Chelsea. She's a major babe.'

On the plane Trevor opted for the window again, and Arlene sat next to him, which put Reuben on the aisle, beside her. It seemed awkward not to talk, but he didn't.

Trevor looked out the window and Reuben fingered the little ring box in his pocket and wondered again why he'd brought it. And wondered, if she knew he'd brought it, would she then understand that his silence wasn't cold, or wasn't meant to be, but rather a trench he'd dug himself into? A trench that only seemed to deepen with his movements. Maybe at some point in the trip he would tell her, just so she would know that for a moment, while packing, he had missed her, and his thoughts had been kind.

But that was a big bite for a man who couldn't even seem to discuss the weather or their itinerary.

The flight was a smooth one, so he read his book.

At the airport, a very young, fresh-faced man in a suit and tie held a sign that read *McKinney Party*. The man, whose name was Frank, loaded their luggage in the trunk of a black American-made car and asked if they'd like to stop at the hotel to freshen up. Arlene said that sounded good, but Trevor looked so crestfallen, they asked what he'd like to do first.

'See things.'

'Well, that's my job today,' Frank said. 'To show the three of you around, get you safely back to your hotel, and then I'll be back to get you tomorrow morning at nine o'clock sharp. We'll take a little tour of the White House until it's time for your appointment with the president.'

'What do we see first?' Trevor said. He and Frank seemed to have formed an instantaneous bond, cutting Reuben and Arlene out of the loop. Which was as it should be, Reuben felt, because this was Trevor's day. 'What all do you want to see?'

'The Washington Monument, the Library of Congress, the Jefferson Memorial, the Lincoln Memorial, the Smithsonian . . .'

'We might not get to all those today,' Frank said. 'But there's tomorrow afternoon. What's first?'

'The Vietnam Memorial.'

Reuben flinched unexpectedly at the mention of the name.

Walking down the Mall, approaching the Vietnam Memorial, Frank dropped back and addressed Reuben by name.

'I understand you're a vet.'

'I am.'

'I'm not going to give the usual tour guide spiel. I've noticed that vets don't always like that. You probably know a lot I don't. You might want a moment to view this by yourself.'

Reuben swallowed past a tight knot in his throat. Until Frank reminded him, he'd avoided focusing on the depths of his own discomfort.

Trevor said, 'We'll wait back here for you a minute, Reuben, and Frank can give *me* the tour guide spiel. I wasn't there.'

Frank's polite laughter echoed in his ears as he walked

toward the Wall. The sound of his own footsteps seemed to reverberate, bigger than life. Seven weeks in Vietnam. Then a week to stabilize in a medical installation and a quick flight to a stateside hospital. The men with names carved into this black granite had known something about the war. Reuben knew only what he saw in the mirror every morning. Maybe, he thought, that was enough.

He studied the index for a time, looking for a specific name. Then he moved along the wall until he found the correct panel, reflecting a time late in the war, and ran his fingers across the names until he found Artie. It jolted him slightly to see it, the reality of it, a recurrent nightmare suddenly become provably real. He reached up and traced the letters with his fingers.

A minute or an hour later he felt Trevor at his right side. In that sudden moment of the child's presence Reuben knew that his wounded pride was harming Trevor as much as or more than Arlene, and causing Reuben to sacrifice far too much in its name.

'Reuben, did you know how many names there are here?'

'About fifty-eight thousand, I think.' It felt strange to talk, and he realized he hadn't for quite a while.

'Fifty-eight thousand, one hundred and eighty-three. Who's Arthur B. Levin?'

'An old buddy of mine.'

Arlene's voice startled him from behind. 'Trevor, maybe Reuben wants to be by himself.'

'No, it's okay Arlene, really.'

'Maybe he doesn't want to talk about Arthur Levin.'

'No, it's okay. He was just someone I got to know in basic training. Artie was the guy voted most likely to screw something up.' He wasn't sure if he was telling this to Trevor, or Arlene, or both. 'First time Artie pulled the pin on a grenade his hands were shaking so much he dropped the grenade. Into high grass. Stood there digging around like he could find it to throw it. I knew he'd never get it in time. He was going to blow himself away. So I ran in and grabbed him, tried to get him to clear the area. Too late, though.'

'He died?' The quiet voice of Trevor.

'Yes.'

'Did you get hurt, Reuben?'

'Can't you tell?' A silence. 'I didn't even know him that well. Just better than anyone else there. He was the only person on the continent who wasn't a total stranger.' He felt Arlene's arms circle his waist from behind. 'Sometimes I look in the mirror and think, What if I had just run? Just saved myself. Artie would be just as dead. And I'd still look like the man in the picture. Just a little older.' But looking at the Wall, he had to wonder. What if it hadn't happened and he hadn't been sent home? Would he be a name carved in granite now?

Arlene's breath tickled his ear. 'That's not the kind of guy you are. Besides, you'd always wonder. If you could've helped.'

'Whereas this way I know I couldn't. Trevor? Go talk to Frank for a minute.'

'Okay, Reuben.'

Reuben turned and held Arlene. Neither said anything for a few minutes.

He took a big breath. 'I've been doing a lot of thinking, Arlene. I'm the kind of person, when I finally let myself love someone, it just goes so deep. You know what I mean? I know you do. I know because you're the same way. So I was thinking. Maybe I can understand that loyalty you felt.'

'What do you mean?' From the sound of her voice he figured she knew but couldn't quite believe he meant it.

'What happened with Ricky. Maybe I should feel lucky to have a woman like that. Because, years from now, when we have that same kind of history, I know I'd get the same level of loyalty from you.'

'You saying what I think you're saying?'

He placed the little velvet box in her hand. 'Look what I just happen to have here.'

She sucked in a breath, shaky with tears that would show in a minute. 'You never took it back for a refund.'

'Funny, isn't it, how I never did that?'

By the time they arrived back at the hotel, Trevor was so fast asleep that Reuben had to haul him in a fireman's carry up to their room. That is, to Trevor and Arlene's room. His own room was just across the hall. He wanted to ask her across the hall with him, but it didn't seem right to leave Trevor alone.

They kissed good night for a long time, and Reuben said they'd have plenty of time, the rest of their lives, to be together. Arlene smiled and said nothing, seeming nervous or sad or both.

In the morning, Trevor came over and said she was sick and throwing up over there, but when Reuben expressed concern, Trevor said it happened all the time.

'It's just stress,' he said. 'She just gets nervous.'

Reuben could certainly relate to nervousness.

They stood anxiously on the red carpet of the main hall. The Cross Hall, Trevor called it, staring up at the presidential seal. Reuben thought they faced the front of the building and Pennsylvania Avenue, but Trevor was quick to point out that Reuben was indicating the south portico, facing the Washington Monument. Reuben had given up on getting his bearings. At one end of the hall, the East Room buzzed with press setting up cameras, and Secret Service, and White House staff. Frank asked Trevor if he was nervous, and Trevor said no, an obvious lie.

The president walked in almost unnoticed, surrounded by Secret Service agents and his press secretary. They just seemed like any other group on first glance. Reuben wondered why he had expected some kind of fanfare.

A moment later the man himself spun off from the group and walked directly to Trevor, looking natural and friendly and unintimidating somehow. He shook Trevor's hand.

'You must be Trevor. Frank treating you okay?'

'Oh, yeah,' Trevor said, seemingly unfazed. 'Sir. I mean, Mr President Clinton, sir.'

Mr President Clinton smiled and said Trevor could call him Bill. Trevor turned and shot a look at his mother.

'The press is still setting up, so this'll take a minute. Everybody wants to get this on the news, Trevor.'

'Okay by me, Bill, sir.'

'So, what have you gotten to see?'

'Everything.'

'What did you like best?'

'The cherry blossoms. No, wait. The Vietnam Memorial. That was the best because my mom and Reuben got engaged.'

'Really?' he said, his smiling eyes coming up to take them in. Reuben felt tongue-tied and wished he could handle himself as smoothly and easily as Trevor did. 'Well, congratulations.'

'Tomorrow's my birthday,' Trevor added. 'Boy, is it ever gonna be a good one.'

'Well, you've just got all kinds of things to celebrate.'

'No kidding.'

A man arrived at Clinton's elbow. 'Mr President, we're ready to get under way.'

Cameras rolled, filling the East Room and filming them with the Cross Hall as backdrop. The president stood beside them, behind a podium, and shook Trevor's hand.

Reuben tried to look natural, but the lights made him want to squint and blink, and between that and his nerves, the whole scene looked and felt surrealistic.

'I'm honored to meet you, Trevor,' the president said.

'Yeah, me too,' Trevor said. 'I mean, I'm honored, too. I was so happy when you won the election.'

'Why, thank you, Trevor.'

'I didn't think you had a prayer.'

Reuben's jaw tightened. In his peripheral vision he saw Arlene's face go suddenly white.

The president threw his head back and laughed, a big, friendly, genuine laugh. Little lines around his eyes crinkled with amusement. A light stir passed through the press corps.

'Well, Trevor, I guess we're both a good example of what happens when you don't give up on your dreams.'

'Yes, sir, Bill, sir. I guess so.'

Trevor was presented with a small plaque. Reuben couldn't read it from where he stood. He felt himself sweating profusely but didn't want to wipe his forehead on camera. Sweat ran into his eye and stung. He heard about one out of every three of the president's words. Something about one person being able to make a difference, and a reference to a child's ability to lead us.

Reuben felt shocked and unprepared when the attention turned to him. He shook Clinton's hand, knowing his palm felt clammy. He nodded humbly when the president said that children were the future and teachers like him shaped that future. He remembered using the word 'sir' a lot and didn't remember much else.

Trevor beamed up at Reuben like this was a birthday party, all fun and no tension, and though it was hardly the moment for the thought, Reuben realized he hadn't known that tomorrow was Trevor's birthday. Why hadn't he known? He would have to buy the boy something.

By the time Reuben had relaxed enough to be fully present, the visit was over and Frank was driving them back to their hotel.

'That was so incredibly cool,' Trevor said.

Reuben felt sorry to have missed it. He consoled himself to know that it would be on the news and his mother would tape it. Maybe he could slow it down and get a better view.

'This has been the best, most incredible day,' Trevor said. 'Do you think there'll ever be a day this good again, Reuben? Or do you just get one of these? I mean, my birthday tomorrow, and meeting the president, and you and Mom getting married. You think I'll ever have another day like this one, Reuben?'

Reuben couldn't answer, because in truth, it seemed unlikely. He couldn't bring himself to tell Trevor he might have hit the peak day of his life just before his fourteenth birthday.

Trevor couldn't allow the silence to stand.

'You know this means I only got one more to do.'

'One more what?' Arlene asked.

'One more person to help. I got Mrs Greenberg, and now you two. That only leaves me one more.'

'You've done plenty, Trevor. Hasn't he, Reuben?'

Reuben was still busy wondering if Trevor would ever match this day. 'I think you can be proud of what you've already done, Trevor.'

'Maybe. But I'll do one more. Somebody else'll need something. Right?'

Reuben and Arlene and Frank all had to agree that it seemed like a reasonably safe bet. Someone always needs something.

Chapter Twenty-Nine

GORDIE

To Gordie, Sandy was a bear of a man. A sweet bear. From a wolf to a bear, he thought. In one easy lesson.

Nothing angry or dangerous. Not that kind of a bear. Just big and husky, a somewhat shaggy, unrefined appearance that overpowered his conservative dress. He'd met Sandy on the Capitol Mall. Sandy was almost forty-two, which gave him a quarter of a century on Gordie, but that didn't matter much, if at all.

Sandy said Gordie was beautiful.

Gordie looked in the mirror sometimes, in the evening before bed. With the door to his room locked. Standing naked in front of the full-length reflection. He appeared wispy and thin to himself, something the wind could carry away. But in another respect, Sandy was right.

Gordie wondered why he had never been given credit for beauty before. Why no one else's eyes had stretched to that truth.

Sandy did not hit, and because he weighed well over two hundred pounds, no one else felt inclined to hit Gordie while Sandy stood close by.

Come live with me, Sandy had said, and Gordie agreed.

He brought no clothing, so his mother and Ralph would not see immediately that he had left for good. Sandy said he would buy more clothes for him later, nice things, and he did.

Sandy gave Gordie another present, a high-quality fake driver's license, making him twenty-one overnight. Sandy frequented upscale bars and key clubs, wearing suits with pilled sweaters for a vest underneath. He wanted Gordie on his arm. He liked to see Gordie dress extravagantly, femininely. The knowledge that Gordie was male underneath his lipstick and silk only added to Sandy's appreciation for him.

It was almost like coming home.

On Saturday nights, Sandy took him dancing. They danced slow and close to a live band, and Gordie had only to follow, which relieved him, because he had been tired. All he really wanted for the time was to follow.

This Saturday, May Day, as Sandy called it, they danced at a bar and grill with an overwhelmingly gay clientele. A uniformed security guard in blue and gray stood at the door and nodded respectfully as he came through on Sandy's arm. The guard didn't have a gun, as far as Gordie could see, but he made a statement by virtue of his presence.

Gordie decided the guard was probably straight. Maybe

he didn't even like or approve of the men he protected, in the most personal sense. But if that was true, he was careful not to show it. Men like Sandy paid his salary, in a roundabout way, and sometimes tipped him on their way out the door. So he appeared to view the male clientele as his professionalism dictated he should. As things of value, to remain unmolested at any cost.

Gordie smiled shyly as he slipped by.

Sandy bought him a steak dinner, and Gordie chewed carefully and watched the men dancing. Halfway through the meal they were joined by Alex and Jay, friends of Sandy's, both of whom worked as congressional pages. Neither cared to eat; both felt they weighed far too much already.

'Gordie doesn't have to worry,' Alex said, lightly pinching Gordie's waist. Gordie smiled at Sandy because he liked Sandy just the way he was. Not fat, but big, overwhelmingly big, and Gordie didn't mind being overwhelmed by someone gentle.

Gordie remained silent, unsure of his ability to join the conversation.

'How the hell do you sneak him in here, Sand?' Jay stage-whispered under his breath.

'What do you mean?' Sandy replied, unfazed. 'He's twenty-one.'

Jay sprayed a sound between his lips, a kind of hybrid

between a laugh and a Bronx cheer. Then he leaned close to Gordie and whispered in his ear.

'Youth is so *attractive*,' he said.

Gordie smiled and watched Sandy buttering his roll. No way was he ever going back home now.

From *The Other Faces Behind the Movement*

I was just getting happy. I was finally happy. But then, I'm happy again now. I think everyone is happy now.

Sandy recovered fully. A couple of cracked ribs and a concussion. We nursed each other back to health.

I just wish the Boy had picked somebody else to help.

But if he had, maybe I wouldn't be here. Unless we'd stayed home that night. But you'll make yourself crazy with that kind of thinking. Isn't it bad enough how many other people used to beat me up? I have to pick up where they left off?

When people read my part of the story, I really hope they'll understand.

I'll tell you as much as I can remember. It's one of those things, though. It happened so fast. The shock sets in so fast. It played out like a dream. So I'll just tell it like a dream.

It happened, though.

★　　★　　★

He hooked his arm through Sandy's as they stepped out into the night. A warm spring night. Gordie turned his head to smile at the guard, but the guard wasn't there.

Then Gordie saw him, off to the left of the awning-covered entryway, his back pressed to the brick wall of the bar. Holding strangely still. A skin-headed young man stood close, pinning him against the brick. The guard's chin jutted out and up, exposing the white of his throat. Gordie's knees felt watery and warm at the flash of the blade. Long and mean and curved, bright with use and care.

It occupied his attention until he heard the sound of Sandy's breath. The sudden evacuation. And felt Sandy's arm pull free as he crumpled away.

Two men stood before Gordie in baggy, low-slung jeans and gang colors. One tapped a baseball bat against his palm. His military-short hair stuck straight up from his white scalp. One eyebrow had been scarred by a cut and had healed back together mismatched.

'Oops,' he said quietly, his face so close that Gordie could smell tobacco on his breath. 'Look what happened to your boyfriend.'

Much to Gordie's surprise and relief, he found the ability to detach had not abandoned him. It would be another beating, like so many before. He would watch it from a distance, and his skin and bones would heal. Or maybe this time not. But he would be elsewhere as it happened, shut down. When you don't care anymore you deprive them of the joy of hurting you. Hard to hit somebody where they live if there's nobody home.

He closed his eyes, not wanting to see the bat swung.

It hit him across his soft underbelly, doubling him. A hand around his throat brought him up straight again, and the bat folded him again.

He was going to pass out now, and then it wouldn't matter.

Noises reached his ears through a tunnel. Like the noises in his grandmother's house, where he'd had to sleep in the living room. Sounds that leak through a veil of half sleep, jarring in a distant, disconnected way. Filtering through the no-man's-land of semiconsciousness.

Just before he sank into it, before muddy gray behind his eyelids turned black, he heard a different sound.

A shouted word.

'Hey!'

It could not have come from either of his tormentors. The word started at a high pitch, the voice of a child, then cracked halfway through. The way Gordie's voice had, the way all boys' voices will when they are changing.

The sound of the bat clattering on the pavement.

Gordie felt himself turn liquid, boneless. Unsupported by himself or his attackers. He fell softly on what he knew by feel to be the big form of Sandy. A comfort. Sparing him from the hard pavement. They would rest here together.

Somehow he remembered feeling Sandy's breathing. Perhaps because its presence was something he really needed to feel.

Chapter Thirty

REUBEN

'Say good-bye to Frank, honey.'

'Good-bye, Frank.'

They stood out on the curb in front of the Washington Arms Hotel, in the light of the street lamps. A warm, comfortable spring night.

'Come on, Trevor,' Frank said. 'Let's help the doorman get all your stuff into the trunk.'

In addition to the baggage they'd brought from home, Trevor had three new heavy boxes, a complete set of encyclopedias he'd received as a birthday gift from the White House. The doorman could surely have handled it all, but Trevor helped supervise as the gift made its way into the trunk of a hotel limousine bound for the airport.

Arlene took hold of Reuben's hand and led him to the front of the car.

'Are you still feeling sick?' he asked her. She seemed

down somehow, distracted, her mood altered by something he couldn't quite name or touch.

'No, I'm okay now. I just need to talk to you about something.'

'Now?'

'I kind of need to get this off my chest.'

'You're not seriously sick, are you?'

'No. I'm just pregnant, is all.'

In the silent moment to follow, Reuben heard the sound of a disturbance, distant, maybe off on the next block. A light scuffle. It didn't really sink in, any more than her words had.

'Could you say something please, Reuben?'

'How far along?'

'I know what you're thinking.'

'Do you?'

It seemed odd to imagine she would. He didn't know what he was thinking, or even if he was thinking. He could only feel his focus on the sound of her voice, and Trevor's voice behind them, and the shouts and thuds on the next block, as if to decide, in a detached way, which seemed more real.

'You're thinking, was it that time I came over in the middle of the night to your house? Or was it right before Ricky left?'

'I forgot about that.' He hadn't forgotten that night, far from it, but it hadn't occurred to him to factor it into this discussion. He had not for a moment considered the idea that this pregnancy could be any of his doing. 'So? Which was it?'

'Well, they were only a week or ten days apart, so it's a little hard to tell.'

'So, how do we know?'

'Well, I guess we don't. Look, if it's too much for you, I understand. I mean, it's not what I want. You know that. I got this ring back now, I'd sort of like to keep it. But I had to tell you, right? But I'll understand, I mean, if you want to wait till we know. I mean, later, you know. Then we'll know.'

But in the confusion of the moment, even having to say whether or not it was too much for him seemed too much.

A split second later Frank appeared at his shoulder. 'Isn't Trevor up here with you?'

Arlene seemed more distracted than alarmed. 'No, we thought he was back there with you.'

'Well, he was just a minute ago . . .'

With a bad dawning that must have been more intuition than observation, Reuben turned his head in the direction of the noises, the muffled shouts and grunts he'd been hearing without attention, without focus, as a backdrop to this confusing exchange.

He saw a small group of figures at the end of the block, outside a restaurant or bar with awnings on the windows. Two men against the building, one on the ground. Two or three standing over the felled man. A baseball bat raised over a head.

And Trevor, running fast in their direction. With a good head start.

Reuben took off after him at a dead sprint.

At the edge of Reuben's vision, the brick facade of their hotel slid by like a dream, a blurred, distorted image through a wide-angle lens. Why couldn't he reach the end of it? He could feel his legs, his heart, opening and straining, yet the distance seemed to stretch out.

Why couldn't he close the gap to the boy?

'Trevor!' he screamed. Screamed. Bellowing, echoing from his lungs, pure panic. Heads turned.

Trevor's head did not.

Reuben's chest ached and burned. How could he be so short of oxygen so fast? He could see Trevor's untucked shirttail flapping out behind him as he ran.

Trevor streaked past the two men pressed against the building. Reuben could see them now, he was almost that close. One of the men wore a blue and gray uniform, like that of a security guard. The other wore baggy jeans, his head shaved, and he seemed to have the guard pinned to the building somehow.

The light from the street lamp glinted off something metal between them, a flash of light in Reuben's eye.

Both men turned their heads as Trevor flew by. The man with the raised bat turned with startled curiosity to watch Trevor's approach.

Without putting on the brakes, Trevor slammed into the man and knocked him down. As he tumbled, he fell against the legs of his accomplice, who also went down. Their second victim crumpled to the sidewalk, untouched, as if an imaginary wind had blown him over. The bat clattered loudly on the sidewalk as Trevor scrambled to his feet.

Reuben had almost drawn level with the men against the building when Trevor turned suddenly, started back in his direction. For what? To head back to Reuben? Or did he think he could knock the last man down?

The skinhead spun away from the guard to block Trevor's path. Trevor's impetus carried him forward to that meeting.

They came together just a foot or two from the end of Reuben's hand. Just a car length from the security guard. Either he or Reuben could almost have reached out and grabbed the man's jacket, if it hadn't all happened so fast.

Almost.

Then, just as suddenly, the skin-headed man ran off into the dark. Past his two partners, who scrambled to their feet and sprinted after him, sliding into the night like a river. Just that fast. Someone threw a switch and they were gone.

Reuben remained the best witness to the sudden collision, yet he failed to comprehend it. He saw it but could not explain it.

It would take him minutes to know what had happened, days to accept that it really had. Most of his life to understand.

1994 interview by Chris Chandler, from
Tracking the Movement

CHRIS: *Just take a big, deep breath. Okay?*
REUBEN: *I'm okay.*
CHRIS: *Take your time with this.*

REUBEN: *I can do this. Just give me a minute.*

CHRIS: *I can give you all day, buddy. We got nothing but time.*

REUBEN: *I saw it from so close. But from a funny angle. I was watching the collision from behind. I had no idea what I'd seen. I just remember seeing the man's right elbow come back, and then fly forward again. It just looked like he'd punched Trevor in the stomach. Not particularly hard. What I can't figure out is, could I really not see what happened? Or was it just so important to me? You know. Not to see.*

CHRIS: *I'm putting this box of Kleenex over by you.*

REUBEN: *Thanks. I just need to breathe for a minute.*

CHRIS: *It hasn't been long enough. They say time heals all wounds, you know? But I'm not sure that's true with all of them. Besides, it takes a ton of time.*

REUBEN: *After they ran off, Trevor was standing there. He looked okay. He had his hands over his stomach. His face was just so open. How do I explain it? He wasn't registering any pain or fear. That I could see. I said, 'Trevor.' It was all I could say. I thought it was over. I thought he was okay. The danger had gone and my family was still all there. Which I guess is how I always thought it would be.*

CHRIS: *You know, if you can't do this—*

REUBEN: *No. I can. I want this on paper. I want this in the book. It's important.*

CHRIS: *Breathe. Take your time.*

REUBEN: *I have to tell you this part. What he said. I'm not even sure what it means, but it stays with me. So I have to say this. I guess I heard footsteps behind me. I think I remember that. Frank's voice, but I never looked around. Trevor looked up at* my face. God only knows what he saw there. I can't even imagine. I don't even know what I was feeling. I couldn't even tell yet. But some of it must have been right there on my face. He could see it. I could see it on him. It was like looking in a mirror. Then I looked down . . . I looked down at Trevor's hands. And then Trevor looked down. It's like he just shifted his eyes down to see where I was looking. And he held his hands out, away from his body, under the light from the street lamp. He looked so surprised.

CHRIS: Because there was blood, you mean?

REUBEN: He looked up at my face again, and he said, 'I'm okay, Reuben. It's okay. Don't worry.'

CHRIS: Was he in shock, do you think?

REUBEN: I don't know. I can't sort that out. I was. But Trevor, I don't know. Sometimes I think he was. Sometimes I think he said he was okay because he didn't know yet that he wasn't. Other times I think he was just trying to comfort me. He didn't want me to be upset.

CHRIS: What do you think motivated him to jump in there? You think he'd just kind of gotten in the habit of trying to help in a big way?

REUBEN: He thought he had to do one more.

CHRIS: We all thought he'd done plenty.

REUBEN: I know. That's what we told him. But he thought Jerry was a failed attempt. He thought he had two down, one to go. So he was on the lookout for somebody who needed something.

CHRIS: If only he'd known about Jerry.

REUBEN: He was having a really good day.

CHRIS: What do you mean?

REUBEN: *He kept saying that. This is the best day ever, he kept saying that. He even asked me if I thought he'd ever have another one like it.*

CHRIS: *Wow. That hurts. Huh?*

REUBEN: *Actually, in a funny sort of way, it's been a consolation to me. That day was the high point of his life. And it probably always would have been. You know what I mean?*

CHRIS: *I think so.*

REUBEN: *He said he was fine. He told me not to worry.*

CHRIS: *Did he say anything else?*

REUBEN: *No. Nothing else.*

Chapter Thirty-One

CHRIS

He lay naked under the covers beside Sally, watching TV.
She had pulled a night shade over her eyes. He couldn't tell
if she was asleep or not.

'Breaking news from Washington,' the anchor an-
nounced to open the eleven o'clock news.

This couldn't be it. Not with the stone face on this
newsman. This is not about Trevor.

'Trevor McKinney, the boy who met with the president
of the United States earlier today, has been hospitalized
tonight in Washington, D.C., not far from the hotel where
his family had been staying. Witnesses say the boy suffered a
single stab wound as he tried to intervene in a mugging on
the street outside the hotel. A hospital spokesperson reports
that Trevor was admitted in critical condition and is under-
going emergency surgery. No further word on his condition
is available at this time.'

Sitting straight up in bed, Chris glanced over to see

Sally slip off the night shade and raise her head.

'President Clinton tonight expressed deep shock and concern for Trevor's condition. The president has issued the following statement. Quote. "It seems unimaginably sad that a boy who came to Washington to be honored for his good deeds and his dedication to promoting kindness in the world should be targeted in a senseless act of violence. My heart goes out to Trevor and his family, and my family will say a prayer tonight for his speedy recovery. We hope the rest of America will join us in a prayer for Trevor's well-being."'

The screen filled with the tape of Trevor's earlier meeting with the president. Chris blinked at it, feeling empty.

He felt her hand on his arm.

He rolled out of bed. Looked for the cordless phone. Finally located it in the living room. She followed after him and drew the curtains closed. It hadn't occurred to him that he'd been standing in front of the apartment windows naked. When he realized, he didn't care.

He punched long distance information, 202 area code. Asked for a listing for every hospital in the Washington, D.C., area.

He hit it on the first try.

The admission desk said yes, Trevor was there. He was in surgery. The woman punched his information up on the computer.

'He's listed as critical.'

'That's all you can tell me?'

'For the present time, yes. I'm sorry. We're getting a lot of calls about him.'

'Where's his mother? Arlene McKinney. She must be there, right?'

'I'm sorry, sir, I couldn't say.'

'Could you page her for me?'

A pause, an audible sigh. He heard the line click onto hold.

He bit the inside of his lip and waited.

He moved into the kitchen with the phone under his chin and poured three fingers of brandy. He looked up to see Sally watching quietly. They both looked away again.

Then a voice on the line. 'Yeah? Who is this?'

'Arlene?'

'Who is this?'

'It's Chris, Arlene. Chris Chandler.'

'Oh, Chris.' Her voice sounded tight and rough.

'What happened, Arlene?'

'Oh, Chris, I don't know. It all happened so fast. He got stabbed. He saw some guys gettin' beat up. He tried to mix in.'

'Is he gonna be okay?'

'They won't tell us, Chris.' Her voice dissolved into sobs. 'He's been in surgery over two hours. They just won't tell us a damn thing. They say we'll know when they do. I gotta go, Chris.'

'Okay. Arlene? Never mind. Okay.'

The dial tone rang in his ear. He clicked the button on the phone to off.

He walked past Sally, back into the bedroom.

'You okay, Chris?'

He slipped back under the covers.

'Hey. Chris. You okay?'

'Did they say anything else about him on the news?'

'Just that they'd update his condition when they had it.'

They sat quietly through the end of the news broadcast. Then into the late-night talk shows. Chris sat awake long after she'd faded, the light from the TV screen flickering on his face, surfing channels. Watching minute-long scraps of late movies.

No updates. Programming seemed to go on.

He jolted awake, surprised he'd ever been asleep.

He looked at the clock and saw it was late morning.

The TV droned on at the end of the bed. He could hear Sally in the kitchen making coffee.

He sat up and rubbed his eyes.

On the screen, President Clinton held a press conference. Or footage from an earlier press conference was being shown.

Chris woke up just in time to hear him say that the flags in Washington would fly at half-mast today and that at noon, the country would stop what it was doing and observe a moment of silence. Edit to news anchor, who said, 'On a sad final note, today would have been Trevor's fourteenth birthday. More news after these messages.'

★　　★　　★

Arlene's front lawn had become a sea of cameras and news teams by the time Chris arrived. He had to park in her driveway behind the GTO. All the street parking had been taken up by television news crew vans.

He cut sideways across her front grass.

'She's not talking to anyone,' a female anchor with stiff, perfect blond hair told him as he stepped onto the front porch.

He rapped hard on the front door. 'Arlene? It's me, Chris.'

The door peeked open and Reuben drew him inside by one elbow. Arlene lay on the couch on her side, a glass of water and a box of Kleenex close by.

'I wish they'd go away,' she said. 'Can you make 'em go away, Chris?'

He sat down on the couch beside her. She patted his hand.

'Everybody cares about this story, Arlene. I've never seen anything like it. I've never seen people mobilize over one story like this.'

'It's not a story, Chris. It happened.'

'I know. I'm sorry. That's just the way I talk.'

'I can't talk to all of them. It's too much.'

'I know, Arlene. I know. Look, you don't have to talk to anybody. But that Citizen of the Month segment is going to run tomorrow. With an update, of course. If there's anything you want to say, I can get one cameraman in here. That's it. Me and one camera. You don't have to do it. But if there's something you want to tell the public about this. They really want to hear from you.'

She sat up, wiped her eyes, and sniffled. 'Like what?'

'I don't know. Anything you want to say.'

'Well, I could just say there's a memorial next Sunday in front of City Hall. We thought maybe even a candlelight march after. You know, if people are interested. If there are people out there who cared about Trevor, they could come and bring a candle. That sort of thing?'

'Yeah. That would be great.' Chris felt tears forming, threatening just behind his eyes. 'I'll go get a cameraman.'

Chapter Thirty-Two

ARLENE

The phone woke them. It was late, after ten in the morning. The sun streamed through the windows onto her face. She wondered how she could have slept through that.

'Let the machine get it,' she said.

He rolled up behind her and slid his left arm under her pillow. Wrapped his good right arm around her and laid his left cheek down against the side of her face. His chest felt warm and solid against her back. His eye patch was off, and she could feel the smooth, empty expanse where his left eye had once been. He didn't work to keep that from her anymore. He knew she didn't mind.

She laced her fingers through his.

The machine picked it up. Again. Arlene had turned the volume all the way down.

'How'd we sleep so long?' she said quietly.

'It's good for us. It's what you do to heal.'

'Take more than a few nights' sleep.'

'I know.'

'So, what're we gonna do until seven o'clock tonight?'

'I don't know. Same thing we've done all week, I guess. Get up. Wash our faces. Eat.'

'Cry.'

'Yeah. That too.'

Neither had cried much in the last twenty-four hours. It was as if they'd struck the bottom of a well. Used up all the tears, leaving an amazing emptiness inside, like a killer case of the flu. They were both tired. Bone tired. Arlene wondered at the place inside her rib cage. Wondered how an empty space could feel so heavy.

She squeezed her eyes closed.

'What if the baby turns out to be Ricky's, Reuben? Sooner or later we gotta talk about that.'

The second or two it took him to answer drew out long and frightening.

'I was willing to sign on to raise Ricky's last kid. Wasn't I? And he turned out pretty good.'

'Yeah, he did. Didn't he? Pretty damn good.'

And to her surprise, that heavy, empty center inside her gave up a few more tears.

She unlaced her fingers from his, reached back, and touched his face. He pressed his right hand onto her belly, big fingers spread to cover the whole area, and held it there. As if to introduce himself.

She could hear a honking of horns, all the way from the Camino. The intermittent red light of a flashing emergency vehicle slipped by their window.

'Wonder what the hell's going on out there,' she said without much genuine curiosity.

'An accident, maybe.'

'That must be it, yeah.'

Reuben unplugged the phone and they fell back asleep for the remainder of the morning.

'How 'bout we take the GTO?'

'Whichever.'

Neither had a strong opinion or was interested in details.

Reuben drove. As he backed out of the driveway, they noticed both sides of the street solid with parked cars. So close together, pushing so hard for space that they slightly overlapped both sides of the driveway, making it a tight fit to get out. And then, when he'd managed to angle straight out between them, he couldn't find a break in traffic. Traffic. On this tiny little residential street.

Arlene got out of the car and personally stopped the procession of cars with her body, giving Reuben a chance to back into the traffic lane.

The GTO crawled an inch or two at a time toward the Camino. For the first few minutes they didn't comment or complain.

Arlene glanced at her watch.

'Why the hell is this happening? I mean, today of all days? We're gonna be late if we can't get out of this jam.'

Reuben chewed on his lower lip and didn't answer.

It was ten minutes after seven when they hit the Camino, only to find traffic police turning cars away at a roadblock. The main drag appeared closed to traffic. Reuben did not turn where the officer told him to. Instead he pulled up to the roadblock and rolled down his window. The sun had dipped to a slant behind the officer's head.

Arlene looked straight through the windshield and saw the Camino clogged with pedestrians. Not just the sidewalks, but the street itself. Hundreds, just in this intersection.

'We don't know what's going on,' Reuben told the officer, 'but we have to get to the memorial at City Hall.'

'Yeah, that's everybody's problem,' he said.

'These people are all here for the memorial?'

'That's right,' he said. 'Your problem is not unique.'

Arlene leaned over Reuben's lap and looked into the officer's face. 'I'm Arlene McKinney,' she said.

His expression changed. 'Right. You are, aren't you? Look, just leave your car here by the barricade and come with me.'

Reuben turned off the motor. They stepped out into the sea of bodies and followed the uniformed officer out onto the Camino. The crowd in their immediate vicinity seemed to notice. To recognize. A silence fell, directly surrounding Reuben and Arlene, and rippled out like a wake on water.

A path opened up to allow them through.

They were escorted into the backseat of a black-and-white patrol car. The officer turned on his lights and siren.

Through the vehicle's loudspeaker, he asked the crowd to open a traffic lane to allow the family to pass.

She sat straight and rigid, squeezing Reuben's hand, staring forward through the windshield, watching the mass of bodies part, watching a ribbon of empty street form ahead of the car.

'This crowd go all the way down to the City Hall?' Arlene asked at last, jarring the silence.

'It goes all over town,' he said. 'We got helicopters in from L.A. We got mounted police coming in with horse trailers right now. Not that there's been any trouble. There hasn't. We just need more personnel. Local rental company donated some sound equipment. Maybe the people in a four- or five-block radius will hear the service. Rest'll have to read about it in the paper. Or see it on TV. We got camera crews coming outta our ears.'

'How many people do you think we have here?' Reuben asked.

'Most recent estimate stands at twenty thousand. But the freeway's backed up thirty miles. It's a parking lot. They're still coming in.'

The patrol car pulled over at the West Mall, and Reuben and Arlene stepped out. She reached for his hand and held it. The officer escorted them through the sea of bodies. A smattering of applause rang in their ears, loudest wherever they happened to walk.

The grassy area overflowed with media equipment. Microphones, cameras, newspeople. They occupied so much space that the nonmedia participants had to squeeze around the edges to allow space for the filming.

It occurred to Arlene that this twenty thousand people might seem like nothing compared to the audience who saw it reported on the news or in the paper. It was all too much to take in at once.

They reached an elevated makeshift stage, where the sound equipment had been set up. Big, heavy, rock-concert speakers stacked on assembled three-level catwalks, framing City Hall. When they stepped onto the stage, the crowd grew quiet. Then a long, steady round of applause broke out.

Chris Chandler slipped up beside her. It felt good to see a familiar face.

'What do you think?' he said.

'Where did all these people come from, Chris?'

'Well, it just so happens you're asking the right person. I've been conducting interviews in the crowd. The people I've talked to are from' – he flipped open his notepad – 'Illinois, Florida, Los Angeles, Las Vegas, Bangladesh, Atascadero, London, San Francisco, Sweden—'

'That little television thing I did went outside the country?'

'A hundred and twenty-four countries around the world. Which is, like, nothing compared to the coverage we've got today. Most of these news crews are sending this out live.'

Arlene raised her eyes to the crowd, knowing she saw only a tiny percentage. Thousands of people, crowding close to hear. A light dusk had begun to settle. They were late getting started. She looked down at the cameras, saw them looking back. She knew by their red lights that everything, everybody was on. Watching.

She stepped up to the microphone. The crowd waited in silence. She opened her mouth to speak. She felt slightly dizzy. The air, the inside of her head, had taken on the qualities of walking in a dream.

'I'm not too good with words,' she said.

Her voice shook and cracked, and the microphone amplified that, ricocheted her tension off the neighboring buildings. The strength of the sound system startled her. The leaves on the oak trees overhead shivered at the sound. All eyes turned up to her in silence.

'I don't even know what I'm doing up here, in front of all these people. I just came here to say good-bye to my boy.' Tears flowed freely at the sound of those words. She let them. Her voice remained steady and she talked through the moment. 'I hope he can see this,' she said. 'Boy, would he be proud.'

The earth seemed to fall out from underneath her. She felt she might pass out. 'I'm gonna turn this over to Reuben,' she said. 'He can talk better than me. I just came here to say good-bye to my boy.'

Reuben's arm slid around her shoulder and held tight. Don't ever let go, she thought. Don't you dare ever let go.

If it wasn't for Reuben, and that tiny presence in her belly, she'd have nothing left worth holding on to.

Except, she thought, maybe for this world that had come here to share this moment with her. Maybe that was something after all.

Chapter Thirty-Three

REUBEN

Reuben lifted the microphone and pulled it up to his lips. The light had begun to fade, and artificial lights glared into his eye from the sea of cameras beneath him. He didn't like lights or cameras or people staring, but it seemed like a minor concern now.

He opened his mouth to speak, prepared to be startled by the sound of his own words amplified into the city dusk.

'The police told me we have more than twenty thousand people here today. Some have traveled from outside the country to share this moment with us. Arlene and I—' His voice cracked slightly and he stopped. Blinked. Swallowed. 'We never expected anything like this.'

Pause. Breathe. He felt light-headed and weak. What did he want to say? What needed to be said? Nothing came into his head.

What would Trevor have wanted him to say? He opened his mouth and the rest flowed easily.

'The freeway is clogged with thousands more people trying to get here. And I'm told this is going out live. To how many viewers? Millions? How many millions of people am I talking to right now?

'What made you all care so much? Why is this such a big story? I think I know. I think you know, too. This is our world. Where is the person who can't relate to that? This is our world. It's the only one we've got. And it's gotten so damn hard to live in. And we care. How can we not care? These are our lives we're talking about.

'And then a little boy came along, and he decided maybe he could change the whole thing. The whole world order. Make it a decent place to live for everybody. Maybe because he was too young and optimistic and inexperienced to know it couldn't be done.

'And it looked for a minute like it could work. So, just for a minute, all these people who care enough to be here or to watch this, just for a minute you thought the world might really change.

'And then Trevor was killed in a senseless, purposeless act of violence. And that's shaken our faith. So now we wonder. Right? Now we don't know if it can ever get better or not.

'But this is my question to all of you. Why are we here asking the question when we could just as easily be here answering it? Do you want a new world? Because it's not just one little boy anymore. Look at all of us. By the time this has been in all the papers, all the news magazines, been repeated on newscasts all over the world . . . the twenty thousand people who made it into the city tonight, that's a drop in the bucket. Twenty million people could hear what I'm about to say.

'So, here it is: If Trevor touched your life that much, then maybe you need to *pay that forward*. In his memory. In his honor. Twenty million people paying it forward. In a few months, that will be sixty million people. And then a hundred and eighty million. In no time at all, that number would be bigger than the population of the world.'

Reuben stopped, scratched his head, breathed. Listened for a moment to the echoing silence.

'I know that sounds kind of mind-boggling. But all it really means is that everybody's life would be touched more than once. Three times, six times someone might pay it forward to you. Every month or two, some miraculous act of kindness for everybody. It just keeps getting bigger. Before you could even pay it forward, someone would pay it forward to you again. We'd all lose track after a while. We'd all be scrambling around trying to find people to do good for. We'd never know for sure if we were caught up. It would just keep going around.

'The question I've been asked more than any other . . . every time I'm interviewed for television. Every time someone talks to me on the street. They say, how was Trevor's idea received when the class first heard it? I tell them the truth. I say it was received with an utter lack of respect. It was seen as ridiculous. Because it requires people to work on the honor system, and because they say they'll do all kinds of things, but in the end, people only help themselves. Because they're selfish. They don't care. They don't follow through. Right? People have no honor.'

He stopped as if expecting the crowd to answer. Paused on the question they'd all come here to explore. The moment felt heavy in the air, a palpable energy.

'Well, then, what are you all doing here? If you don't care. Don't ask me if people will really pay it forward. Tell me. Will you? Will each of you really do it? It's your world. So, you decide. I'm getting a little overwrought here. I think I need to drink a glass of water and sit down. We're going to have a candlelight march in a few minutes, when it's dark. So, think about it, and join us then.'

The cameras stayed on. Nobody moved. Faces watched him in silence. Applause came up like thunder, spreading down and across the street in all directions, farther than Reuben could see, farther than he knew he could be heard. The whole world, applauding Trevor's idea.

Reuben recognized Chris's face in the candlelight.

Arlene clung tightly to Reuben's hand.

'It's like this,' Chris said. 'It's not exactly going to be a candlelight march. I mean, everybody brought a candle. But we've got, maybe, thirty-five thousand people here. How you going to march that many people? I mean, from where to where? The city's full. So, they're just going to line the street. Like they're doing. And you and Arlene are going to walk. You know? They'll open up a path for you to walk. Right down the middle of the Camino.'

'You come with us, Chris,' Arlene said suddenly, grabbing at his sleeve.

'No. No way. I don't belong there.'

'The hell you don't. Who do you think told all these people about Trevor?'

'I'm not family, though.'

'I'm not family by blood, either,' Reuben said. 'She's right. You come along.'

Two uniformed policemen walked on either side. Reuben slipped his arm through Arlene's. Their candles flickered in the still night as they moved forward.

The streetlights had not come on. On purpose? he wondered. It didn't seem to matter. On every block thousands of candles glowed, lighting up the streets like the full moon that would rise momentarily.

A thin dark ribbon stretched ahead, a path down the middle of the street, left open for them.

Here and there a hand reached out to lightly touch his shoulder or his sleeve. Round, soft moons of faces shone in the circles of each candle.

A woman reached out and touched Reuben's hand.

'I will,' she said.

Then the man beside her said the same. 'I will.'

They passed a mounted policeman on a big bay horse. Sitting still and straight, watching. In one hand he held the reins, in the other, a candle. 'I will,' he said, looking down as they passed.

It spread like a ripple along the route, echoing ten and twenty deep, like the crowd. The simple words followed them along their path, lighting up to their passing. One commitment for every candle.

Everyone said they would.

Epilogue

A photographer had stationed himself on the third floor of a building along the route. He'd set up a tripod and opened the shutter for a long exposure, and caught the thousands of candle flames in two solid bands down the main street of town, with a thin dark path along the center. A ribbon of candle points stretching off into the distance, curving with the street, narrowing to a pinprick of light in the background.

It won an award for the photographer, who printed and framed a blown-up copy as a wedding gift for Reuben and Arlene. They hung it on their living room wall as proof of the Boy's continued existence. It graced the cover of Chris's biography of Trevor, which hit the bookstores in the summer of 1994. It appeared on the cover of three weekly newsmagazines and was quickly issued in poster form to stores all over the world, earning over $7 million for the photographer. He gave half to Reuben and Arlene, the rest to charity. Reuben and Arlene gave their half away as well.

It found its way onto the front pages of newspapers worldwide, above the special extra sections most papers added to cover stories of reported acts of kindness. The early stories. In a few weeks the stories became too voluminous to print. In a few months acts of kindness were no longer considered news.

In December of that year, the first holiday season they would have to spend without him, Reuben and Arlene attended, by special invitation, the National Christmas Tree lighting ceremony on the ellipse of the White House lawn.

They were placed in the front row, bundled against the cold, the new baby dressed in her freshly bought leggings and hooded coat, waiting for the moment in the president's speech that might define why they had been invited.

When the moment came, when the president said, 'I want us to all turn our attention to the memory of a very special young man,' a light was trained onto Reuben and Arlene, and a camera swung around and took a tight shot of them. Arlene turned the baby's face into her shoulder to shield her sensitive little eyes from the light. 'Trevor McKinney is not able to be with us tonight,' the president continued. 'Or maybe he is here. I don't know.' A comfortable smile. 'But he left us all with a very special gift this holiday season. He wasn't even fourteen years old yet, but he was a visionary and a hero, and I want everyone within the sound of my voice to look into your hearts and make sure you haven't forgotten your promise to that boy. If he were here tonight I'd ask him to throw the switch and light this tree. But I'll have to do it in his honor. In a small, symbolic way I'm going to do what Trevor did in a very big and very real way: light up the world.'

The baby began to fuss, and Reuben lifted her from Arlene's arms and turned her to face the tree. The lights were off them now, the cameras faced away. All eyes were on the president, throwing the switch. When the tree sprang to light, a rush of breath and sound escaped the crowd, and just as Reuben had hoped, the baby fell silent. Her eyes and mouth opened wide, frozen in a moment of pure, unguarded awe. Reuben could see the multicolored points of light reflected in her eyes.

A few days before Christmas, Ricky showed up at their door late at night, unexpectedly, as was his way. Arlene stayed in bed while Reuben put on his robe and answered the knock.

They stared at each other in a measured silence.

'I think I got a right to see my kid,' Ricky said.

'Whose kid?'

'Look, I don't care what you say. Blood is blood. Now come on, where is she?'

By this time Arlene was up and standing in the living

room behind him in one of Reuben's big shirts. Her face seemed unafraid.

'He just wants to see the baby, Arlene.'

'Okay, fine. Come see her.' She swung one arm wide to motion Ricky into the nursery.

They walked in together and Reuben turned on a soft light over the crib.

She lay curled on her side, knees tucked up, her thumb in her mouth. Her lips and cheeks moved in a suckling motion in her sleep. It struck a spot inside Reuben, the way it always had, probably always would. An excruciating blend of sorrow and joy, springing from who she was and from who she was not. He reached in and ran the back of his fingers over her smooth, caramel-colored cheek.

When he looked up, Ricky's face had changed. Now he looked pale and helpless.

'Okay. I guess maybe I was wrong.' That was all he said for the moment.

'When she was being born,' Arlene said, her voice soft with respect, 'Reuben's parents came all the way from Chicago to be with us. Pretty nice of 'em to do, I thought, since nobody really knew which way it would go. They brought a picture of Reuben when he was just a baby. Just about the age she is now. I wish you could've seen it. Like a mirror image. Gave me goose bumps.'

Before she finished with the telling of this, Ricky had excused himself from the room. Reuben found him in the living room, sitting on the couch with his head in his hands, looking desperate and small.

Reuben took a deep breath and sat down beside him. In his peripheral vision he could see Arlene standing in the bedroom doorway. Nothing was said for the longest time.

Then Ricky spoke up in a small voice. 'I hear tell Deion Sanders is gonna leave Atlanta. Go off as a free agent. Can't say as I blame him. He wants a Super Bowl ring. He's gonna sign with the team most likely to get him one. People figure that'll mean San Francisco.' He laughed nervously and shifted his eyes to the ceiling. 'I ain't a superstitious man, but I tell you now . . . day Deion Sanders signs on with the 49ers, I got to look up at the sky and wonder if that boy don't have some kinda pull up there.' He allowed an awkward silence. 'I know I hardly knew that boy,' he said. His forehead creased. 'Something about his bein' mine. Like blood, you know? Like the part of your own life you think might actually keep going.'

They talked quietly for a few minutes, Reuben saying that life can start over out of the worst circumstances, and he wasn't just preaching that, he'd proven it.

Ricky said Cheryl had thrown him out. 'Right before Christmas,' he said. 'How cold is that?' And he had no job, no place to stay, nothing to even start over from or with. Yet it was hard not to notice that Ricky wore a very expensive coat, new-looking heavy suede with a sheepskin lining. Reuben never mentioned that.

Though Ricky never said it straight out, Reuben heard some dashed hope that fatherhood of that girl might have given him an anchor in somebody's life. If he had been the father of the girl, that is.

Reuben listened for a while, then rose and walked to the living room desk and got the checkbook, because he remembered something that Trevor had said.

'*If you help somebody you really want to help, then that's not very big. You know? But if you're all mad at my mom, and you helped her. That would be a big thing.*' At the time Reuben hadn't felt that big. But maybe the past few months had stretched him, painfully so, torn him and broken him in such a way as to leave more room inside him now than before.

'Honey,' he said to Arlene, 'I'm going to write Ricky a check to help him get started, okay?'

'I guess,' she said. 'How much?'

'Well, we've got about four thousand in the bank. How about if I give him half?'

'Sure, I guess. We'll get by.'

He left the name blank, because he didn't know Ricky's last name, or need to.

While he was writing it out, Ricky said, 'This is a joke. Right?'

He tore the check off the pad and held it out in Ricky's direction. Ricky half rose from the couch, not quite reaching for it, as though somehow it could hurt him.

'No, it's not a joke. Take it.'

Ricky took it. 'What's the catch?'

'No catch. You just have to pay it forward. Do you know how to do that?'

Ricky let out a nervous little laugh. 'Shoot, everybody in the country knows that by now. Maybe the whole world.

Last night I had to sleep in the park 'cause Cheryl threw me out with just the clothes on my back. Guy come and stood over me in the middle of the night. I thought he was gonna roll me. Instead he looks down and says, "You look cold." Takes this coat right off his back and gives it to me. Got to be, like, a five-hundred-dollar coat, right? Takes it off his own back. So then *he* was cold. Things like that, they're not even a big deal anymore, you know?'

He shuffled quickly for the door, as if Reuben might still change his mind.

'Uh . . .' He opened the front door and paused.

Reuben moved back into the bedroom doorway with Arlene and stood with an arm around her shoulder. Not a proud or defensive posture. Just something he wanted, needed, to do.

'I'm obliged.'

'But not to us,' Reuben said.

Ricky just stood a moment, as though there must be one more thing to say, if only he knew where to look for it. Then he said, barely audibly, 'Merry Christmas to the both of you,' and closed the door behind him.

Reuben kissed his little girl good night gently, careful not to wake her, before joining Arlene in bed.

THE END

LOVE IN THE PRESENT TENSE
Catherine Ryan Hyde

'So much of how it started was when that cop got out and came up to me. But I didn't know all this when it first happened. I didn't know there would ever be a Leonard, or that this man would be his father, or that anyone would have to die . . .'

Leonard is an eerily wise five-year-old-boy with asthma, terrible eyesight, and the ability to captivate everyone he meets.

Pearl is Leonard's devoted teenage mother, desperately trying to hide a violent secret from her past.

Mitch is Leonard's 25-year-old next-door neighbour, busy running his own company and entertaining the Mayor's wife.

Then one day Pearl drops Leonard off with Mitch, and never returns.

How do you go on loving someone who isn't there? As truth and fiction, memory and dreams collide, Mitch finds himself learning from a surprising source the true, magical definition of love.

'A SWEET AND HONEST LOOK AT THE PAINS AND PLEASURES OF LOVE, AND WHO COULD NOT FALL IN LOVE WITH LEONARD – WHAT A BEAUTIFULLY DRAWN CHARACTER'
Jane Green

'A WORK OF ART . . . ENCHANTING'
San Francisco Chronicle

'HAUNTING'
Washington Post

9780552773645

BLACK SWAN

LOVE AND OTHER IMPOSSIBLE PURSUITS
Ayelet Waldman

'WICKED STEPMOTHERS EVERYWHERE HAVE
CAUSE TO CHEER . . . TOUGH, TOUCHING, AND
VERY, VERY FUNNY'
Bella Pollen

Falling in love with Jack was so easy, I had assumed that falling
in love with his son would be just as effortless . . .

Who says you have to love your step-child?

Wouldn't *you* dislike a precocious five-year old who corrected
your French pronunciation, and who calculated your
Body Mass Index when you were halfway through
a piece of cheesecake?

Does that make you a 'wicked stepmother'? Even *if* you feed
him dairy products while he's lactose intolerant? Even *if* you
push him (accidentally) into the pond in Central Park?

How far do you have to go before it starts to be right?

'MOVING AND DARKLY FUNNY, ROMANTIC,
SHOCKING, PAINFUL PAGE-TURNER . . . SAYS
SOMETHING NEW AND INTERESTING ABOUT
WOMEN, FAMILIES AND LOVE'
New York Times

'ONE MOMENT I WAS LAUGHING OUT LOUD, THE
NEXT I HAD TEARS POURING DOWN . . . WHETHER
YOU'RE A PARENT OR NOT, YOU CAN'T
FAIL TO BE MOVED'
Daily Express

9780552772921

BLACK SWAN

THE MOTHER-IN-LAW
Eve Makis

Electra and Adam are living proof that opposites attract.

Electra is warm, passionate and creative.
She wants to have a baby.

Adam is calm, reasonable and very English. He doesn't.

Enter the mother-in-law . . .

Cold, critical and snobbish, she disapproves of
her son's marriage.

And then she moves in with them.

Will their relationship survive?

A darkly funny, insightful and cautionary tale that will
make you question where *your* loyalties lie.

'WITH SIZEABLE PINCHES OF LOVE,
TRAGEDY AND HUMOUR, THIS IS
DELICIOUSLY SATISFYING'
Cosmopolitan

'ENGAGING, DELICATELY OBSERVED
AND BELIEVABLE'
Good Housekeeping

9780552773249

BLACK SWAN

YOU, ME & HIM
Alice Peterson

Josie and Finn seem to lead a charmed life, with successful careers, an enviable relationship and an adorable son. But parenthood is no easy ride when your adorable son is hyperactive . . .

When Josie unexpectedly finds herself pregnant again, her feelings are mixed. How can you love your child yet fear to have another who might be just like him? Finn thinks she's over-reacting – so she turns to her best friend, **Clarky**. He's always been there for her – even if Finn suspects ulterior motives.

As she and Clarky become ever closer, Josie's world is suddenly thrown into doubt. What if she and **Finn** aren't the perfect couple after all? Is there such a thing as a straightforward friendship between a man and a woman? But most importantly: is she prepared to risk everything to find out?

'A GREAT SUMMER READ THAT'S ENLIGHTENING AND PROVOCATIVE'
Easy Living

9780552773034

BLACK SWAN